A HAZARD OF LOSERS

LLOYD BIGGLE, JR.

A BROWN BAG MYSTERY
FROM COUNCIL OAK BOOKS

T U L S A

Council Oak Books
Tulsa, Oklahoma 74120
© 1991 by Lloyd Biggle, Jr.
All rights reserved. Published 1991
Printed in the United States of America
98 97 96 95 94 93 92 91   5 4 3 2 1

Library of Congress Catalog Card Number 91-70229
ISBN 0-933031-38-6

Designed by Carol Haralson

The City and the Stars, by Arthur C. Clarke,
is quoted with the kind permission of the author.

Americans All and Nevada 2100 are wholly fictitious, as
are Diamond D's hotel and casino, Lon's 24-Hour-Cafe,
the L D and Farnby Apartments, Forrie's Bistro, the
Preswick and Lyonce Advertising Agency, and their
locations.

All of the characters in this book are fictitious, and any
resemblance to actual persons, living or dead, is purely
coincidental.

Books By Lloyd Biggle, Jr.

Mystery Novels

Memoirs of Sherlock Holmes:
The Quallsford Inheritance
The Glendower Conspiracy

J. Pletcher Detective Novels:
Interface For Murder
A Hazard of Losers

Science Fiction Novels

The Angry Espers
All the Colors of Darkness
The Fury Out of Time
Watchers of the Dark
The Still, Small Voice of Trumpets
The World Menders
The Light That Never Was
Monument
This Darkening Universe
Silence Is Deadly
The Whirligig of Time
(with T. L. Sherred) *Alien Main*

Science Fiction Short Stories

The Rule of The Door, and Other Fanciful Regulations
The Metallic Muse
A Galaxy of Strangers
(As Editor) *Nebula Award Stories Seven*

This book was made possible by the friendly interest and generous assistance of a number of Las Vegas residents who, in official or unofficial capacities, were unfailingly considerate and hospitable to an inquiring stranger. As with all of the more interesting localities in the world, Las Vegas presents many faces to its visitors—each of which, if scrutinized with care, proves to be a mirror.

1

BEFORE I CHECKED IN AT LOS ANGELES IN-
ternational Airport that Tuesday morning, I bought
a paperback science fiction novel, *The City and the
Stars*, by Arthur C. Clarke. The first paragraph
read:

> Like a glowing jewel, the city lay upon
> the breast of the desert. Once it had
> known change and alteration, but now
> Time passed it by. Night and day fled
> across the desert's face, but in the
> streets of Diaspar it was always after-
> noon, and darkness never came. The
> long winter nights might dust the des-
> ert with frost, as the last moisture left
> in the thin air of Earth congealed —
> but the city knew neither heat nor cold.
> It had no contact with the outer world;
> it was a universe itself.

Less than an hour after takeoff, as my plane
pointed downward for its landing, the meandering
arms of Lake Mead were elongated shards of blue-

tinted mirror strung across the eastern horizon, and Las Vegas lay upon the breast of its mountain-rimmed desert like a glowing jewel. It was a sprawling, patchwork city. Sections of new suburbs, distinctly marked off by their colors — red-tiled roofs in one housing development, green roofs in another — alternated with sections of desert ornamented only with sage brush.

McCarran International Airport, which surely is the busiest in the world for cities of a million or less, is the gateway to fantasy for multi-millions of visitors each year. The Las Vegas wonderland begins here, with metal palm trees casting a luminous shade under a chromium-plated sky, and with ranks of slot machines, single arms raised in salute, that grab the visitors' attention the moment they emerge from the exit gates. One could blow the savings of a lifetime at the terminal and return home broke without seeing a casino.

I ignored all of it. As soon as the baggage carousel completed the usual stress and endurance tests on my suitcases, I followed signs pointing the way to ground transportation. Outside I found a sunny but incongruously chilly morning. During summer, the parching heat reaches 115 degrees — and higher — and hangs over Las Vegas like a tangible thing that could be sliced and exported to Siberia. Winter weather, with low humidity, midday temperatures that may reach the sixties, and invigoratingly cool nights, can be lovely. Some would call it ideal. At nine o'clock on a January morning, however, the day was cool enough to make a top-coat feel welcome.

The cab driver greeted me with a Brooklyn accent, a reminder that fewer than a sixth of the people living in Las Vegas are natives. I told him, "Diamond D's." We drove away, and I leaned back and thought about the similarities between Las Vegas and Diaspar. Day might singe the desert; night might dust it with frost; but within the vibrant, jewel-like city, Las Vegas's seething casinos never close, and the city's residents know neither heat nor cold except when they flit from one environmentally controlled building to another.

Unlike Arthur C. Clarke's city, however, Las Vegas is not a universe unto itself. It survives, it is able to give a modicum of substance to the illusions it fosters, only because of a constant flow of pleasure-seeking tourists bringing money.

The Las Vegas fantasy permeates the city in surprising ways. I wouldn't have been surprised to find a slot machine in the back seat of the cab. Why not? One sees them in restaurants, convenience stores, even car washes, but it takes most tourists only a few hours — or perhaps a day or two if they are slow learners — to infer that the entire Las Vegas scenario has been artfully contrived for no other reason than to separate them from their money.

This insight should surprise no one. Any tourist

3

attraction, anywhere, has a similar objective, but a fantasy world offers only fantasy values in return.

We headed up Las Vegas Boulevard, the famous "Strip," and casino names celebrated in entertainment lore rolled past: Tropicana . . . Excalibur . . . Aladdin . . . Dunes . . . Bally's . . . Caesar's Palace . . . Flamingo . . . Mirage . . . Sands . . . Desert Inn . . . Frontier . . . Stardust . . . Riviera . . . Circus Circus . . . Sahara . . .

I found all of these legendary establishments disappointing. Without the dazzling nighttime splashes of light and color, the gigantic signs and marquees seemed starkly two-dimensional and purposeless, like debris left over from a motion picture company that finished shooting last week. Even the Mirage's spectacular waterfalls were so unlikely in that desert setting that they looked like props someone hadn't got around to disassembling. The crowds of tourists — sparse at nine in the morning — completed the illusion; they behaved like extras mistakenly left behind, and they milled about the abandoned sets, hurrying from ancient Rome to the Old West, from desert oasis to oriental palace, from Arabian Nights to Gay Nineties to Roaring Twenties to Medieval England, as though they were frantically searching for jobs in the next film sequence. The only structures that seemed permanent were the scaffoldings. At any moment of any year, new casinos are being built, old ones are being enlarged or remodeled, and still older ones are being torn down. Locals joke that Nevada's state bird is the crane.

I asked the cab driver about Diamond D's. He shrugged. "It's a drag of a hotel, but it's your money and your vacation."

"Right," I said. "What I want is a quiet week with very little action."

He sent a suspicious glance at me by way of the rear-view mirror. "I guess Diamond D's is okay if you're looking for a cheap place to stay. Most people don't spend much time in their hotels anyway."

We turned onto a side street and found Diamond D's, which some ancient business eddy had left stranded a short distance south of the Casino Center and a light year from the high rolling action on the Strip. It had been refurbished within recent memory, and it had the look of being well-maintained and well-run, but I suspected that it was exactly what the driver had called it, a drag of a hotel, the kind that is filled with elderly bargain hunters who have to save up for their vacations. In Las Vegas, having to save for a vacation is considered a lesser form of destitution. The favorite Las Vegas visitor is the "George," the high-rolling tourist who tokes — or tips — flamboyantly. The vacationer with so little financial margin that he has to save for the trip is likely to be a "Stiff," a cheapskate who doesn't toke at all.

The casino of any Las Vegas hotel is the tail

5

that wags everything. Finding the registration desk by way of the hotel's front entrance, which invariably opens into the casino, can become a major expedition requiring maps and a compass, but the cab driver thoughtfully swung around to a side entrance that led directly into Diamond D's small hotel lobby. I tipped him enough to bring a note of sincerity into his "Have a nice day," surrendered my suitcases to an ancient retainer who tottered with them despite the fact that I have learned to travel lightly, and strode into the lobby.

"I have a reservation," I told the room clerk. "The name is Pletcher."

I filled out a form while he looked up the reservation.

"Mr. J. Pletcher?" he asked finally.

"Correct. The 'J' stands for 'Jawohl,' but I never use it."

He shot a puzzled glance at me but managed to keep his smile in place. "You'll be staying for a week?"

"At least a week if my plans don't change."

The elderly bellhop claimed my suitcases again, took the room key, and escorted me to an elevator. Renovated hotels can look brightly new — Diamond D's did — but inevitably their elevators give them away. We creaked our way to the sixth floor. The bellhop placed my suitcases on racks, took a quick turn around the room to make certain the previous occupant hadn't stolen the bed and plumbing fixtures, accepted my tip, and left. I allowed him time to get off the floor before I followed him. The room was comfortably sized and neatly and attractively furnished, but for the amount of time I expected to spend there, none of that mattered.

Downstairs, I turned toward the casino and was immediately overwhelmed by pounding noise and cigarette smoke. Casinos may differ in size, in the ages of their slot machines, in the tone and quantity of the ballyhoo they dispense, in the stylishness of their décor, and in the thickness of their carpets, but behind all of that is a generic casino atmosphere that none of them can escape: Music, either canned or live, provides a throbbing background against which coins rattle into slot machine collection pans like the sound of a corps of different drummers. The machines emit their own kaleidoscopic range of sounds and music when they pay off and sometimes when they don't. All of that is drowned out by regular, grating blasts on the PA system announcing that a lucky lady from Vermont has won five hundred dollars or a luckier gentleman from Texas has won a thousand. The lady from Wisconsin whose losses have just passed the seven hundred mark, and the man from Idaho who just dropped his third thousand, are not commemorated.

I am mildly allergic to cigarette smoke. I can tolerate it when I must, but the atmosphere of any Las Vegas casino inflicts a severe test of endurance on me. Even a non-smoker's clothing will be permeated with smoke after a few hours of carefree gambling. In the interest of public health and safety, every casino should be required to post environmental ratings on both air and sound pollution.

Diamond D's hostess, whose name was of course Miss Diamond Dee, greeted me effusively. She was pertly blonde and very, very cute. She surely had to be twenty-one and prove it in order to work in a casino, but she looked like a high school cheerleader despite the sensational maturity of her frontal elevation. Splashes of sequins masqueraded as diamonds on her 1890s-style dance hall gown. At that time of morning, the room's bleary gambling population would have required more than a cheerleader to excite it, and her enthusiasm seemed not only ineffectual but downright silly.

She tried to present me with a sheaf of coupons entitling me to discounts and freebies, including a free pull on a slot machine. I shook my head gently. "My religion forbids me to gamble," I told her. "I only came here to gloat over the certain fate of these sinners." She gave me a blank look, but after that she directed her effusiveness elsewhere.

The bar, located at one side of the casino, had a row of video poker games built into it. While waiting for the bartender to mix a drink for me, I pondered the losing hand left behind by the last player. It provided a much more emphatic argument against gambling than my fictitious religion. I carried my drink to the keno lounge and found a chair where I could study the mechanics of the game as closely as possible while pretending to watch the sinners.

I was not in Las Vegas for a holiday. Even in fantasy cities, people get into trouble, or they develop itches they can't scratch. If the police fail them, or if the irritation is personal enough and hurts badly enough, they turn to private detectives.

Joel Eckling, the owner of Diamond D's, had trouble that was too serious, or too confidential, to entrust to a local detective agency. He thought there was something wrong with his keno game.

Keno is one of the oldest known games of chance. It is a lottery type game similar to the many government-run state lotteries that are impoverishing people so successfully, and it was operated as a national lottery in China a couple of thousand years ago. The original game, which employed a hundred and twenty Chinese characters, was brought to the United States in the nineteenth century by Chinese laborers. Eventually it was Americanized using eighty Arabic numbers.

From a gambler's viewpoint, the game is easy to play and easy to understand. It requires very little skill. You simply cross off as few as one or as many as twenty of your favorite numbers on a keno ticket — which has numbers from one to eighty

— present the ticket at the counter, pay your money, and sit back to wait until the current game's twenty winning numbers have been posted. There is no other game in which one can win so much by betting so little.

There are two methods used by casinos for selecting the winning numbers. Eighty Ping-Pong-type balls, bearing numbers from 1 to 80, are mixed by a blower that forces air through a transparent chamber called a goose — actually, it is a large glass fishbowl-like container, sometimes referred to as a crystal ball with ears — or they are mixed in a rotating wire cage. For each game, the twenty winning numbers are mechanically selected at random from this random mix, and with either system they are kicked up into two appendages positioned like a wide V at the top of the aparatus, ten into each. The winning numbers are announced on the PA system as they are selected. Lighted keno boards display them throughout the casino. If you so desire, you can play keno while having dinner, playing the slots, or shooting craps. Keno runners will take your money and tickets to the keno counter and bring back your copies, and you can follow the game on the nearest keno board.

Unlike people who play the state lotteries, you don't have to wait for the weekend drawing to find out you didn't win anything. There is a new game every few minutes, twenty-four hours a day. The games run faster late at night or during the morning hours because the lounges are less crowded and it takes the writers less time to record the tickets.

I spent almost an hour in Diamond D's keno lounge studying the selection of winning numbers and the handling of the tickets. Diamond D's used the transparent mixing chamber with a blower. The air pressure made a miniature fountain of the balls, and the winning numbers were caught by a mechanism placed in the center. It looked like a completely random process, and casino security certainly included an arrangement of cameras that automatically took still photos at crucial moments or videotaped the entire process. Venerable dodges such as faking the draw or announcing numbers other than those drawn were impossible. Further, tickets were recorded on a computer before the game began. They were numbered consecutively and photographed in the order in which they were played, and I could see no way that anyone, even an employee, could slip a ticket into a game after play was closed and the numbers had been called.

Behind the keno counter was a raised desk where the supervisors did their paperwork. From that vantage point, they could see everything that transpired.

When I had studied the system thoroughly, I left. I passed Miss Diamond Dee again on the way out. She ignored me.

I toured the Casino Center — the term refers to downtown Las Vegas and the concentration of casinos along Fremont Street from Main to Fourth with overspills a block north on Ogden and varying distances south and west — visiting all the casinos within walking distance and watching the keno play. The more I saw, the more baffled I felt. The security seemed impeccable, and the precautions I could glimpse from the customer's side of the counter would be no more than surface indications. With so much money at stake in every game, it was understandable that casinos would go to great lengths to avoid being cheated.

At the same time, the situation was complicated enormously by the fact that casinos expect their customers to win. When that happens, they brag about it. Some of them post signs: Keno Payouts: Yesterday, $36,842. Last Month, $697,366. Some display copies of winning keno tickets.

This cheerful surrender of money is not motivated by beneficent impulses. Jackpots are good publicity for casinos. They encourage gambling, and the more money bet, the higher the profits. Regardless of how much the gamblers win, time and mathematics are on the casinos' side. In Las Vegas, the law of averages is an Eleventh Commandment promulgated for the benefit of casino owners. Further, much of the money won in gambling casinos is also lost there. A slot machine winner will greedily keep playing in expectation of more or larger jackpots and lose it all. A winner at keno may drop the bundle at roulette on his way out of the casino.

Mathematics to the contrary, someone had rigged Diamond D's keno game so expertly that jackpots were being paid with impossible frequency. A freakish run of big winners can happen at any casino, but that inexorable law of averages should provide compensating periods during which there are none. At Diamond D's, this hadn't happened.

I watched until my eyes became bleary, I racked my imagination, and at each casino I reached the same unshakable conclusion: There was absolutely no way to tamper with a game of keno.

2

IT WAS ALMOST TWO O'CLOCK WHEN I ABAN-
doned the keno lounges. I had a quick lunch at a
casino snack bar and then strolled two blocks north
to the City Hall, pausing along the way to buy a
map of Las Vegas. The City Hall, whose tower has
a curving facade and a shape like a thick wedge of
pie, is Las Vegas's most distinctive landmark north
of Fremont Street. If you ever chance to pass that
way, the mayor would be pleased to make your
acquaintance, especially if you are a distinguished
visitor with questions about the feasibility of moving your corporate headquarters to Las Vegas or
holding a major convention there. My business was
with the Las Vegas Metropolitan Police, who don't
get many distinguished visitors. I handed in my
card and asked for Lt. David McCarney.

The lieutenant came to the lobby to meet me,
which was nice of him. He shook hands politely,
escorted me to his office, and got me seated beside
his desk. He was a man of medium height, plump,
round-faced, with thinning curly hair. There was a

faint twang to his speech that I couldn't place. He looked like a very tired businessman.

He examined my card, which — below the fine print that lists the phone numbers of our Los Angeles and New York offices and their addresses, the Klemmer Building in Los Angeles, and Mayly Plaza in New York — states boldly:

LAMBERT AND ASSOCIATES
Investigative consultants

J. Pletcher

"Very nice," he said. "We don't often see an engraved business card. So you're J. Pletcher."

"The 'J' stands for Jeronimo," I told him.

"Sure it does. We don't receive many visits from Investigative Consultants, either. This is indeed an honor. Ed Barnes, of the Los Angeles Police, telephoned me this morning — at your request, I understand — and he told me all about you and your various names. He says you're very bright, and very capable, and you cooperate fully and keep all of your cards on the table. Lambert and Associates must be an unusual outfit."

"We are. We work for wealthy people, who are referred to us by other wealthy people. Publicity is the last thing we — or our clients — want. We let the police take the credit. When there is any."

"That's uncommonly nice of you. How long have

you been here?"

"I caught an early flight from L.A. and got in shortly after eight-thirty."

"Don't tell me you've landed yourself in trouble already!"

I shook my head. "I haven't even started. I've been handed a peculiar gambit, and I have a hunch it might get sticky."

"In what way?"

"Diamond D's Casino is having problems with its keno game. Is anything similar happening in the other casinos?"

McCarney frowned and tilted back in his chair. "For that kind of information, you'll have to talk with people at the State of Nevada Gaming Control Board. The board has its own investigative division, and if it suspects a scam, it'll keep extremely quiet about it until it's ready to break the case. Did Diamond D's give you any details?"

"None. Joel Eckling, who owns the place, telephoned my boss yesterday afternoon. In recent months, his losses — meaning his customers' winnings — have been enormous, and of course such a blatant defiance of the laws of mathematics is sheer blasphemy to a casino owner. My boss gave Eckling my name and phone number. One of his subordinates was to get in touch with me and furnish the necessary background information. Shortly after eight last evening, I received a call from one Harley Dantzil."

McCarney shook his head. "I don't know him. There's a Florence Stevens-Dantzil who is a pillar, and also a pill, on the local social scene. Is he connected?"

"The only thing I know about him is that he called himself Eckling's assistant. He gave me a page of instructions and nothing more." I got out my notebook. "He insisted that I take a Southwest Airlines flight from L.A. to Phoenix and change there to another Southwest flight that would put me in Las Vegas shortly after one o'clock today, thus inflating what should be a fifty-minute flight into an expedition lasting more than three hours. After that, his instructions get complicated. I quote: 'Bring with you some kind of bright yellow flower — artificial if you prefer. Before you leave the plane in Las Vegas, attach the flower to your left lapel. Check your luggage at the airport — you can pick it up later. Take a cab to the corner of Fremont and Second Street and enter the Four Queens Casino by its west entrance. Walk the entire block from Second to Third Street *inside* the casino, exiting by its east front door at Third and Fremont. Cross Third Street and enter Fitzgerald's Casino. Wait until a cab is available at the stand outside. Then dash out and grab it. Take the cab to the Showboat Casino, pretend to play the slots there, have a drink. Then take a cab back to the Casino Center and get out at Lady Luck Casino. Walk the block south from Ogden to Fre-

17

mont and turn west on Fremont, entering each casino and exiting by a different door if possible, checking frequently to make certain you're not being followed. If you're early, stop in any casino along the way and play the slots. Try to arrive at the corner of Fremont and Main, just outside the Golden Gate Casino, precisely at four o'clock.'"

I paused. "At that point, I finally get to meet Dantzil — perhaps. He described himself, told me what he would be wearing, and gave me instructions as to what to do if he doesn't show. All of that rigamarole, he said, is to make certain I'm not tailed to our meeting, and he cautioned me to keep looking over my shoulder every step of the way."

McCarney's eyebrows had arched impressively. He sat twiddling his thumbs for a moment. "It sounds like something lifted from John le Carré. Moscow Rules and such. This guy has been reading too many spy novels. All of that fuss when no one except him knew you were coming? Of course you took a direct flight instead of the roundabout one he chose for you. Are you actually going to act out the rest of that nonsense?"

I shook my head. "I'll wear the yellow flower when I meet him, since that seemed important to him, but I refuse to trek through those casinos, and I'm not going to take a cab out to the Showboat. I have my own methods for dealing with tails. I asked him what difference it made if someone does follow me. We aren't going to discuss state

18

secrets — at least, I hope we're not — and those who rigged the keno scam know it's certain to be investigated sooner or later. He told me again how important it is to be positive I'm not tailed when I meet him."

"It certainly does sound odd, but I can understand why Eckling would call in outside investigators. Casinos like to handle this kind of trouble themselves, and Diamond D's doesn't have a large security force. A complicated scheme for rigging one of its games would cause problems for it."

I shook my head. "There's more to it than that, I'm sure. Dantzil is behaving like a man who knows something."

"You figure he's scared?"

"He's in a panic. That's why I thought I ought to check with you. I enjoy complicated investigations, but I prefer a bit of advance warning if I'm about to walk into a combat zone."

"I don't blame you," McCarney said. "But I haven't heard a thing. For what it's worth, I have no notion at all of how one would go about cheating at keno — but the casinos aren't my beat, and my information about gambling comes mostly from personal experience."

"I watched the play at Diamond D's and several other places. The game looked invulnerable to me, but then — I'm just getting started."

"The casino security people aren't fools, and they've already seen everything. This must be a really ingenious scheme if it has them stumped. If there's any weakness at all in a security system, though, eventually a crook will spot it and find a way to take advantage of it."

I passed my notebook across the desk. "This is a telephone number I'm supposed to use if Dantzil fails to show. Could you give it a name and address?"

"Glad to," he said. He picked up his phone, asked the question, waited for the answer, and then wrote briefly before he pushed the notebook back to me. "Listed in the name of John Swailey. Swoboda Street — that's a bit of a surprise. It isn't the nicest part of Las Vegas. Where are you staying?"

"Diamond D's, of course." I got out my new map of Las Vegas. "What do you mean — not the nicest part?"

He showed me where we were and where Swoboda Street was. "As neighborhoods go, that one is rather run down. Nothing like what New York and L.A. have to offer, but it does seem like an odd place for an assistant to a casino owner to be hanging out. I am sure you're able to look after yourself. Keep me informed, will you?"

I promised to do so, shook his hand, and left.

The most curious instruction Dantzil had given to me was his insistence that I don my yellow flower the moment my plane arrived. Since he wouldn't be seeing me until we met on a street corner almost three hours later, it seemed unnecessary for me to identify myself flagrantly before I got off the airplane. I could only conclude that Dantzil had arranged for someone to follow me from the airport.

Having set me up for that, he then provided me with an absurdly complicated agenda designed to lose this tail several times over before I reached the corner of Fremont and Main. I had been severely tempted to return to the airport, join the crowd arriving on the plane I was supposed to take, and flaunt my yellow flower just to see whether anyone took the bait.

But all of that was Harley Dantzil's problem. Mine was simply to meet him, find out what he had to tell me, and get on with the case.

When I left City Hall, I walked down Las Vegas Boulevard to the corner of Fremont Street, where I stood in the doorway of an old-fashioned Woolworth store for several minutes watching passing cars and cabs and scrutinizing dawdling pedestrians. The store, with its many aisles, high displays of merchandise, and dual exits, was an ideal place for losing a tail. Unfortunately, I had none to lose. I paused there long enough to make certain I hadn't acquired one through divine intervention, parthenogenesis, or some related miracle like regeneration, which enables a lizard to grow a new tail, and then I slowly walked the five blocks to Fremont and Main Street.

The Las Vegas Club occupies the northeast corner of that intersection. Its floor layout follows the common casino pattern. The rows of slot machines angle away from the entrance, and every aisle is an uncharted passage into a bizarre unknown where the novice is surrounded and overwhelmed by gambling apparatus. Casinos seem to be deliberately designed to prevent a customer from escaping once he is safely hooked. The fire in the MGM Casino is still talked about in Las Vegas. Considering the difficulties I had in finding my way to the keno lounges of several casinos and then trying to find my way out again, I wondered how anyone had been able to escape from a burning casino. The aisles run in strange directions and take jogs. Whenever I thought I had a clear path to an exit, I would fetch up against a mirrored partition that was showing me where I had come from.

The Las Vegas Club offered the usual casino atmosphere of cigarette smoke and noise. Just inside the door was a double row of console video poker games, massive desk-like contrivances whose arrays of controls give gamblers the illusion of piloting a 747. I settled myself at the console nearest the door; flagged down a shapely, scantily costumed young lady who was taking orders for free drinks, a standard perk for Las Vegas gamblers, and asked for a gin and tonic; converted a five-dollar bill into quarters with the assistance of a less shapely and more fully clothed change girl; and set about losing money as slowly as possible while watching pedestrian traffic outside the door and looking across at the corner where my rendezvous was to take place.

My drink arrived, which gave me an excuse to interrupt my gambling until I had finished it. While I drank, I watched the other gamblers. Fewer than half the machines were in use, but people were drifting in, and by evening the place would be crowded. A little old lady in tennis shoes was taking advantage of the slack by playing three slot machines in rapid succession. She carried her coins in a plastic cup embellished with the Las Vegas Club's logo and the motto, "House of Jackpots since 1961," another perk for gamblers, and she ran back and forth, inserting money and jerking the handle of each machine as she passed it. She never paused to look at the result. The machine of course dropped down any winnings automatically. When four o'clock approached, I tabulated $4.25 worth of losses, attached the synthetic yellow flower to my left lapel, gave a final salute to the little old lady — who was much too engrossed to notice — and sauntered out to see what complicated mystery Las Vegas had prepared for me.

The west end of Las Vegas's Fremont Street has been called the most brightly lighted three-block area in the world. It is also disrespectfully known as "Glitter Gulch" because of the unrestrained exuberance with which electric signs and ornamentation have been applied. A fifty foot high animated, cigarette smoking, electric neon cowboy called Vegas Vic towers over the Pioneer Club at Fremont and First Street and booms out, "Howdy, podner, welcome to downtown Las Vegas," every few minutes. He is the cigarette manufacturers' ideal advertisement. He was erected in 1951, years before the Surgeon General's warning, and he has been smoking twenty-four hours a day ever since without a hint of lung cancer. Probably he does not inhale. He smokes and talks and waves and welcomes visitors without a break. His girl friend, the cowgirl atop the Glitter Gulch Casino across the street, has a much more relaxed attitude toward life. She does nothing at all, and she does it sitting down. Both of them ignore Old King Cole, who is perched on the Coin Castle, and the snobbery is mutual. The king is far too busy counting his money to indulge in social relationships.

At night, the flashing, whirling, flowing colored lights animate the multi-storied logos and come-ons and bestow rainbow complexions on the pedestrians who crowd the walks below. The bulky tower of the Union Plaza, with its splashes of red neon whipped-cream topping, looms at the end of Fremont Street like an advertising man's conception of an occidental Taj Mahal. Like so many things in Las Vegas, the topping is overdone. The Plaza would be rich enough without it.

24

At four in the afternoon, under the harsh reality of desert sunlight, one receives the unmistakable impression that this fantasy landscape was wrought of converted W. T. Grant and J. C. Penney emporiums. Glitter Gulch's unlit facades look as unattractive and spurious as the store fronts of the synthetic ghost towns that are such a thriving industry in the West. Without the distracting dazzle and movement of colored illumination, all of the magic of Las Vegas is reduced to foot-high letters that deliver such timeless proclamations as **NEVADA'S LOOSEST VIDEO POKER;** and **97.4% PAYBACK ON SLOTS;** and **MOST LIBERAL "21" IN THE WORLD;** and **DOUBLE ODDS ON CRAPS.**

The moment my foot touched the curb of the southeast corner, a young man pushed diagonally through the throng of pedestrians and accosted me. Such is my deductive skill that I had reached two conclusions about him before he opened his mouth. First, his name was not Harley Dantzil. There was no part of him that matched the description Dantzil had given of himself. Second, if I ever needed an inconspicuous messenger, this one would be a desperate last choice. He was six feet two inches tall with the biceps and reach of a prize fighter. His nose had been broken at least twice. His conservative suit and necktie contrasted sharply with the casual dress of the tourists who crowded past us. Despite his bulk, he was reasonably presentable, and a young lady who wasn't overly discriminating might have considered him handsome.

He spoke in tones that were barely audible above the talk and traffic noises that swirled around us. "Mr. Pletcher?"

I nodded.

"Harley can't make it." He pressed a slip of paper into my hand. "This corner is being watched. Go to your hotel. Call this number at five o'clock, and you'll be given new instructions."

He turned away, waited briefly for a green light, and headed across Main Street. The last I saw of him was his back moving toward the Union Plaza. I had to go through the motions of following his instructions, just in case he found himself an observation post across the street and watched me, so I mingled with the thronging tourists for a stroll east as far as First Street.

Downtown Las Vegas is too remote from the fabled Strip for anyone but a masochistic athlete to hike back and forth, but in either location, tourists may be seen swarming in all directions at almost any time of day and far into the night. The really dedicated gamblers attempt to leave money in every casino within walking distance like wild animals marking their territories.

I moved with the crowd, paused long enough at First Street to give my unexpected messenger the impression that I had believed him, and then returned to the Fremont and Main intersection. Mr. Harley Dantzil's instructions had been clear enough, and I wasn't about to run off at the behest of an unknown passerby who contradicted them.

Unlike the Las Vegas Club on the other side of Fremont, the Golden Gate Casino doesn't have a corner entrance. There was no way I could stand on the Fremont side without obstructing the flow of traffic, so I took up a position just around the corner on Main Street and waited for something to happen. There is an unmistakable air about a person who has to meet someone he has never seen before. He anxiously scrutinizes everyone who remotely matches the description he has been given. No one sent hopeful glances in my direction. The passing pedestrians, hurrying about their businesses of gambling or whatever, ignored me. My only accomplishment was the discovery of a plaque in the sidewalk on the Fremont Street side of the corner: *At this site the first telephone was installed in Las Vegas. Dedicated during Las Vegas' Diamond Jubilee October 1980. Central Telephone — Nevada.*

I briefly returned to the north side of Fremont Street and the enticing invitations of the Las Vegas Club, just in case Dantzil had got his own instructions twisted. He had described himself as short, thin, and balding, which made him as unlike the mysterious messenger as possible, and he had promised to wear dark-brown slacks and a yellow sport shirt splashed with bright red flowers under an unbuttoned brown sport coat. That combination would have stood out in most of America's downtown areas and especially so in a January Las Vegas where the tourists affected drab sweaters and souvenir sweat shirts. The temperature was already dropping. A few brave young ladies had paraded on Fremont Street in shorts under the noonday sun, but by four o'clock, they had long since run for cover. I saw no one with the slightest resemblance to the mental image I had fashioned of Dantzil, and I saw no one who appeared to be looking for me.

I crossed the street again and waited. Still no Harley Dantzil.

I had started toward First Street a second time when I suddenly discovered that my anonymous informant was right. The corner *was* being watched, and so was I. A woman had taken up a position at the door to the Golden Gate Casino, which was located a dozen paces from the corner, and she was observing my every move.

I was positive no one had followed me to Main and Fremont. Like the messenger, she must have been waiting for me. Since no one but Dantzil and I were supposed to know where I was meeting him, all of this was extremely interesting.

Las Vegas is abundantly populated with beautiful women for a very simple reason. Sex is part of the fantasy commodity it purveys. The show girls are gorgeous, and every casino has highly attractive girls who serve free drinks and encourage the gamblers by wearing the sexiest costumes seen anywhere since harems went out of fashion.

Prostitution is a local option in Nevada, and it can be an ostentatious big business where it is legal. In Las Vegas, where it is not, there are periodic police crackdowns, and it has to make do with the status of a quiet home — or motel — industry. One way or another, a lot of sex gets peddled, and a lot of attractive women come to Las Vegas to do the peddling. A girl with good looks and style has plenty of opportunities open to her if she doesn't mind the obvious risks. The style is more important than the good looks. Exquisitely handled, it can create a stunning illusion of beauty, and Las Vegas's beauties tend to be dazzlingly stylish.

The woman who had been observing me from the Golden Gate Casino's doorway was neither stylish nor beautiful. She was just a cut above being homely, and though I saw nothing wrong with her shopping for clothing bargains at K-Mart, she should have exercised a modicum of good taste in making her selections. Insipid pastels do nothing for hair that is a nondescript shade between blonde and brunette, and the appearance of a lanky female with thin, unattractive legs is not enhanced by short skirts.

I had noticed her shortly after I arrived — not because she was particularly noticeable, but because I have trained myself to observe. She appeared to be waiting for someone, and at first I placed no sinister interpretation on the surreptitious glances she sent in my direction. It is not a sign of perversion for a woman in her mid-thirties to openly appraise the men who drift into her orbit.

When I started my second trip toward First Street, however, I saw her hurrying after me. She did it in installments, moving from one doorway to another and anxiously trying to keep an eye on me while pretending to look into the casinos she passed. I amused myself by walking briskly all the way to Second Street while she alternately hurried and then lingered in doorways.

When I turned back, she waited until I passed her, and then she drifted after me, again moving from one doorway to another. As much as I wanted to find out who she was, I had far more important business on my mind: What had become of Mr. Harley Dantzil? I had to wait for him until four-thirty, another eight minutes, and — now that I knew I had a tail — the longer I waited, the more exposed I felt. The looming, booming Vegas Vic began to get on my nerves.

I was considering yet another walk to First Street when I found myself face to face with a girl. This one was genuinely beautiful without being stylish. She was dressed neatly and with good taste in a light-blue suit, and she had long black hair that no beautician had meddled with recently.

There was about her none of the pretentiousness, the air of having been dressed and coiffured by a Hollywood make-up man, that is present in so many of the girls who place themselves on display in Las Vegas. She might have been the receptionist in a dentist's office in Minneapolis, where the glow of her presence would have lent pleasurable overtones to the most severe toothache.

She said quietly, "Mr. Pletcher? I'm Joletta Eckling. Harley asked me to meet you."

I pointed at the Las Vegas Club across the street. In doing so, I took a sidewise step to make certain that the woman following me wouldn't be able to lip-read either of us. "I'm being followed," I said quietly. "Pretend you're asking me for directions." I pointed across the street again. "Go over to the Las Vegas Club, find yourself a slot machine near the door, order a drink, and wait. I'll join you as soon as I ditch my tail."

Not only was she beautiful, but she was bright enough to catch all of that on the first pass without having a picture drawn for her. She said, "Thank you," turned, made a dignified sprint across the street on a yellow light, and vanished into the Las Vegas Club.

I resumed my pacing and meditated what I should do with the gawky female tailing me. Losing her would be no problem, but it behooved me to find out as much as I could about her. I had a hunch we would meet again.

I waited for the next green light, and then I crossed to the massive complex of the Union Plaza, which has hotel, casino, restaurants, a theater, and an Amtrak station all in one building. My tail had to abandon her coyness when I started across the street. She took two uncertain steps and then put on a spurt that brought her within a couple of yards of me. I strode along with a steady pace and paid no attention to her.

Once inside the Plaza, I walked the whole length of the casino — past the stage where a male and a female performer were offering something intended as vocal entertainment while gyrating approximately in time with the music; past the almost empty arena of table games where only a few people were playing craps, roulette, or blackjack at that time of day; past scattered stands of slot machines — and went directly to the men's room. There I tossed my yellow flower into a wastebasket and sought the ultimate privacy available, where I quickly removed coat and necktie, leaving my shirt open at the collar. On my way out, I restyled my hair, parting it in the middle and giving it an unruly, ruffled look in front. All of this took less than twenty seconds. I was emerging, coat over my arm, appearance altered, before my tail had settled on an observation post. She was still looking about for one while trying to keep an eye on the men's room door.

I passed within three feet of her, and she didn't

give me a second glance. She was such a novice that she had no awareness at all of what I actually looked like. All of her concentration had been focused on the patterned sport coat with the highly conspicuous yellow flower, and she was poised to react the moment she saw it again. I wondered how long she would wait for me. I hoped sincerely that having to watch an unending procession of males giving their flies one last check as they emerged from the rest room would not permanently warp her psyche.

Before I left the Plaza, I found a pay telephone and dialed the number Harley Dantzil had given to me. I waited for twelve rings before I hung up. The phone call had been included in my instructions. If he failed to meet me, I was to call at any time after four-thirty.

The twelve unanswered rings were not part of his plan. He had promised to be waiting for the call.

The young man who presented me with a phone number, and the beautiful young lady who was supposed to be waiting for me in the Las Vegas Club, posed problems I most emphatically did not like. Already my case was a tangled mess, and I hadn't even made a beginning.

Harley Dantzel had been afraid of something. I still had no idea what it was, but I was beginning to feel decidedly uneasy myself.

3

JOLETTA ECKLING WAS SEATED AT THE SAME video poker console I had used, but she was making no pretense of playing it. She had been watching for me anxiously, and she sprang to her feet the moment she saw me. I continued to give her high marks. Not only did she recognize me at once, but she made no mention of the change in my appearance.

"Why aren't you having a drink?" I asked her with mock sternness.

"I don't drink," she said. She made it sound like a confession of wrongdoing. We stood facing each other with the clamor of the casino vibrating around us. Music blared; slots beeped and honked; jackpots rattled down with an artfully contrived slowness that made them sound far larger than they were. Casinos practice audio psychology with their slots. A jackpot never gushes out in a sudden Niagara of wealth. It comes haltingly, almost reluctantly, in the form of a stuttering dribble, with each coin producing its own distinct metallic reverberation. If the sound continues, and even a middling jackpot seems to go on and on and on, passing gamblers begin edging toward it with avid curiosity — one might even say greed — in their faces.

A casino is an excellent setting for the study of psychology — that of casino owners as well as gamblers — but it is a lousy place for getting acquainted with someone or even for carrying on a serious conversation.

Joletta asked anxiously, "Why would anyone be tailing you? You just arrived, didn't you? I thought no one except us knew you were coming."

"I've been wondering about that myself. Maybe Harley talks in his sleep. When we see him, we'll ask him about it. Just in case someone else is hanging around this corner waiting for me, I suggest that we talk somewhere else."

We walked east on Fremont with me striding quickly and her keeping up with small, hurried steps. I had no idea where we were going, but I wanted to put the congested corner of Main and Fremont behind me as quickly as possible. What we needed was a quiet lounge where no one would think it the least unusual if a man and a woman sat apart from the other customers and conversed in hushed tones.

Unfortunately, there was none available. Las Vegas has the strangest "downtown" in America. The stores and shops and services one normally would expect to find within walking distance simply don't exist. There are no independent restaurants except on the fringes where one can find a McDonald's or a scattering of small take-out places in various dialects of Chinese. There are no bars or lounges. All of these functions have been taken over by the casinos, which operate them as adjuncts to their gambling businesses. You cannot shop in downtown Las Vegas except at Woolworth's or an assortment of souvenir stores. If you want refreshment and quiet conversation without the casino clamor, you must grab a cab and head for the outskirts.

I mentioned the problem to Joletta, and she led me to the Horseshoe Casino's downstairs coffee shop. It was moderately busy, but I spotted a booth that offered relative privacy, and the hostess, scenting a romantic tryst, smiled and seated us there. It was horseshoe-shaped, which seemed appropriate, and large enough for five or six diners. We sat close together at the rear and kept our voices low. Although it was not a classy setting, at least it offered an escape from the casino racket.

The waiter brought menus. Neither of us wanted food, so Joletta asked for orange juice, and I ordered coffee. When the drinks arrived, she took a deep sip and sighed. The tension of meeting me, of being chased away, of worrying about whether I would show up again, and finally of our gallop to this nondescript rendezvous, had unsettled her, but now she was able to relax.

I was not. My case was still a tangled mess, and I very urgently wanted to know what had happened to Harley Dantzil.

"Are you related to Joel Eckling?" I asked. Eckling not only was the owner of Diamond D's, but when Lambert and Associates got around to submitting a bill, it would be sent to him. A meddling relative of his could be a problem, and I needed to know exactly who Joletta was and whether she was meddling with our client's permission.

"He's my father," she said. "I manage Diamond D's Casino."

It sounded like a big job for a girl her age, but I kept the thought to myself. "When did you see Harley last?" I asked.

"Last night. I was working late, and he came to my office and talked about this problem before he telephoned you."

"What's the problem?" I wanted to find out how much she knew about it. I also wanted to make certain she really was Joletta Eckling.

Her eyes widened. "Didn't Harley tell you?"

"He gave me detailed instructions for meeting him. I was to be briefed after we met." This was true. Dantzil hadn't mentioned the problem. My boss, Raina Lambert, had told me about it, and she got the information directly from Joel Eckling. I asked again, "What's the problem?"

"There's something funny going on with the keno game at Diamond D's."

"Someone has rigged the game?"

She nodded. "It must be that. The winnings have been unusually high for some time. During the past six months they suddenly got much worse. The casino has taken a beating. It makes no sense at all. It's as if the laws of mathematics have been suspended."

"It sounds unbelievable," I agreed. "When did Harley tell you to meet me?"

"It must have been almost four o'clock when he telephoned. He said he wouldn't be able to make it. I was to meet you and take you to my office, and he'd come there as soon as he could."

"Did he give you a reason?"

"No. I was frantically busy, telephones ringing, people waiting to see me, customers' complaints to handle." She sighed. "I was so afraid I'd be late."

"Harley gave me a phone number to call if we missed connections," I said. I showed it to her. "Do you recognize it?"

She shook her head. "It isn't a Diamond D's number."

"He promised to wait there for my call. Please excuse me a moment. I'll see if I can reach him now."

She was enjoying the relaxation too much to protest.

Casinos have taken great pains to eliminate anything extraneous that might be a distraction to gamblers. There are no clocks in a casino. Anyone worried about the time is not properly concentrating on losing money. The newer casinos don't even have outside windows. In the older buildings, windows are blocked off by slot machines or other paraphernalia. Some casinos even banish the rest rooms to out-of-sight, out-of-mind locations.

That ultimate distraction, the telephone, can be located only with persistence and luck, but I already knew where the Horseshoe's telephones were. On our way to the coffee shop, I had seen them hidden under a stairway near the point where the Horseshoe ostentatiously displays a million dollars for the consolation of gamblers who have just lost their shirts.

I dialed Harley's number and counted eight rings before I hung up. It was almost five o'clock, so I waited until the digital display on my watch showed a five and two zeros, and then I dialed the number the mysterious messenger had handed to me. I got a busy signal. After thirty seconds I dialed again. Another busy signal. Third try, ditto. On my fourth attempt, the phone rang. A woman's voice answered immediately.

"Pletcher," I said. "Calling as instructed."

She said uncertainly, "This is a pay telephone. I was about to use it when it rang."

"Thank you," I told her.

I'd never had an opportunity to see a million dollars all at once, so I paused for a look before I returned to the coffee shop. I found it disappointing. The display consists of a hundred ten-thousand-dollar bills secured between thick sheets of plastic. A million of anything sounds like quite a lot, but reduce it to a mere hundred, five rows with twenty bills in each, and it becomes something that could be stuffed into a pocket.

Joletta Eckling was contentedly nursing her orange juice when I returned. She greeted me with a smile. "This tastes good. I didn't realize how thirsty I was."

A bus boy was clearing off a nearby table. I waited until he had finished and moved out of hearing before I spoke. "Please don't feel offended," I said. "I have to make certain you really are Joletta Eckling. What was your mother's maiden name?"

"Rogers," she said. She seemed more puzzled than resentful.

"Where was she born?"

"Sioux Falls, South Dakota."

"Does your father have a middle name?"

"It's Oliver, but he hates it."

"Where was he born?"

"Somewhere in Wisconsin. I never can remember the name of that place. Fond something."

"Fond du Lac?"

"That's it."

"When is his birthday?"

"July 9." She straightened up suddenly and gave me a perplexed look. "How do you happen to know all those things?"

"I don't," I said.

"Then — I could have told you anything at all!"

"Of course, but if you did, it would only take one phone call to make a liar of you. You sound genuine to me, so I won't bother to check."

She relaxed again and sipped her drink. "It's nice to get away from the casino for awhile. They're all alike, aren't they?"

"They certainly have all of their worst features in common, including atmosphere. I would enjoy discussing them with you. Unfortunately, right now I have work to do. Harley's failure to meet me is only one of several things that are decidedly wrong about this keno problem of yours."

"I can't imagine what could have happened to him — he's one of the most dependable people I know. But he did sound odd on the telephone."

"He sounded odd last night when he talked with me on the phone. Why this elaborate folderol for a business meeting? Why not simply meet in his office at Diamond D's? You say he called you just before four?"

She nodded. She said uneasily, "He didn't mention anything being wrong, just that he couldn't make it, but I know he was worried about meeting you."

"How long have you known him?"

"Since I was a child. He's worked for Diamond D's longer than I am old. Where could he be?"

41

"That's what I intend to find out. You go back to Diamond D's, and I'll meet you there."

"What are you going to do?"

"Look for him."

"Where?"

"Swoboda Street."

She frowned. "*Swoboda* Street? I don't know it. What is it near?"

"It's out Fremont," I told her. "Somewhere in the vicinity of Eastern Avenue."

She wrinkled her nose. She wrinkled it very nicely. "That's a run-down part of town, isn't it? Why would Harley be there?"

"It's the address for the telephone number he gave me."

"I'll come with you."

I looked at her levelly. She returned the look without flinching. The hardness in her eyes suggested dimensions to her character that belied her sweet-young-girl appearance.

I decided to let her come. She was, after all, the daughter of the man who would pay the bill, and I preferred to have her on my side. She would be exposed to nothing more dangerous than a cab ride in Las Vegas, which according to the *Las Vegas Review-Journal*, or maybe it was the *Las Vegas Sun*, is the most civilized city in the world.

But of course I said no. She said yes, very firmly.

"We may be dealing with a crime, and criminals

42

play rough," I warned.

"I'm not afraid."

"Come along, then, but be prepared to follow orders. If I say 'Jump!' I want you to jump. Instantly. Leave the arguments for later."

"Why do you think criminals are involved?"

"Because there's money involved. Let's go."

Dusk was already upon us, and the air was cooling rapidly. I had left my topcoat at Diamond D's, and I felt chilly without it. Joletta had forgotten hers in the rush to meet me. Fortunately there was a taxi stand outside the Horseshoe with a cab waiting.

"Take us east on Fremont and let us out just before we get to Swoboda," I told the driver.

"There's nothing there!" he protested. I thought for a moment he was going to argue, and so did he, but he subsided and drove off. A cab driver has to be a philosopher in order to survive. If he cultivated psychology instead, and tried to figure his customers out, he would be in therapy before the end of the first week.

In the Casino Center, Fremont is a one-way street for westbound traffic, so we drove north to Ogden Street and east all the way to Twelfth before we returned to Fremont. The driver was right — there was nothing in the bleak neighborhood around Swoboda that any rational person would pay money to get to. Flotsam from an earlier age had settled there. Fremont Street, which eventually

43

becomes Boulder Highway, was at one time a major route into Las Vegas. The usual clutter of businesses grew up along it, among them auto courts — later called motels — and cut-rate hamburger emporiums dating all the way back to the days of the great depression. Some of those early businesses, or their descendants, have survived, including a scattering of motels that extends almost to Glitter Gulch.

Some have not. The failed motels were small and Spartan compared with modern establishments. Their rooms were cramped and poorly furnished. They lacked amenities such as swimming pools, and their air conditioning was primitive. It was increasingly difficult for them to compete with the newer motels, and when interstate highways cut the flow of potential customers along Fremont, they fell on evil days. They were torn down, boarded up, or converted into apartments that were every bit as unattractive as the motels had been.

The driver plainly doubted the sanity of anyone making a call in that neighborhood. After I had looked about, I agreed with him. "You'd better wait for us," I said. I tore a page from my notebook and scribbled Harley Dantzil's address on it. I handed it to him along with a hundred-dollar bill. If you want a cab driver to do something out of the ordinary, you must start by letting him know you have plenty of money and aren't bashful about spending it. "This is where we're going. Find yourself a parking place. Give us half an hour and then come looking for us."

He glanced at the address. "Is that the former motel around the corner?"

"I don't know. I've never been here before."

"They didn't waste much remodeling on it when they changed it to apartments," he said grimly. "It's still a dump."

"Right. We may be back in a moment or two. If we aren't, come looking for us in half an hour."

At the corner we turned south on Swoboda, walking on the opposite side of the street from the run-down former motel. I hoped that anyone seeing us would mistake us for a pair of tourists in pursuit of a wrong address.

On the corner was a boarded-up gasoline station. Behind the station, a much-deteriorated sign celebrated the Lazi-Daze Motel, a name that surely deserved its present fate of peeling paint and missing letters. There was a single-story structure on Swoboda that had served as the motel office. It was now the office for the apartments, and it bore a carelessly lettered sign over the door, "L D Apartments, Furnished, Weekly or Monthly." The vacancy sign was nailed in place; the L D Apartments had permanent vacancies. Behind and perpendicular to the office were the former motel units, two long two-story buildings. They were back to back, and their backs were blank walls with a narrow space between them. On the front side each unit had porches the length of the building on both levels. An outside stairway at each end gave access to the upper story.

On the other side of the street, the one we were walking on, there were a few one- and two-story houses, also dilapidated. I could understand McCarney's remark that this was not a nice neighborhood.

There was no clue as to how the apartment numbers ran. The mysterious John Swailey, whose telephone number Dantzil had given me, occupied 212A. The two hundred had to mean the upper level, but the *A* could have indicated either building. It should have been easy to stroll over and find out, but nothing about this case was turning out to be simple.

I spoke softly to Joletta. "That apple-green Volkswagen parked just ahead of us has two men sitting in it. *Don't stare at it!* As we walk past, take a casual glance in that direction and tell me whether you've ever seen them before."

She nodded.

"Just one quick look, mind you," I warned her. "Pretend you aren't really interested."

We passed the parked car. She took her one look; I was directing my attention at a house number on our side of the street, but I also snatched a glance just in case I encountered the men again in less casual circumstances. In the growing dusk

46

it was difficult to see them well, and I had noticed them from a distance only because one of them lit a cigarette, but even in dim light, their size made them memorable. They were huge. Seated together in a Volkswagen, they were like two carp in a sardine can.

"No," she said when we had walked another twenty feet. "I've never seen either of them. Why do you ask?"

"Because they're watching the apartment buildings."

Their interest was reason enough to look for another approach to the apartments, perhaps by way of an alley if there was one. We walked on. Beyond the former motel, there were run-down houses on both sides of the street. We went all the way to the end of the block, where I paused to record the Volkswagen's license number in my notebook. Then we turned, crossed Swoboda, and continued along Cutler Street. Joletta glanced at me a couple of times, but she was astute enough to say nothing.

The Volkswagen was an antique — 1950s vintage — and only rank amateurs would take such a conspicuous car for a stake-out. Further, the two men weren't displaying newspapers or any of the usual trappings for camouflage. They were so intent on watching the apartments that they hadn't even turned their heads when a pretty girl walked past.

47

Whatever their experience in the stake-out business, they obviously were tough characters, and I was liking the situation less and less. I regretted bringing Joletta along, but it would have been a waste of breath to try to send her back to Diamond D's now.

We found an alley that ran down the center of the block and connected with one I had seen behind the closed gasoline station. I turned into it. Joletta hesitated and then hurried to catch up.

"Detectives do very little walking on clouds," I told her. "When you go out with one, you have to expect an alley now and then."

Both of us were feeling cold, so we moved as quickly as we could. The alley was unpaved, and we had to pick our way around puddles, probably left where someone had washed a car. Most of the fences were of the rickety-picket variety, but one stretch of woven-wire was in better shape than the buildings it was protecting. There were sagging garages whose peeling roofs were incongruously moss-covered. Several were being used as living quarters. Some of the larger houses had been divided into apartments. The telltale clues were the number of mailboxes in front and the walks that led around the house to various entrances.

Across the alley from the L D Apartments was a large, relatively new complex of single-story structures containing rows of small apartments. The looming L D buildings looked huge by comparison. Lights were appearing here and there, and a bright light had been turned on over each of the L D stairways. Fortunately the stairs were attached to the ends of the buildings, and those at the rear were not visible from the street.

I made out a large *B* on one building. We moved on and approached the next stairway without being challenged. The first-floor apartment had a window that was just above our heads as we started up the stairs, but no face looked out.

When we reached the second-floor porch, 212 was the end apartment. There was a light on inside. I knocked twice, then three times, then twice. The code meant nothing at all, but any neighbor who heard it might assume that a caller who rapped an obvious signal was expected. When you invade a strange building, it is important to create the impression that you belong there. I knocked a second time, same code. There was no response.

An expert locksmith could have opened the door's antique lock with a hairpin. So could I, but I was in a hurry. I depressed the catch with my pen knife and swung the door open. All the curtains were drawn, and a dim overhead light was on. I quickly checked to see whether anyone was lurking behind the door, and then I pulled Joletta inside and closed it, touching only the edge and leaving it slightly ajar because I didn't know how quickly we might have to leave. Joletta gasped as she entered. I had already seen the thin little man who lay at the far end of the living room. His contorted posture could only mean death.

I had to make certain there was no one else in the apartment before I gave him my attention. Not until I had inspected the bedroom and turned on a massive table lamp — which had another dim bulb — did I kneel beside him. Joletta remained standing by the door.

A private detective's options with a newly discovered corpse are limited. He is well advised to look quickly and keep his hands off. Perhaps an astute operative who dabbled in psychology could have prepared a ten-page character study based on the fact that the victim had chosen a black tie with an orange pattern to go with a blue suit and a pink shirt, but I wasn't qualified. It was much more important to me that Mr. Harley Dantzil, if this were he, had been bashed on the head before he changed into the outfit he promised to wear when he met me.

I noted several pronounced indentations in the balding skull. The dead man had not merely been struck; he had been battered. There was no blood, but the forensic surgeon who performed the autopsy would find quantities when he opened the skull. A disarrangement of the shirt collar suggested strangulation as well.

"Is it Harley Dantzil?" I asked.

Joletta nodded. She whispered, "Is he . . ."

50

He was. I placed the back of my hand against his face. It was cold. He had been dead for many hours. I checked an arm and then an eyelid. Rigor was fully established. My new job had become a police case the night before while I was still in Los Angeles.

"Didn't you say he called you just before four and told you to meet me?" I asked her.

She nodded dumbly.

"Better give some very careful thought to that telephone call," I said. "The police will have questions about it. They may even want to talk about it for hours. At a quarter to four, Harley was extremely dead. Probably he was murdered before midnight last night."

4

JOLETTA SEATED HERSELF ON THE SAGGING sofa and tried not to look in the direction of the corpse. I picked up the telephone, using my handkerchief to grip the handset by one end while I dialed with a ball-point pen. The voice that answered had that detached matter-of-factness that only a police operator can achieve. I asked if Lieutenant McCarney was still in the building.

"Pletcher," I said when the lieutenant's voice responded. "Dantzil didn't show, so I went to the Swoboda Street address. That's where I'm calling from. Dantzil has been murdered."

McCarney exhaled a sharp whistle. "How long has he been dead?"

"Hours. Probably since last night."

"You said you talked with him last night. What time was that?"

"Shortly after eight o'clock. One item of interest. This place is being watched. Two men in a vintage green Volkswagen." I read the license number.

"Is the address that former motel just off Fremont?" he asked.

"Right. The 'A' building is on the left, and 212 is upstairs at the far end. There's access from the alley as well as from Swoboda Street."

"Sit tight. You'll have company shortly."

"One more item. A stranger was waiting for me when I went to meet Dantzil. He recognized me immediately, probably from the yellow flower. He told me Dantzil couldn't make it and handed me a phone number to call at five o'clock for new instructions. It turned out to be a pay phone — first I got nothing but busy signals, and then a woman who'd stopped to use the phone answered. You might send a car to see if anyone is still waiting there for the phone to ring. You might even send someone to watch the phone and then have someone else call the number to see if anyone runs to answer it."

"Will do," he said.

I read the phone number to him. Then I hung up and took a quick turn around the apartment. Despite the shabby furniture and worn vinyl floor covering, the place looked so neat and clean that it had an unlived-in air about it. Even the murder had been done neatly. There was no mess, no sign of a struggle. Dantzil had admitted the murderer and led him to the far end of the room, probably to talk. Three chairs stood there in a conversational grouping. He offered his visitor one of them,

53

unwisely turned his back to take one himself, and was struck once, viciously, from behind. He collapsed, and while he lay on the floor, the murderer hit him at least three more times just to make it emphatic. The strangling came at the end because he was still breathing.

The apartment had been fashioned from two motel rooms by the simple expedient of cutting a connecting door. The unit we were in had served as a living room, and its bathroom had been transformed into a tiny kitchen by substituting a counter and cupboards for the bathtub and a small range for the toilet. There was insufficient room for a refrigerator — that was in the living room. Except for the three chairs already mentioned, which looked like refugees from a good dining room suite, the furniture would have garnered no bids at a public auction. Everything was worn, or sagging, or teetering, or all three; table tops were cracked and scarred; the antique refrigerator was scratched as though someone had tried to play ice hockey on it. Obviously the landlord placed a minimal interpretation on the word "furnished."

I restrained my curiosity about the contents of cupboards and drawers. If I were patient and cooperative, I would get all of that from the police.

I sank into the room's one overstuffed chair — the word *sank* was literally correct — and studied the corpse of Harley Dantzil for a moment. Joletta watched me and said nothing. I continued to think

54

highly of her. A woman who knows when to keep her mouth shut has mastered one of the most difficult problems in human relationships.

"What was Harley's position at Diamond D's?" I asked.

"He didn't have a 'position.' He was just an employee."

He had been at everyone's beck and call, she said. He was stuck with the jobs no one else wanted or had time for. He did them ineptly, he did everything ineptly, but apparently no one at Diamond D's expected this kind of thing to be done well. Other than that, he frequently had to poke around and look for things to do just to pretend he was earning his pay.

"He called himself your father's assistant," I said.

"He was father's lackey. He really wasn't good at anything except maybe personal errands. He was an expert Christmas shopper. He'd put in a lot of time and find things no one else would think of. Sometimes father let him do little favors for the casino customers or the hotel guests. He enjoyed that. He was so concerned and thoughtful, and people really liked him."

Dantzil had tried to dabble in casino security. He would get himself up in a silly disguise and wander about watching the gambling and pretending he was a spotter, an employee who mingled with the customers and kept a close check on what was going on. His disguises were a joke and an instant giveaway. If he'd had the astuteness to be himself, everyone would have taken him for a vacationing Sunday school teacher from Terre Haute.

Joletta knew very little about his personal life except that he had an extremely rich wife who was regularly featured in the society pages — but always as Florence Stevens-Dantzil, never as Mrs. Harley Dantzil.

I got down on my knees and looked under the sofa and the overstuffed chair with my penlight. There was no accumulated dust and dirt. The vinyl had been waxed recently. The standard of housekeeping seemed entirely inappropriate for the address.

One small object caught my eye. I slipped a shoe off and raked it out without touching it. It was a partially used book of matches from Lon's 24-Hour-Cafe on Las Vegas Boulevard.

I looked about for ashtrays and then asked, "Did Harley smoke?"

She shook her head. "He had emphysema. He quit smoking years ago. The smoke can get pretty thick in the casino, and sometimes it gave him problems."

I sat down again and resumed my thinking.

When I finally heard footsteps on the stairs, my mental agitation had accomplished nothing at all.

A sergeant named Dunkor and two detectives were the first arrivals. Lieutenant McCarney had paid me a compliment. Normally a patrol car would have been dispatched. If the officers confirmed that the case looked like a 420, a homicide, their sergeant would have investigated the matter himself and then requested a homicide detail. McCarney took my word for it and sent the homicide officers immediately.

Dunkor questioned Joletta and me with polite formality. Credentials and recommendations aside, those who discover a corpse can expect the investigating detective to experience twitches of curiosity about them. He would be remiss if he did not. Since I had been in Los Angeles the previous night, and Joletta had worked until after midnight within sight of whatever late crowds Diamond D's could muster, the interrogation wasn't a long one.

The sergeant politely inquired into my motives for manipulating the lock on the door. "I'll give it to you in as much detail as you like," I said, "but surely you don't need the young lady any longer. She'll be available at any reasonable time, and she'd prefer to be interrogated without a corpse on the floor."

"You'll be at Diamond D's?" he asked her.

She nodded.

"All right. You can go."

"What about the Volkswagen?" I asked.

"Lieutenant McCarney is looking after that."

"I'd rather the men in the Volkswagen don't see her leave. Would you mind if I check on the lieutenant's progress before she goes?"

He raised his eyebrows. "One of those cases. I'll find out for you."

He got only as far as the door. Lieutenant Mc-Carney opened it and then stepped aside to admit the technicians. Dunkor spoke quietly to him. Mc-Carney scrutinized Joletta Eckling before he turned to me. "You came in the back way?" he asked.

I nodded. "I didn't want those characters to see us coming here. What'd you do with them?"

"I let them go. I know both of them, though they aren't aware of that. They gave me Seattle addresses, but they come from Frisco. Frisco told us they might touch down here, and we've kept an eye on them since they arrived. The one in the driver's seat was Robert Smith. When he first came here I thought he was calling himself that for protective coloration — there must be two or three dozen Robert Smiths in this city — but no. Frisco claims it really is his name. He's also known as Breezy Bob — he always does the talking. The other calls himself Ben Bolt, and I'd love to know where he got that. They claimed to be waiting for a friend named Joe Esset, who was calling on someone in the house across the street, and of course Joe Esset really was calling on someone there.

"Esset has been hanging around for several years without doing anything we could prove. He was upstairs in the apartment of one Jesse Derman. The place is a two-family house, though it doesn't look it, and Derman and his wife have the upstairs apartment. As far as we know, they're law-abiding. I think our three friends picked Derman up because he has a convenient address for watching this place. Any time Esset showed up there with a couple of six-packs, he had squatter's rights on the front window for as long as the beer lasted. Do you figure those characters are important?"

I was entering the names in my notebook. "Right now everything is too muddled for figuring. I have a cab waiting around the corner. If you'll excuse me for a few minutes, I'll escort Miss Eckling down to it."

"It's downstairs," McCarney said. "The driver got curious when he saw us arrive. I told him to wait here."

The driver was afraid he had put his foot into something. I assured him both of us were innocent and rewarded his diligence. Then I sent Joletta back to Diamond D's with him.

I went upstairs again and was interviewed by Dunkor. There were repeated flashes in the background as the technicians photographed the murder scene. When Dunkor was finally convinced that he knew everything I could tell him, I waited with McCarney for a report from the patrol car sent to check the pay telephone. When it finally came, he swore bitterly.

"They blew it," he said. "They drove right up to the phone and got out. Naturally they didn't see anyone waiting there. While they were scratching their heads and wondering what to do next, a car parked a short distance up the street suddenly roared away. They didn't even get the license number."

"When I called, there must have been a line waiting to use the phone," I said. "A woman standing there answered before they could get to it. They were still hanging around just in case I might try again, which is interesting. It'd be nice to know why."

I regretted the wasted opportunity, but I'd suddenly had more lines to reel in than I could handle.

I asked about Lon's 24-Hour-Cafe.

"Cheap food but good for the price," McCarney said. "The place is clean and well-run. It's a long way from here, though. People in this neighborhood wouldn't be likely to go all the way to Las Vegas Boulevard just to eat at Lon's. There are other places a lot closer. But if one of them happened to be in that vicinity when he got hungry, he'd probably eat there."

"The question is how Harley Dantzil comes into it," I said. "He doesn't belong at this address. He looks out-of-place here even as a corpse. He functioned as a kind of supernumerary at Diamond D's, but he must have been paid a decent salary in addition to which he had a rich wife. Also, he worked in the Casino Center where bargain meals and buffets are a menace to the waist line. Surely there was no reason for him to eat at Lon's. And since he didn't smoke, he had no use for matches. So who brought them?"

The lieutenant had a question he liked better. "Whose apartment is it?"

One of the detectives had gone looking for the manager. He finally found him at a neighbor's house and brought him up to us — a gaunt, elderly man named Chris Olsen. Olsen squeamishly identified Harley Dantzil as one John Swailey, who had rented the apartment a month before. Olsen knew virtually nothing about him except that he had seemed like a decent, quiet person, and he had paid a month's rent plus a deposit with no problem and no protest. Olsen hadn't seen him since he rented the place. His month wasn't up until Saturday, and there had been no complaints about him from the other tenants.

The manager was permitted to leave, and Dunkor intimated that I was free to follow him.

"I'm waiting," I said, "to see whether you turn up a murder weapon. Whatever dented Dantzil's skull wasn't the sort of thing that's normally carried in a vest pocket. If the murderer picked it up here and used it on the spur of the moment, I'm wondering why he didn't leave it. I make it out to be about the diameter of a broomstick but very heavy

— a piece of galvanized iron pipe sounds ideal. Eighteen inches would provide the proper leverage, but he could have managed with less. Was it someone who normally has a piece of pipe about him — a plumber, for example — or was it someone who just happened to have one with him last night? Or did Dantzil keep it on that rickety coffee table to use for mixing drinks?"

Lieutenant McCarney grinned at Dunkor. "Send someone to check the alley," he said.

Detectives were canvassing other tenants for information. No one responded to their knocking at the next apartment, number 210, but they reported lights on and music playing softly. McCarney went to see for himself, and I followed him. He marched past 211 — now an outside entrance to the bedroom of Harley Dantzil's apartment — and kicked resoundingly on the door of 210. There was still no response. He kicked again. And again. He shook the building. He was about to give up when the door jerked open and a man faced us angrily. "What is it?" he demanded.

He was a heavyset, overweight, balding man wearing a dirty white shirt and baggy, stained trousers. His shirt was open at the collar, and both sleeves were carelessly pushed up above his elbows. From the room behind him came the relentless beat of rock music. The volume was turned so low that the music was an indistinct mutter, but the throbbing beat had a life of its own.

"Police," McCarney told him curtly. "Lieutenant McCarney. Your neighbor has had an accident. I'd like to ask you some questions about him."

"What neighbor is that?" the man asked.

"Next door. John Swailey."

The man frowned perplexedly. "I have a lousy memory for names. John . . . Swailey, you say? I'm not sure I know him."

"You don't know a person who's lived next door to you for a month?"

"People come and go in a place like this," the man said with a shrug. "Some only rent for a week. I might know him if I saw him, but I wouldn't know what his name was. What sort of an accident did he have?"

"A fatal one. Come and see if you can identify him."

The man trailed after McCarney, and I brought up the rear. In Swailey's — or Dantzil's — apartment, Dantzil had been turned onto his back. The man took one quick look.

"Oh," he said. "So that's who he is."

He retreated all the way to his own apartment without another word. At the door, he turned and faced us. "Come in," he said.

He occupied a larger apartment than Dantzil's, one that had been fashioned of three motel rooms. He gave us the freedom of a cluttered living room with a gesture and went to turn off the music. In the next room, an enormous, paper-littered table served as a desk. At one end was a computer. Two large hi-fi speakers were aimed at a swivel chair. Whoever worked there floated in sound.

On top of each speaker was a glass cage. There was an iguana in one, and I caught a glimpse of a snake in the other.

The room beyond was the bedroom.

This apartment's furniture was in good condition, but the walls were a mess — they were shedding wall paper — and the vinyl floor covering was curled and cracked. Newspapers piled in the corner were still folded as the newsboy had left them. Obviously our host had very little interest in current events.

The music halted abruptly, and the man returned, mopping his face with a soiled handkerchief. He dropped into a chair and peered first at the lieutenant and then at me. "John — what did you say that name was?"

"Swailey," McCarney said. "Incidentally, who are you?"

"Excuse me. I'm Wilbert Kuyper. About this Swailey . . ."

He paused. McCarney finally asked, "Did you hear any unusual noises last night — say between 10:00 P.M. and 2:00 A.M.?"

Kuyper shook his head. He pointed at the speaker arrangement in the next room. "I'm a computer programmer," he said. "Self-employed. I write software for business firms. When I'm working, I have to concentrate totally. Any time my train of thought is derailed, it can cost me hours or even days of work. So I play music when I'm working, or I wear ear plugs. Or both."

"Were you working last night?" McCarney asked.

Kuyper nodded. "Working today, too." He added resentfully, "You interrupted me. When I have a job, I work until I finish it. I do damned little sleeping and eating until it's done."

"I see. While you work, you're blind and deaf. A man lived next door to you for a month, and you never saw him or heard his name before."

"That isn't what I said," Kuyper said plaintively. "I've seen him before, but I never heard him called — what was that name?"

"Swailey. John Swailey."

Kuyper shook his head. "No. I never heard that. How long did you say he'd lived here?"

"The superintendent said a month on Saturday."

"He's been around a lot longer than that. I wouldn't say that I 'knew' him, but I've been seeing him now and then for — oh, for a year or more. Maybe almost two years."

"Seeing him where?" McCarney demanded.

"Here. In this neighborhood. Sometimes in this apartment. But I never heard him called John Swailey."

"How about 'Harley Dantzil'?" McCarney asked.

Kuyper pondered that. "Not 'Dantzil,'" he said finally. "I don't remember that. But 'Harley . . .'" He paused. "Yeah. Maybe it was 'Harley,' but I wouldn't swear to it. I just don't remember names."

"Suppose you tell us about it," McCarney suggested.

Kuyper had little to tell. Since he was self-employed and had all the jobs he wanted — with a waiting list — he took one at a time and worked on it nonstop, barely pausing for necessities until he finished it.

He got rid of the accumulated tension by giving a party for himself. He would pass the word — "Tonight I'm celebrating" — and his neighbors, most of whom were barely acquaintances, would drop in and drink his beer and liquor and consume his food and make merry. They were people who lived in that apartment building or in others nearby, but occasionally total strangers who happened to be visiting in the neighborhood would join them. When he'd had his fill of partying, he threw everyone out, cleaned up the mess, and went to bed and slept for about twenty hours. Then he started his next job.

That was how he met the man he had seen lying on the floor next door. Either Swailey had been living somewhere nearby, heard about Kuyper's parties, and came when he got the word; or several times he had chanced to be visiting in the neighborhood when Kuyper announced a party. "I may never have heard his name," Kuyper said. "There's no reason why I should at a party."

"I suppose no one gets introduced at your parties."

"Hell, no. As far as I'm concerned, I don't want to know who they are. All I want is people around me for a few hours — someone who'll talk and laugh and never mention computer programs."

"Any girls come?"

Kuyper snorted. "We don't have 'girls' in this neighborhood. Leastways, I've never met any. No ladies, either. Women come now and then. Mostly someone brings them. Why not? They like to drink and eat, too."

"Did Swailey ever bring a woman with him?"

Kuyper leaned back with his eyes closed, thinking. "Not that I recall," he said finally. "I don't even remember seeing him talk to one of the women. He said very little. Sat in a corner munching on something. Didn't even drink much. He was one of those guys you know at a glance has never had any fun and is never going to have any."

McCarney thanked him and told him there certainly would be more questions later. We returned to Dantzil's apartment. The officer Dunkor had sent to prowl the alley was still at it, from which the sergeant concluded that the murder weapon hadn't been found. Another detective had discovered Dantzil's four-year-old car parked at the end of the block on Cutler Street. He noted nothing unusual about it except its location. He offered a neat theory that Dantzil had left his car there the previous evening and sneaked to his apartment by way of the alley because the building was being watched, but that collapsed when another detective turned up the information that Dantzil always parked there.

I'd had my curiosity aroused on a couple of points, but I preferred to find the answers myself. When I told McCarney I was leaving, he wanted to know what I thought.

"I would very much like to know whether this is connected with the problem I'm supposed to be investigating, or whether it's the result of an extracurricular activity," I said.

"I'd like to know that, too," McCarney said.

"Dantzil doesn't seem like the type," I went on, "but when a man of his age and position hangs out in this neighborhood and rents this dump of an apartment under an assumed name, either he has something extracurricular going or he's doing a lot of wishful thinking. But he still could have been knocked on the head because of Diamond D's keno problem. I need to go somewhere and cogitate. I have a hunch this case is going to require a lot of that."

"I feel the same way," McCarney said. "If you solve it, you will let us know, won't you?"

I promised to do that and left.

5

ONE OF THE PATROL CARS GAVE ME A LIFT
as far as the cab stand at the Showboat Casino. I
told the cab driver what I wanted, and then I had
to repeat it twice. Cabbies develop a "here to
there" mentality, and the notion of going from A
to B by way of C and D takes time to penetrate.

First we returned to the neighborhood of
Dantzil's apartment and drove slowly through the
nearby streets. I wanted to get the feel of the area
and perhaps arrive at a fumbling understanding of
why Harley Dantzil had sought refuge there. The
neighborhood was as run-down as I'd thought.
Eventually a developer would buy up the crumbling
buildings and move in bulldozers. That already had
been done with the land occupied by the new apartment complex behind the L D Apartments. It faced
Farnby Street, the next street over, and was ap-
propriately called Farnby Apartments. The neat
brick buildings looked well cared for, and the management was even trying to grow lawns and trees.
Otherwise, as Lieutenant McCarney had said, this

was not the nicest part of the city, and I picked up no clue as to why Dantzil had chosen it.

When I had seen enough, we headed for Las Vegas Boulevard by way of Charleston and found Lon's 24-Hour-Cafe. It shared an old-fashioned commercial block with four other business establishments: a pawn shop, which in Las Vegas is an institution almost as ubiquitous as the slot machine; a hardware store; a liquor store; and a dry-cleaning establishment. Across the street was a vacant structure that once had been occupied by an auto repair shop. That stretch of Las Vegas Boulevard showed the inevitable signs of decay, destruction, and renovation that alternately blight and regenerate a city's major traffic arteries.

I asked the driver to pull to the curb a short distance past Lon's, and I walked back slowly and pretended to read the bill of fare posted in the window while I studied the interior and tried to get an idea of the clientele. I strolled to the end of the row of stores and back again, pausing to look at the menu a second time before I returned to the cab. The food was generic greasy-spoon-Americana with a Mex touch, but I wasn't looking for a place to eat.

Large city police forces have resources in personnel and equipment, and in technicians and laboratories, that no private detective can compete with, but these assets sometimes constitute a severe disadvantage because they must be used. The

70

police must investigate every clue, at least until clear-cut lines of investigation emerge. The private investigator can follow the most wildly improbable hunches. If he is wrong, no harm is done. The methodically plodding police will sift the clues his flights of fancy left behind. If he makes a lucky guess, he can advance the case by a quantum leap.

An up-to-date criminologist might apologize to himself for bothering to notice a hackneyed clue like a book of matches, but I had a hunch about this cafe. I saw no reason for Dantzil to go slumming so far from his usual orbit when he felt hungry. Since he was a non-smoker, he certainly wouldn't be picking up matches for his own use. Therefore the matches in his apartment must have been dropped by a visitor. Because the room had been cleaned regularly, it had to be a recent visitor.

At that point, my brilliant chain of deduction snapped. The restaurant kept a box of match books on the counter by the cash register. Customers helped themselves. Dantzil's visitor could have eaten at Lon's only once, months earlier, or he could have asked a total stranger for a light. I knew the probable reaction if I were to question the elderly woman at the cash register about people who had picked up matches during the past year. I decided to save Lon's 24-Hour-Cafe as a last resort.

I rode the cab back to the Casino Center and paid the driver what was rapidly becoming a king's ransom. Even for a city where money is thrown about recklessly, Las Vegas's cab fares raise eyebrows and tax the credulity of expense account auditors.

I didn't know what to do next. I needed orders, but they wouldn't be available until after 9:00 P.M. Glitter Gulch was now awash with splashes of multicolored illumination except for the block-long facade of the Golden Nugget, whose subdued lighting and simplicity of design make it an unexpected oasis in a garish wasteland. I began a second tour of the keno lounges, wondering what Harley Dantzil had known that made someone want to murder him.

Most casinos strive to make keno one of their most attractive pastimes. They supply comfortable lounges, and they are lavish with bargain food, bargain tickets, and free drinks. Why not? At twenty-five to thirty percent, the house's take is greater on keno than on any other game the casinos offer, and millions of dollars pass over the Las Vegas keno counters each year.

Keno is a leisurely pastime when compared with other casino games. Most bets are small, and there is ample time between games to check results and search for a new set of lucky numbers. You can lose a fortune at blackjack or craps during the time it takes you to work your way through a couple of twenty-dollar bills at keno unless you insist on buying several tickets for each game.

Keno is a game for the elderly. As I went from casino to casino, I saw few young people in keno lounges. Often every player was a senior citizen. The pace is slow, especially during the busy hours, and playing it for long periods of time requires patience. It is a passive game that makes little demand on the players. There are no handles to pull as with slots, no dice to throw as with craps, no cards to finger as with blackjack, no chips to keep track of. There are no quick decisions to make. Some casinos let you play the same numbers for ten or even twenty consecutive games — which the casinos like to call "races" — with one trip to the keno counter. Then all you have to do is relax, enjoy the free drinks that a charming young lady will bring to you from time to time, and check your ticket after the winning numbers are called for each game. It is by far the most comfortable and relaxing way to lose money that Las Vegas offers.

Keno customers don't hit or score — they "catch." Bet eight numbers, catch five. Bet five numbers, catch four. In my case, the game gave me plenty of time to think about Harley Dantzil, but I caught nothing at all.

I moved to another casino and thought again with no better result. Apart from the two kinds of chambers for mixing the numbered balls and selecting the winners, there also were differences in the ways the casinos handled the tickets, but every casino had what looked like a foolproof system for registering and copying them, and every casino kept the ticket the customer had marked and gave the customer a copy of it.

A keno ticket is divided into two rectangles. The numbers 1 through 40 are arranged in four rows in the upper rectangle, and the numbers 41 through 80 are arranged in four rows in the lower. This plan has little significance for modern players, but the Chinese are said to have ascribed deep psychological meaning to the selection of characters in one half of the ticket as opposed to the other.

Casinos that think they have more affluent customers may require higher minimum bets than a place with a proletarian clientele like Diamond D's. Every casino has its own special keno promotions with fancy names. The "Incredible Seven" was a game one casino offered where the player picked seven numbers. He could win $20,000 on a two-dollar bet if he hit — or "caught," as the casinos prefer to say — all seven, thus beating odds of about 41,000 to 1. He won only $800 for catching six of the seven. The "Remarkable Twenty" was a game where the player picked twenty numbers for a five-dollar bet. He had to catch 10 or more to win a noticeable amount of money, but from that point his winnings rose sharply — $200 for 11, $1,000 for 12, $5,000 for 13, $12,500 for 14, and $25,000 for 15. If he caught 17 or more, beating odds beyond the capacity of a pocket calculator, he won $50,000, which is not a bad return on a five-dollar investment. There even was a booby prize of $500 if he managed to pick 20 numbers and not catch any.

There are "way" or "combination" or "split" tickets in which multiple arrangements of numbers are played on the same ticket. These provide a mental challenge for those who scorn the simplified gambling that a straight ticket makes possible, but to keno purists they are unnecessary complications.

Eventually I found myself back at the Las Vegas Club. The video poker game both Joletta and I had sat at was unoccupied, so I reclaimed it, watched the flickering tracery of artificial lights on the passersby outside, sipped a free drink, and meditated while absently inserting coins and pushing buttons.

As I watched the passing pedestrians, I became increasingly puzzled. Las Vegas had to equal the sum of its parts, and tourists surely constituted only one of those parts. Some seventy percent of the population of Nevada lives in this small corner of the state. There had to be large numbers of secretaries, attorneys, construction workers, clerks, real estate agents, salespersons, school teachers, plumbers, factory workers, janitors, and every other employment classification — not to mention bargain-hunting housewives — traveling to and from jobs, going to lunch, eating out, shopping, and finding ways to entertain themselves.

75

There should have been a rich mix of local residents in the flow of tourists, and I hadn't been able to recognize any.

The tourists would have been easy to distinguish had there been anyone to distinguish them from. During the day, many of them have the look of having just got out of bed. And why not? They were up all night gambling or watching the high-rollers, and now they must wallow in the throes of groggy indecision as to which casino to hit for a late bargain breakfast or an early bargain supper.

The absence in that flow of foot traffic of anyone who appeared to be a resident puzzled me. I saw an unending stream of tourists punctuated only by an occasional panhandler. Except for casino employees, local residents were leaving the Las Vegas fantasy to the visitors. I wondered whether there existed somewhere within the all-embracing tentacles of this glittering, artificial city a normal, homey, bustling town struggling to get out.

The question was relevant. I felt certain that the murderer I sought was not a tourist. I couldn't imagine one of these dazed movie set extras finding his way to a shabby building in a remote, run-down part of Las Vegas and denting Harley Dantzil's skull with a piece of iron pipe he just happened to have up his sleeve.

A life had been crushed out with brutal force, and that kind of murder has to be done in great anger or with enormous purpose — or both. Dantzil seemed like a meek, unimaginative type who followed orders and asked no questions. Such types don't ordinarily incite friends or even enemies to overpowering rage — only to great contempt, which rarely terminates in skull bashing; but neither do such types rent slum hideaways or create elaborate spy story scenarios for meeting a visitor. I very much wanted to know whether Harley Dantzil was equally fanciful in the company he kept.

I got to my feet, picked up the five quarters the machine returned to me, noted a gambling loss of a dollar seventy-five, and left. As I paused for a moment in the doorway, a different kind of movie set extra strode past. This one was a refugee from an outer space film — *The Perils of Planet Q* or some such thing — and he was wearing sleek knee boots, a tight-fitting, one-piece silvery suit that looked as though it had no fastenings, and a short cape. There was a wide raised collar that could have functioned as the base for a space helmet when one was needed. I stared after him for a moment, and then I took off in pursuit like a child following the Pied Piper.

The Old West theme is so common and so commonly celebrated in Nevada that a mounted posse picking its way through and around the Fremont Street traffic or a herd of longhorn cattle moving down the Strip with cowboys in attendance would be accepted without a raised eyebrow as either a celebration or an advertisement. Reincarnations of Old Western towns or forts are prominent sightseeing attractions, and they offer dramatized shoot-outs and even simulated hangings for the titillation of tourists. Museums dedicated to the good old days when insanitary violence raged unchecked are to be found everywhere. Rodeos are big business throughout the state. I have mentioned Vegas Vic, the animated, cigarette-smoking cowboy who presides over the Fremont and First Street intersection and welcomes visitors to downtown Las Vegas. Most souvenir stores offer Western "cowboy" hats.

A spaceman seemed unreal even among the crowds of motion picture extras, and this one definitely interested me. I had seen, hanging from a leather loop on his belt, a metallic tube some eighteen inches long and slightly larger around than a broomstick with a bulge at one end — an ideal size and shape, in fact, for producing the kind of dents left in Harley Dantzil's skull.

I followed him a block north to Ogden Street and then along Ogden Street to a parking structure. There he shattered my illusion by joining two similarly dressed spacemen who appeared to be waiting for him. I was expecting something like the starship *Enterprise*, but he climbed into the rear seat of an ordinary Ford Escort that was several years old and badly in need of washing. As the car made its leisurely way out of the parking structure,

I wrote down the license number, though I felt foolish in doing so. I also copied the logo painted on the side of the car: NEVADA 2100.

I returned to Diamond D's. There was a new Diamond Dee exercising her wiles in the casino. She was older and much more poised than the one I had seen earlier but so similarly proportioned that she could have been wearing the same sequin-spattered gown.

I avoided her. I still didn't want a free pull on a slot machine. I wanted to know what Harley Dantzil had known about rigging the keno game. I went to my room, slipped my shoes off, and sat down in the room's one chair with my feet on the bed. This elegantly relaxed posture did nothing to stimulate my thinking processes. Shortly after nine o'clock, I was back downstairs at a pay telephone.

I dialed the number I had been given. The familiar voice of Raina Lambert, the guiding genius of Lambert and Associates, answered. I rarely meet with her, though we communicate frequently. She firmly believes that close contact between co-workers results in the type of familiarity that breeds contempt. Whenever we work together, my link with her is a telephone number. She always arranges in advance to occupy a hotel suite or an apartment with a private telephone — she refuses to talk business on any contrivance connected with a switchboard. She rarely bothers to tell me where she is staying, and I have learned not to ask.

I said, "I want to go home. I can't seem to get the right perspective on this place. It's starting to look real to me, and that means the real world has gone bonkers."

"Have you turned up anything?" she asked.

"Too much," I said. I described the adventures that had culminated in the discovery of Harley Dantzil's body.

She said, "Damn. I suppose the murder has to be connected with the gambling scam."

"Not guaranteed but likely. Dantzil was behaving like a man who knew something. Unfortunately, he tried to act on it himself."

"We don't know that. Perhaps he intended to tell you all about it."

"Someone thought he intended to," I said.

"What are you going to do next?"

"Browse around unless you have something in mind. I won't be able to function effectively until I get the feel of this place."

"Has it occurred to you that an ambitious crook with a successful keno scam would certainly try it on more than one casino?"

"Of course, and the scam would go unnoticed longer in the larger casinos. A side street place like Diamond D's is much quicker to scream for help when the odds don't seem to work out. All the casinos should be checked, but that isn't my kind of problem."

"I've already taken steps," she said.

"Is the State of Nevada Gaming Control Board your beat or mine?"

"I talked with a member of the board this afternoon. It was the board's auditors who discovered the problem for Diamond D's. The casino's win percentage on its keno game was way out of whack. The board put in undercover people to try to figure out what was going on. The casino hired them in the usual way, and they worked with its regular employees. They couldn't find a thing wrong. They thought it was a mathematical fluke that would correct itself. They were wrong. It not only continued, but it got much worse."

"Then the experts had a shot at it before we were called in."

"That's right."

"I watched a lot of keno today. The only thing I could think of that would influence the outcome of a game would be telekinesis — controlling the the Ping-Pong balls by mind power. You wouldn't even have to be efficient. Eight balls out of the twenty chosen are only forty percent, but that would win you fifty thousand dollars on a two-dollar bet. Pick eight and catch eight once every two months, and you'd have an annual income of three hundred thousand dollars. You could play at a different casino each time and no one would suspect a thing."

"It's impossible to see the numbers on the balls while they're in motion," she said. "Telekinesis wouldn't work, but we may find ourselves investigating stranger things before we're finished. Browse around, then, and see what you can come up with. Call me in the morning between eight and nine. If you lose more than a hundred dollars gambling, it's your own money."

"How can I get the feel of this place by losing a lousy hundred dollars?" I protested, but she had already hung up.

In the interest of research, I inflicted dinner on myself in Diamond D's restaurant. My first taste convinced me that Harley Dantzil had ample cause for patronizing Lon's 24-Hour-Cafe. I still didn't believe he had, but he would have been justified in doing so. The evening buffet at Diamond D's was inexpensive, inelegant, and inedible. Tourist literature touts the many buffets offered by Las Vegas's casinos as excellent dining bargains, but the quality can vary considerably. Diamond D's lasagna was flavored with taco sauce, and that put me in a mood to go rig a few keno games myself. I left my plate barely touched and went to consume a couple of passable hot dogs at the snack bar.

I called at the casino office to see whether Joletta Eckling was working late. She was, and she immediately told me she was extremely busy. There was no one waiting to see her, her phone wasn't ringing, and her desk was bare. She looked like an executive with plenty of time on her hands. Because I'm a detective, I instantly deduced that her feigned busyness was an excuse to avoid talking with me. I didn't want to talk with her, either, so my feelings remained unscarred. I needed to meet a veteran employee who could tell me something about casino operations.

"Who knows everything about the casino?" I asked.

"Mildred Comptom," she said instantly.

"Is she here now?"

Joletta nodded, blinking her long lashes at me.

"Would you introduce me to her and give me an imprimatur so I can ask questions and get answers?"

"Of course," she said. She jumped to her feet, left her pressing business to manage itself, and led me into the seething clamor of the casino.

I expected Mildred Comptom to be the current version of Miss Diamond Dee, but she turned out to be my maiden aunt. She wore a sedate dress, and she stayed behind the scenes or at one side, never crossing the center of a gaming area when she could circle around it, floating quietly in the background, and keeping an eye on everything. She was in fact Joel Eckling's special assistant and had been for years; and she had been acting as a spotter and working enormously long hours, Joletta said, because she was worried about the keno game.

Her slender, almost boyish figure and graying hair probably were assets in the sensitive job she held. The guests weren't likely to look twice at her, but employees were very much aware of her constant presence. Joletta Eckling was called the manager, several men with subordinate titles were actually running the place — I had seen them — but Mildred Comptom, who probably didn't appear in the table of organization at all, was the boss.

Joletta spoke into her ear briefly, gave me a nod, and left. Mildred Comptom guided me to a tiny office and closed the door on the pounding music, the honks and beeps of slot machines, the rattle of dropping coins. She got me seated, and then she perched on the edge of the chair behind the desk. "What can I do for you?" she asked.

"Were you here earlier today when I came in?"

She smiled faintly and nodded. My appraisal of her had been correct. She missed absolutely nothing. "I must have impressed you as a suspicious character," I said.

Her smile broadened. "Actually, you did. But after a few minutes I decided you were harmless. I see, now, that I was wrong. What is it you want?"

I was wondering why I hadn't noticed her. A crook would have instantly labeled her the most dangerous person in the casino — the more so because she was so inconspicuous. "For a start, tell me what the keno game looks like from the other side of the counter," I said. "Who are the people working on it, and what are they doing?"

"There are first, second, and sometimes third

shift bosses. They work at the raised desk behind the counter. The first shift boss runs the shift. He makes out work schedules, runs the games, supervises everything. He approves complimentary drinks and meals for gamblers or special guests. He has to approve all wins of ten dollars or more. He deals with any problems that come up. His assistants help with the paperwork and run the game in his absence. The people working at the counter are called writers. They copy the customers' tickets, register them, punch the draws — these are tickets with the winning numbers punched out so winners can be checked easily — and they pay off the winners. They may operate the keno machine and call the game."

"Are keno workers well-paid?"

"In comparison with other casino workers, they are very well paid, but they actually earn less money. That's because keno gamblers don't toke as much as the gamblers in other games. A blackjack dealer is paid less than a keno writer, for example, but he earns far more because blackjack winners toke the dealer generously."

"Tell me about the security precautions," I said. "Obviously there must be two kinds. One would involve the tickets — the paperwork."

She nodded. "Every customer's ticket is copied, as you must have noticed. In some casinos, the writers make the copies; with others, a computer prints copies. In any case, the casino always keeps the original, the ticket filled out by the customer. That's the 'inside copy.' It stays behind the counter, and the customer receives the copy the casino makes, which is the 'outside copy' — it goes outside the counter. Inside and outside copies are stamped with the game number, the date, the ticket's own unique number, and the time. There's another backup copy for emergency use, a copy of the copy. At Diamond D's, it is made by the computer. As soon as a game is closed, the writers close their stations, meaning that they accept no more tickets for that game. Each writer puts a yellow or blank sheet in the box — tray, actually — to open a game, with the number of the station and the writer's initials on it. While the game is open, all inside copies the writer accepts are placed in the box in order. Another yellow sheet goes into the tray to close the game. The tickets for each station are then photographed and stapled together."

"All of that happens before the numbers are called?"

"Of course. Obviously the paperwork must be completed first."

"The system looks impregnable," I said. "If the customer tries to tamper with his outside copy, he accomplishes nothing because the rules clearly state that the payoff will be made on the basis of the original ticket, which remains behind the counter. And I don't see how anyone, even an employee, could sneak a ticket into a game after the game was called — there's the stamped number and the sequence of photographs, not to mention the fact that it wouldn't be a part of the stapled group. I take it there have been no paperwork irregularities."

"None," she said.

"Very well. What's the security with the machine?"

"When the machine is turned on to start the game, three pictures are taken of it from different angles. Our first concern is to make certain that the ears are actually empty. If a sleight-of-hand were worked so that one ball remained in each ear and was counted in the next game, that would give a gambler a considerable advantage."

"In fact, two advantages out of twenty," I said. "Ten percent. If the circumstances were right, that could make someone a big winner."

"Indeed it could. So we make certain that the ears are empty at the start of a game — or, to put the problem another way, we make certain that all the balls have been returned to the goose, since several instances of employee cheating in casinos have involved manipulations of this kind. More photographs are taken automatically when the machine is turned off — in other words, when all twenty numbers have been caught."

"Do the photos show the numbers?"

"They do."

"Then the employee calling the game couldn't call his own set of numbers or even substitute one now and then."

"He could not. There are other checks when the game has a winner of a hundred dollars or more. We have to be constantly alert to the possibility of fraud. Years ago, the Gaming Control Board uncovered a scam in which a syringe was used to inject a fluid into some of the balls. There also have been attempts to use a heavy paint on the numbers of some balls. Both ploys would have increased the probability of those balls being selected. If employees are properly trained to watch for such things, this kind of tampering is quickly detected."

"Very well. I'm a winner. I marked eight numbers on a dollar bet and caught all eight. I return to the desk to claim my twenty-five thousand dollars. What happens?"

"First, the inside ticket is checked. The writer calls the ticket number and station number. At the desk, someone pulls the write for the game, finds your copy in the stapled group, and checks it with a draw — a ticket with the winning numbers punched. If it is indeed a winner, then the ticket is pulled from the group, leaving the stapled corner in place to prove where it came from so its numerical order in the group can be rechecked if necessary.

"Next, a ball report is made. This is done on a

88

special form if there's a winner of a hundred dollars or more. The form shows the position in the ears of each winning number. For a really large payoff, the balls are rechecked by the keno manager or — if he isn't available — a pit boss may be called in from another department to do it. He'll sign the report and indicate which writer called the game and who punched the draws. The winning ticket is stapled together with the customer's copy, the ball report, and a copy of the draw. If there's any problem at all, the films can be removed from the cameras and developed — we develop them ourselves."

"Say there's no problem," I said. "I chose my numbers, I paid my money, and I won, and now I'm standing here waiting while you go through all that rigamarole. When do I get paid?"

"As soon as the paperwork is finished, but you must identify yourself if the amount is fifteen hundred dollars or more. Internal Revenue requires it. You must furnish two forms of ID — a driver's license and a Social Security card. Then you have to fill out an Internal Revenue form W2G. After that, we can pay you."

"I see," I said. "You certainly cover every angle."

I was reminded of insurance company claim procedures. Insurance companies accept your premiums in a friendly and trusting manner, just as casinos accept bets; but the moment you have a claim, they get huffy and suspicious and demand all kinds of supporting documents. Few people think of an insurance policy as a form of gambling, but it is. You bet the insurance company that you'll have a fire. The insurance company bets that you won't. If you do have one, it calls in the equivalent of a pit boss and checks everything very carefully.

"What else do you want to know?" she asked.

"Please walk over to the keno lounge with me," I said. "I may have some questions there."

"Are you after anything in particular?" she asked bluntly.

"I don't know enough — yet — to have even an inkling of what I'm after."

At the keno lounge, she identified the people working that shift. It was called the swing shift, and at Diamond D's its hours were from five in the afternoon until 1:00 A.M. The grave shift worked from one to nine and the day shift from nine to five.

The shift boss, working at the raised desk behind the counter, was a middle-aged man named Clyde Goodler. The second shift boss was a younger man, Paval Jordanne. There were four stations open at the counter, and the writers working there were Seth Hollange, a young man in his early twenties, and three women: Tamara Johnson, Linda Bartkowiak, and Eloise Smith. I hoped the latter was not related to Breezy Bob Smith, the thug in the Volkswagen. That would have been what is called a complicating coincidence.

I wrote the information in my notebook though I had no immediate use for it. Raina Lambert would work through the personnel department to investigate the net worth of all of these employees and find out whether any of them were concealing an affluence beyond their visible means of support.

We had finished our conversation, and both of us were absently watching the activity around the keno desk, when someone called, "Mildred!"

It was a youth with a mop of blond, curly hair and an open, good-looking face. He was wearing a college sweat shirt with the message, *Runnin' Rebels*, but he looked far too young to be patronizing a casino.

He hurried up to us and asked in hushed tones, "Is it really true? Harley's dead?"

Mildred Comptom nodded.

"Murdered?"

She nodded again.

He stared at her. "That can't be! Why would anyone . . ." Then he turned away, tossed a mumbled, "Thanks," over his shoulder, and stumbled over to the nearest empty chair. He sat down and stared at the carpet, which at that time of day was cluttered with discarded keno tickets and litter from spilled ashtrays.

"Friend of Harley's?" I asked quietly.

She shrugged. "I'd call him an acquaintance. I doubt that anyone knew Harley well. He's Wes

Zerin, a former employee. Bright and very capable, but unfortunately he picked up the gambling habit. We discourage it. We won't let employees gamble here, but of course we can't control what they do elsewhere."

"So he ruined himself gambling?"

"No. He hit a jackpot down at Hacienda and won three thousand dollars. He quit his job and enrolled at the university. That isn't enough money to carry a university student very far, so he's trying to support himself by gambling while he finishes his education."

"Is that possible?"

"It's possible to try. Since he's still taking classes, I suppose it's worked for him — so far." She didn't sound optimistic about his future.

"How old is he?" I asked.

"At least twenty-five."

I wrote Zerin's name in my notebook with a reminder to investigate this original method of financing a college education. Then I thanked Mildred Comptom for the information. I certainly would need more later, but for the present, I wanted to watch the game and digest what she'd told me.

She resumed her inconspicuous prowling, and I studied the keno operation and asked myself how I would go about cheating. The casino's own security people, as well as those of the State of Nevada Gaming Control Board, hadn't found anything wrong. The scam that fooled those experts had to be extremely complicated or so simple as to be easily overlooked. Either way, I didn't think it could be managed without the collusion, if not the active assistance, of an employee.

Clyde Goodler was my nominee. If fraud had been perpetrated on Diamond D's keno game during his shift, he had to be involved. The other shift bosses came and went, helped the writers, ran errands. He remained at the raised desk where he could see everything that happened. He was a long-time employee and must know the game thoroughly.

That conclusion took me nowhere. Since he was the most obvious suspect, Goodler certainly had been investigated by the the casino's own security officers as well as the Gaming Control Board.

Harley Dantzil's unfortunate murder had been a stroke of luck for Lambert and Associates. It was unlikely that novice outsiders such as ourselves could figure out a gambling scam that had the local experts bollixed, but murder was something we understood. The Keno scam ought to come unglued the moment we cornered Dantzil's murderer.

Even so, I didn't see how it was possible to cheat at keno.

6

WHEN THE BLEAK SAMENESS OF ONE KENO
game after another got on my nerves, I wandered
about the casino until the noise overwhelmed me,
at which point I returned to the keno lounge.

Shortly after eleven, a group of drunken aristo-
crats staggered in, denizens of the much plusher
casinos on the Strip who were out slumming. The
men, plump millionaires all, were in evening dress;
the jewel-bedecked women were in low-cut evening
gowns. The contrast with Diamond D's casually
dressed regulars was startling.

The laughing, joking newcomers staggered toward a roulette table, bumping into slot machines
or each other along the way. They'd just had a hell
of a good time at a stage show, and now they were
ready to gamble. This is the allure of Fun City.
Most people win a little and lose a lot, but if they're
rich enough, they can even enjoy losing.

One of the women was a tiny, dynamic redhead,
far younger than the others, more stylish, and
much more attractive. It was my boss, Raina Lam-

bert, and her presence was a better indication of the net worth of these men than anything Dunn and Bradstreet could have offered. She collected millionaires, and while she gathered evidence for the current case, she would be subtly brainwashing her escorts. These wealthy men would never forget the tiny, beautiful, brilliant young woman who ran a detective agency named Lambert and Associates and called her operatives "Investigative Consultants." The next time they were confronted with a sudden threat to life, reputation, or business, they would know where to turn. If one of them made the drunken mistake of thinking her an ornamental plaything, however, his enlightenment would be both emphatic and painful. She was a master practitioner of every known form of armed and unarmed mayhem along with several unknown varieties she had invented herself.

Her group kept the casino in an uproar for an hour, lost enough money to make the management purr when the day's receipts were totaled, and then left in the same staggering rush with which it had entered. Relative quiet ensued, and it was possible to hear the pounding music and dropping coins again.

Except for the keno lounge, there is no place in a casino where one can sit down, relax, and watch what is going on, and keno lounges are usually placed in out-of-the-way corners where there is nothing to watch but keno. On my seventeenth circuit of Diamond D's, I noticed that the restaurant, which was separated from the casino by a low partition, had two rows of tables at the back that were elevated, so I persuaded the hostess to seat me at one of them. It gave me a partial view of the casino's main room.

I ordered a sandwich and a drink, and I had just settled back to review the day's strange events when a woman passing my table dropped her handbag. The contents spilled wildly. I politely helped her retrieve the clutter; in the process, she bumped her knee against the table leg and came up limping, so of course I invited her to sit down until she recovered, and I ordered a drink for her.

It was my unattractive friend from the corner of Fremont and Main, whom I'd last seen outside the men's room in the Union Plaza Casino, and I couldn't remember a more blatant pickup of anyone, anywhere. She was so much an amateur that she hadn't bothered to change her clothing, but I had been wrong on one point. She was able to recognize me without the yellow flower as long as I had my coat and tie on and my hair combed.

The back of the restaurant was almost quiet enough for conversation. My new acquaintance, who told me her name was Phoebe Wallark, tried to engage me in casual small talk, but for some reason her heart didn't seem to be in it. I wasn't as cooperative as I should have been because my mind wasn't in it. I was being entertained by the reaction of Mildred Comptom, who was watching with stern disapproval from a position just beyond the blackjack tables. She suspected me of playing when I was supposed to be working, and she should have known better. Any impartial judge would have listed Phoebe Wallark's playmate potential in negative numbers, and Phoebe seemed to be regarding me in the same light. She had managed to pick me up, but she had no idea what she was going to do with me.

Our conversation expired of mutual boredom. I turned my thoughts elsewhere, and she sat looking at me awkwardly. In another minute or two, she would have felt sufficiently embarrassed to thank me and move along.

Then I made an absent-minded remark contrasting the cheap glitter of Las Vegas with the barren desert that surrounds it. For some reason not entirely clear to me, this was an insult to the state she loved. She straightened her shoulders, looked me squarely in the eyes, and began to talk about her pioneer ancestors. They had survived enormous hardships to settle this harsh land, where they had to contend with drought and starvation, with Indian raids and the cussedness of what seemed like a grotesquely alien world to settlers from more favored regions in the East. They'd not only had to bring in water for their crops, but they had to learn how to make the most effective use of it in a soil perversely laced with boron and salt. They'd had to deal with strange new kinds of weed pests like tumbleweed, dock, and ticklegrass. They'd had to learn uses for whatever odds and ends nature condescended to provide in that bleak land — including that strange tree-plant, mesquite, which could be shaped into fence posts and tool handles and whose pods made a nutritive stock feed. Pioneers who turned to ranching had to master a whole new botany of poisonous plants, usually by costly trial and error when they found animals dead or in convulsions from eating an unlikely list of things I had never heard of, such as greasewood, or rabbit bush, or locoweed. Some of these had the confusing attribute of being dangerous only at certain times of the year. The pioneers persisted, and as they conquered their rigorous environment, they came to love it.

To my immense surprise, Phoebe Wallark was an articulate and interesting conversationalist as long as I didn't try to sneak in personal questions. She was willing to discuss anything except herself. She painted a nostalgic picture, from her mother's recollections, of what Nevada had been like before the modern casino boom — a friendly, small-town state where everyone knew everyone, with a strong interest in education and churches and an unrestrained talent for neighborliness. With its benign climate and its boundless economic potential, the bleak world the pioneers had conquered became the most favored land on earth. The towns, with tree-lined streets, lovely flowers, and lush grass lawns, rivaled anything New England could offer.

Never mind the gambling signs in Glitter Gulch, or the divorce mills, or the assembly line marriage chapels, or the prostitution. Those were seamy things imposed on Nevada by outsiders because of the residents' open-mindedness and refusal to poke their noses into someone else's business. Instead, one should think of Las Vegas as a place surrounded by awesome natural beauty with more churches per capita than any other city in the world.

I listened to this outpouring of civic pride with astonishment because Phoebe Wallark was offering no indication at all of having designs on me beyond the enjoyment of my company. We finished our drinks, and I ordered another round. I began to like her.

Her face would not launch any ships or even leaky rowboats. In any kind of topographic competition, she would represent the Great Plains states whereas the two Diamond Dees would proudly symbolize the High Sierras. I even doubted that she could make feet hit brake pedals by walking down Las Vegas Boulevard in excessively tight shorts, no matter how excessively tight they were, but she kept her brown eyes fixed on my face with deep sincerity, she leaned across the table as though I were the only male in the entire casino who mattered to her, and her behavior gave every indication of a desire to have her intelligence appreciated because she knew she didn't have much else going for her. Her face, when the crinkle of a smile touched it, became actually attractive, and laughter transformed it completely. I almost felt tempted to spend the rest of the evening trying to keep her laughing.

If I hadn't already seen her in action, I might have tagged her as a woman of quality who had been shamefully neglected in a city that fanatically emphasizes pulchritude over character. Beauty is only skin deep, and Las Vegas, in its grosser aspects, is a skin-deep city. But I had seen her, and I am anyway able to recognize a line before one end is tied firmly around my throat. Even so, the temptation to ask her how she had made out watching the men's room at the Union Plaza lessened as my liking for her grew.

Then she ruined her performance with one short sentence. She said, "Why don't we have the next drinks at my place?"

Joletta Eckling's beauty, topped with globs of the best glamour dished out by the two Diamond Dees, couldn't entice me into a parlor when I have already identified the spider, but Phoebe's performance entitled her to be let down easily. I leaned across the table and took her hot, oversized hand in mine. Warm hands may mean a warm heart, but hot, oversized hands are more likely to symbolize perspiring, oversized feet.

"I don't want to point," I said. "but there's a jolly fat man sitting alone in a booth on the far side of the room. Have you noticed him?"

I had been watching him ever since he came in on the chance that he might prove useful to me. He was a businessman from Albany or Albuquerque and the most important member of a group of people who had arrived at the restaurant together. They came and went from his table, pausing to exchange a few words with him. Occasionally a man would sit down and talk briefly. Women laughed with him and bent low as though reporting for a cleavage inspection. During an unnatural lull, I heard him addressed as "Elmer."

Phoebe Wallark looked in his direction and nodded.

"That," I said, speaking with the distaste I certainly would have felt if it had been true, "is my boss. Any minute, now, he will signal to me, and I will march over to his table, stand at attention, and receive my orders. If he tells me I'm through for the day . . ." I paused significantly and squeezed her hand. "Unfortunately, he's much more likely to contrive something that will keep me occupied all night. Everyone knows that life is unfair, but few men have that fact driven home to them as frequently as I do."

"But . . . what can he make you do at this time of night?"

"Probably something silly," I said. "Whatever it is, that's what I'm going to be doing. If he tells me Vegas Vic's cigarette has gone out, you will, shortly afterward, see me at the corner of Fremont and First Street climbing up with a lighter."

Our conversation expired a second time. She was anxiously watching the fat man. I watched him, too, hoping he would do something I could interpret as a signal. Eventually he made a stabbing gesture in our direction.

"That's it," I said. "If I come back, you'll know all is well. If I don't, I may be on my way to Upper Alaska to set up a new wholesale operation for peddling artificial snow to the Eskimos."

I waited until the man he was talking with left. Then I strode across the room, called him Elmer, shook his hand, said I was glad to see him again, was invited to sit down, did so, and exchanged impressions of Las Vegas with him for all of four minutes — after which I got to my feet, told him I hoped he would continue to enjoy his visit, shook his hand again, and left, leaving him to sift his memory with a perplexed expression on his face. I headed toward a casino exit without looking in the direction of Phoebe Wallark.

Outside, the cool night air revived me. The sudden stillness was as much an auditory shock as a blast of noise can be. There was little traffic of any kind at that hour; streets and sidewalks were deserted. Then a man with a familiar face stepped into the light flooding from the casino. It was Clyde Goodler, the keno shift boss, who probably was treating his lungs to a few gulps of smoke-free air. I'd had a long and frustrating day, and I was in my most choice *Why-not-throw-an-egg-in-the-fan?* mood. Ever since I had opened the door on Harley Dantzil's body, I had been wondering whether he was murdered because he was investigating the keno scam or because he was a part of it. As Goodler approached me, I thought of a way to find out. I extended a hand and stopped him.

I looked about as though making certain we weren't being overheard. "You know Harley is dead, don't you?" I asked him guardedly. Joletta had brought news of the murder, and everyone at Diamond D's knew it by this time.

He nodded. He was still in his late forties with a slender figure, but there were flecks of gray in his hair. He seemed far too intelligent to get involved in anything stupid like a keno scam, but all evening he had looked extremely worried. Now that worry took on an overlay of perplexity.

"I'm taking over," I said. "Don't do anything at all until you hear from me."

His perplexity vanished. He nodded, muttered, "Got you," and walked on.

I took another deep gulp of Las Vegas's cool night air and remarked to myself, "I really wish I knew what that was all about."

Phoebe Wallark remained in the casino for another hour. She was watching fat Elmer, the man I had called my boss. Eventually he collected his fat wife, who had been jollying a group of much younger men at a nearby table, and the two of them went up to bed. Phoebe trailed after them as far as the elevator. They boarded it; she stood there for a full minute thoughtfully contemplating the closed elevator door. Then she left the hotel.

I anticipated her and grabbed the only available cab before she got outside. We waited around the corner. She took the next cab that arrived, and my driver followed her.

In an ordinary passenger car, it would have been a routine job of tailing. With one taxicab following another through deserted residential streets, it was tricky, but my driver was a veteran and equal to anything.

Then I made a monumental discovery. I wasn't the only one following her. In concentrating on the cab ahead, I had failed to notice the car behind.

We were a block away when Phoebe Wallark's cab pulled to the curb and let her out at an apartment building on Gottford Street between Eighth and Ninth. My driver swung over as though to let out a fare of his own. The car roared past us and swung in behind Phoebe's cab. She was halfway to the building and didn't look back.

I shouted an order, and my driver jammed down his accelerator. I didn't know whether I was trying to prevent an abduction or a murder, but I had stupidly left her wide open for either. Her cab pulled away; we swung in ahead of the car and I jumped out, gun in hand. Phoebe had reached the doorway.

But nothing happened. The car pulled away, and I found I had committed a second stupidity in placing myself where I couldn't get the license number. Her "tail" had been seeing her home — or maybe making certain that she reached home safely.

My pulse returned to normal. I sent the cab around the corner to wait for me while I performed some routine snooping. It was a pleasant neighborhood of single-family houses, and even at night, the apartment building's shadowy mass looked strangely out of place. I had noticed other instances of isolated office or apartment buildings located in residential areas, and I could only reflect that Las Vegas must have curious zoning regulations.

It was a two-story building, stuccoed, with the fake Spanish touches that are popular in Las Vegas. In the glare of the one outside light that was on, it seemed to be yellow or cream-colored. There were several tall palms in the small yard. There was an entrance at each corner of the building with two doorways — one for a ground level apartment and one for stairs to an apartment on the second floor. Without even counting on my fingers, I was able to deduce that there were eight apartments in the building.

I went from entrance to entrance with my pen-light, writing down the names I found posted above the doorbells. "Wallark" wasn't among them, and only three of the eight seemed to be the names of single women. Phoebe Wallark hadn't worn a wedding ring, but I was taking nothing for granted where she was concerned. I copied all eight names. Then I returned to Diamond D's.

Mildred Comptom was making her rounds as energetically as she had earlier in the evening, but there were lines of weariness in her face. I asked her if she could spare a moment, and we returned to her small office.

"I am going to read some names to you," I said. "Tell me if you recognize any of them." I began with the single women. "Jane Miller . . . Rachel Kabeloff . . . Leda Rauchman . . ."

"Leda was an employee of Diamond D's up to a couple of weeks ago, when she was fired. I saw you talking with her."

"Bull's eye," I breathed. "What was her job?"

"She was Mr. Eckling's secretary for several years. Before that, she did general office work."

"How long did she work for Diamond D's?"

"Ten years or more."

"Competent?"

"I never heard anything to the contrary. I thought she was extremely competent and a very likable person, but she and Joletta didn't get along. What was she up to tonight?"

106

"I left before she got around to confiding that. If I'd known who she was, I would have stayed."

"You should have asked me," she said reproachfully.

"I should have. I don't know why I'm so slow on the uptake this week. It must be the low humidity. Next time, I'll ask. What do you know about Harley Dantzil's private life?"

"Next to nothing. His wife is a tartar and a snob — a very rich snob — but as far as I know, she's never been inside Diamond D's."

"Was there anyone among the employees he might have confided his personal affairs to?"

"I doubt it. I saw him talking with Wes Zerin a few times during breaks, but Harley wouldn't have confided in him, and I'm certain they never saw each other away from work. Harley seemed to have no private life at all. He never kept track of hours. He hung around Diamond D's as long as anyone wanted him to or would let him. Mr. Eckling would review his time card occasionally and make him take time off to compensate for his overtime."

"No private life," I mused. "If that's true, his murder must have had something to do with his work."

"I don't see how it could have. He kept himself busy after a fashion, but he never did anything important. I just thought of something." She paused and frowned at me.

107

I waited.

"Several years ago, Harley was involved in a fight on the sidewalk in front of Diamond D's. Someone beat him up."

"You fascinate me. Tell me more."

She laughed and blushed almost prettily. "I can't remember the last time a man said that to me — if one ever did. There isn't much more to tell. Someone attacked him when he got off work one night. He was beaten rather badly — both his eyes were swollen shut, his nose and mouth were bloody, and the back of his head was cut where he fell against the curb. I remember all that because I was the one who performed the first aid. A bystander called the police, but by the time they arrived, Harley was inside being bandaged, and his assailant had disappeared. Harley told them it was all due to a misunderstanding, and he wouldn't press charges. They offered to take him to a hospital, but he refused, so they left. So did Harley as soon as he felt a little better. Someone called a cab for him."

"Did he recover quickly?"

"He missed several days' work."

"How long ago was this?"

"Five or six years, I'm sure. Possibly even longer."

"Was there any subsequent trouble?"

"I never heard of any, and Harley never mentioned the incident again."

"If you think of anything else," I said, "please let me know."

A beating that happened five or six years before and was perhaps due to a misunderstanding probably had no connection with his murder, but taken with Dantzil's frequenting of a shabby neighborhood and renting an apartment there, it did suggest that he'd had a considerable amount of private life his coworkers knew nothing about.

So had Leda Rauchman, alias Phoebe Wallark. I still had no notion of what was going on, but I was beginning to see the glimmerings of a case.

At eight o'clock the next morning, I was at one of the hotel lobby's telephones listening to Joletta Eckling's phone ring unanswered. I wanted to ask a few questions about the mysterious phone call Harley had made after he was murdered. The hotel clerk had given me her home telephone number without an argument, which meant that someone — my guess made it Joel Eckling, prompted by Raina Lambert — had passed the word that the guest registered as J. Pletcher was privileged.

She didn't answer, and after several tries, I gave up. The clerk was watching me. He said apologetically, "She usually leaves early and stops for breakfast somewhere on her way to work." It was another nonendorsement of Diamond D's restaurant.

I called Raina Lambert, who answered on the first ring. I told her about Leda Rauchman and about Dantzil's beating. I also described the reaction of the keno shift boss, Clyde Goodler, to my improvised message.

"Certainly Dantzil was involved in the keno scam," she said. "Why else would he produce all of that mystification? The moment word got around that Eckling had hired detectives, everyone concerned started feeling the heat."

"You don't buy the extracurricular activity theory?"

"It's asking too much of coincidence to have him murdered for an entirely different reason shortly after he made an appointment with a detective to talk about the keno scam. Do you?"

"I have problems fitting that slum apartment into a scheme that's taking huge sums of money from the casinos."

"Perhaps he was gay and that was his love nest."

"I also have problems imagining him with a rich society butterfly for a wife. According to my correspondence course in practical scientific detection, a murder victim's spouse is always the prime suspect. This could be a 'do-it-yourself' divorce, no connection with the keno scam. I want to talk to the widow and ask her."

Raina planned to spend the morning checking employees' credit ratings to see whether one of them had been foolish enough to sock away illegal gains under his own name. "There's a lot of money involved in this case, and thus far we haven't caught a whiff of it," she said.

"Don't forget Joel Eckling," I told her. "Stealing from himself could be a very neat tax dodge."

"Phone at noon," she said and hung up.

I went outside and took a turn around the block, enjoying the cool, invigorating morning air. The sky was clear and sparkling, and there was promise of another ideal winter day, sunny and warm — in fact, one of the 320 sunny days each year that the Chamber of Commerce claims for Las Vegas. After my first circuit, I took a wider turn, down a block, south for two blocks, east for four, and so back toward the hotel. The streets of downtown Las Vegas are sparsely populated before the tourists begin straggling forth. I had the sidewalks to myself, and I strolled along briskly, lost in thought. I was still trying to develop a feel for Las Vegas. The problem, I decided, was that the motion picture set Las Vegas and the real Las Vegas were completely dissimilar but linked like Siamese twins who shared a number of vital organs. They couldn't be separated and survive in anything like their present health. Without the hype and the gambling, the closed hotels and casinos would turn Las Vegas into a large-scale Nevada ghost town.

A short distance ahead of me a car swung to the curb, the young lady in the passenger seat flung herself at the driver for a frenzied embrace, slipped out, threw him a kiss, was thrown one in

111

return, and hurried away with a fine, swinging stride. This is a scene repeated millions of times every morning all over America as lovers and spouses part on the way to their respective jobs, and only a cantankerous cad would see anything objectionable in it. I had no cause for disapproval, but I did find it remarkably interesting.

The young lady was Joletta Eckling, whose beauty and intelligence, combined with youthful innocence, had made her my previous day's All-American Girl nominee. The driver who calmly received her volcanic embrace was wearing a silver space uniform that looked identical to those I had seen the day before. I now understood Joletta's unanswered telephone. Either she hadn't been at home or she had been far too occupied to receive calls. I marked for further investigation the fact that her sweetheart had let her out more than two blocks from the place she worked. My crassly suspicious mind immediately deduced that she didn't want to be seen with him.

Our case was adding complications faster than I could handle them. I had no notion of what role Joletta Eckling was fated to play in it, but my complete misreading of her character disturbed me. I decided to give up my study of Las Vegas and concentrate on being a detective.

I telephoned Lieutenant McCarney. The lieutenant was out, but Sergeant Dunkor summarized the police reports for me. Dantzil had been an anonymous man living an anonymous life, and the police hadn't learned much about him. He had moved about Diamond D's like a wraith. The other employees poked fun at him, but they all seemed to like him. He was pathetically eager to be nice to everyone. If anyone was in trouble or needed a favor, Dantzil would go to ridiculous lengths to help him out.

Tenants at the Swoboda Street apartments confirmed that Dantzil had been hanging about the neighborhood for at least a year and probably longer. None of them remembered back as far as two years because none of them had been living there that long, but several remembered seeing Dantzil at Kuyper's parties or elsewhere in the neighborhood, walking or driving.

No one had seen a stranger near the building on the night of the murder. The tenant turnover was so large that probably few of the residents could distinguish between tenants and outsiders anyway. Anyone could have climbed the stairs and manipulated Dantzil's lock.

The police had found no connection — yet — between Dantzil and the pair of Frisco thugs in the Volkswagen, but that investigation was just getting started. Detectives had already searched Dantzil's office at the casino and his den and bedroom in his home. Their reports were as devoid of interest as a police report could possibly be. Most victims' possessions retain strong auras of their owners' personalities. They may even hint at secrets skillfully concealed from prying eyes. As far as the police could determine, Dantzil's did neither.

I was disappointed but not surprised to learn that the fingerprints on the book of matches were too smudged to be useful. Fingerprints found at the scene of a crime usually vary from badly smudged to totally smeared.

Obviously the Las Vegas Metropolitan Police were conducting a skillful and meticulous investigation. If the dirt under Dantzil's fingernails, or the dust in his pockets, or the scuffs on his shoes provided vital clues, the police would quickly solve his murder. My hunch said that none of them would.

"I'm going to call on the grieving widow," I told Dunkor. "Do you have any suggestions?"

"She may not see you. She talked to me last night but only with great reluctance and after receiving a very pointed legal threat."

"What was her attitude toward her husband?"

"She ignored him as completely as possible. She actually behaved as though the man didn't exist. Several people who knew them say they had an unwritten agreement that Harley would do absolutely nothing to call attention to himself — either from her or from anyone else. I've never experienced such a 'so what?' attitude on the part of a new widow. That was before it suddenly occurred to her that social conventions impose certain obli-

114

gations on her. Then she became angry. Not only will she have to hold a suitable funeral for him, but she'll also have to go through the motions of observing a period of mourning, which is certain to play hob with her social calendar. She hadn't quite grasped all of the implications last night, but by this morning she'll have everything figured out, and she'll be hopping mad."

I thanked him and went to see her.

The Harley Dantzils — or, as his wife would have preferred it, the Florence Stevens-Dantzils, lived in the Rancho-Bonanza area to the northwest of Las Vegas, one of the older residential suburbs. The money that built the houses there arrived before the casino boom. The lots were much larger — some houses had a couple of acres or more. The trees were taller than in the newer suburbs because they had been growing longer.

The Stevens-Dantzil estate had clusters of towering palms and a lavish scattering of oleander and olive bushes. It was a motion-picture-set house, a mock brick castle with arrow slits, turrets, and even a fake drawbridge at the front door, all of which seemed appropriate enough for Las Vegas. There was a two-car garage incorporated into it, and the two cars were parked in the driveway — a Mercedes that was at least ten years old but looked as though it had just left the dealer's showroom, and a recent-model Toyota. A man in patched work pants and a ragged shirt was washing them. He was of wiry build with a head of thinning gray hair. He paid no attention to me as I walked up to the house.

There was no wreath on the front door, but any attempt to draw conclusions from that would have been unfair to the widow. She hadn't had time to cover all of the proprieties.

I pressed the doorbell button. A speaker installed just above it gave forth a strident female voice. "This is the Stevens-Dantzil residence. Deliveries are accepted at the rear entrance only. Soliciting is not permitted at this address, and solicitors are reported to the police. If you have a legitimate reason for calling, please ring the bell a second time."

I firmly rang the bell again. I expected to be greeted by a butler, but a very young black maid opened the door. Perhaps in Las Vegas, butlers can make far more money driving cabs or dealing blackjack than Florence Stevens-Dantzil would have been willing to pay for butlering. Mildred Comptom had called her a rich snob, and like every member of that species I've had the displeasure of knowing, she was certain to be a tightwad.

The maid was a recent import from the Deep South, and her rich, lazy accent evoked Spanish moss and mint juleps. She was extremely polite, and she took obvious pride in her neat white apron, but she had been carefully indoctrinated in the Stevens-Dantzil brand of snobbery. I spent several

116

minutes trying to persuade her that I had a legitimate reason for bothering her mistress at this tragic time.

"If she doesn't want to see me," I said finally, "she'll want to tell me so herself."

The maid closed the door and went to ask. Several more minutes passed before I finally faced Florence Stevens-Dantzil. Her appearance matched the harsh voice I had already heard. She was tall, thin, and hatchet-faced. Popular rumor had it that her complexion was anemic, but I never saw it in that condition. When she was angry or otherwise emotionally disturbed, her face flushed to a vivid red and remained so. As Sergeant Dunkor had predicted, I found her hopping mad, and my interview with her was brief and totally one-sided. She'd had to tolerate the police, but she knew how to tell off a private detective who had no official status.

"Mr. Pletcher," she said icily. "I want to make my position perfectly clear." She proceeded to do so. Fate had saddled her with a lazy, worthless husband, but she had supported him, provided a lovely home for him, and been as good a wife to him as his shiftless character made possible, and if that wasn't disgrace enough, now he had humiliated her further by getting himself murdered. She announced, after talking nonstop for five minutes, that she didn't want to talk about it. She stepped inside and slammed the door.

Calling her a society butterfly had been a serious entomological error. She was a praying mantis.

As I turned away, a new black Mercedes coasted down the driveway. The driver, a short, tubby man in an expensive suit and an incongruous Stetson hat, got out and waddled toward the front door. He gave me a polite nod as we passed. His face was wrinkled; what I could see of his hair was a youthful, shining black and certainly dyed. I slowed my pace and managed to eavesdrop on his reception. The widow had been watching to make certain I left, and she saw him arrive. She opened the door before he could ring the bell.

"Florence!" he exclaimed. "I just got back from Chicago. What a tragedy! I came the moment I heard."

Her murmured reply was indistinguishable. The door closed behind them, and I walked back up the drive, pausing only to note the license number of the caller's Mercedes. The widow's lack of enthusiasm for private detectives hadn't taken me by surprise; I had asked my cab driver to wait. I returned to Diamond D's, sat down at a slot machine, and procured a drink for myself.

I had an expense account limit of a hundred dollars for gambling, but nothing had been said about liquor, which in casinos can be had for a nominal tip to the waitress. This case already seemed like the kind that turns iron-willed teetotalers into lushes.

7

THE HOTEL DESK HAD A MESSAGE FOR ME. Lieutenant McCarney wanted to see me. I returned to police headquarters in a rush, expecting sensational developments, or at least developments, but it turned out that McCarney merely wanted to know what I had been doing.

"Have you turned up anything at all?" he asked.

I told him about the beating Dantzil had received. He listened with a scowl.

"Five or six years ago, you say? If the officers got there after the fight was over, and Dantzil refused to sign a complaint, it may be impossible to find out anything, but I'll try."

"His conduct made no sense to me until I saw his wife," I said. "Now I understand why he wouldn't press charges. He was terrified about getting his name in the papers. Florence would have given him hell. The husband of a Stevens-Dantzil does not get beaten up on a public street. How'd she happen to marry him?"

"I wondered about that myself, so I inquired.

119

She was Little Miss Nobody from a poor family and on the verge of spinsterhood. Harley wasn't doing well himself, but Mrs. Stevens, Florence's mother, was Joel Eckling's housekeeper, and she spoke to Joel about him, and Harley was given a sort of job at Diamond D's, mostly doing things no one else could be bothered with. That was twenty-five years ago. His job never changed.

"A short time after the marriage, Mrs. Stevens was left a fortune by a remote relative she didn't know she had. She died a couple of years later and passed the whole bundle to Florence, who quickly discovered advantages in having a nonentity husband. It gave her the social status of a married woman with none of the obligations."

I asked about the refugees from a science fiction film and the strange weapon that seemed designed to fit the dents in Harley Dantzil's skull. He dismissed that notion with one emphatic monosyllable.

"The spacemen are from Nevada 2100 — the 'Frontier Town of the Future.' What connection could Dantzil — or Diamond D's — have with those characters?"

"All I know is that Joletta Eckling is on a basis of close familiarity with one of them." I told him about her ride to work and gave him the license number. I also gave him the numbers of the car the spacemen had been using the day before and the Mercedes of Florence Stevens-Dantzil's caller.

He grimaced, but he made his phone call.

The spacemen's cars were registered to Nevada 2100. The widow's caller had been one Edwin Morabin. Morabin, McCarney informed me, was a distinguished citizen from an old Las Vegas family. He had been professor of something at the University of Nevada, Las Vegas before he retired.

I have known several murderers who were distinguished citizens, so I recorded Morabin's name in my notebook and asked about the frontier town of the future.

"It's a tourist trap with an original twist. Kids love it. Lots of plastic, geodesic domes, solar power panels, far-out electronic games, and the playground of the future, with live entertainment in the form of laser gun duels. Those characters have 'laser shields' in the backs of their capes. They whip them out and start dueling at the drop of an electron. They catch laser beams on the shields and reflect them back, or pretend to do so, and they put on a good show. Nevada 2100 is supposed to be what a pioneer village would have been like if Nevada hadn't been settled until 2100. Or if aliens from outer space had settled it. There are plenty of ghost towns and pioneer villages that dramatize the spirit of the Old West. Nevada 2100 claims to catch the spirit of the future. Or the New West. The only complaint I've heard about it came from a friend of mine who says the casino's slot machines don't pay off, but losers say that about

121

every casino in Las Vegas."

"Does the law require them to pay off?" I asked.

"No, but the Gaming Control Board encourages them to pay back seventy-five percent or more. So does the competition. Customers will go elsewhere if they don't. Also, frequent jackpots are good psychology. They keep people betting. What does any of this have to do with Harley Dantzil's murder?"

"Probably nothing. You don't think the laser guns are capable of smashing a skull?"

"They look like metal, but they're hollow tubes made of light plastic with nothing inside except flashlight batteries. I was inveigled into a laser duel myself, once, and the spaceman made me look silly. If one of those tubes collided with a skull, the tube would be wrecked."

"They could have filled one with cement for skull-bashing purposes, but I won't belabor that unless I turn up a reason for their wanting Harley Dantzil dead. What can you tell me about Joletta Eckling?"

"She was a wild kid. She grew up without a mother and caused her father no end of grief. Ten years ago, or even five, I wouldn't have bet a losing keno ticket on her future, but she seems to have straightened out. There's been no scandal at all about her for several years. Don't tell me you're trying to tag her with robbing her father!"

I shook my head. "I can't get the feel of this

place. I wouldn't have tagged her as an ex-wild kid. She certainly looks and acts sweet and innocent."

"That's how she was able to get away with it."

"In that case, maybe I will tag her with robbing her father. How about putting a police guard on Leda Rauchman?"

McCarney wanted to know who Leda Rauchman was, and I told him. "I want her watched," I said, "because someone thinks she's worth tailing."

He started a lecture on police economics, and I left before he finished it.

At noon I telephoned Raina Lambert. "Following orders," I announced. "Nothing to report."

"Nothing? What have you been doing all morning?"

I told her about Joletta Eckling's warm farewell to the spaceman, my interview with Florence Stevens-Dantzil, and my conversation with McCarney.

She said thoughtfully, "I suppose Mrs. Stevens-Dantzil would be reluctant to give you permission to search her husband's den and bedroom."

"If 'reluctant' means 'over my dead body,' I suppose she would. Anyway, the police just did that. McCarney could get me in, but it wouldn't be polite to suggest that his detectives have to be swept up after."

"I'll see if I can arrange it with someone higher up. You won't need special permission to search Dantzil's office. I'll telephone Eckling now, and you can do that right away. If you find anything, follow it up. When you finish with that, go out to the University of Nevada, Las Vegas and have a chat with a Professor Quilley. That's Dr. Harold Quilley, Professor of Physics. Tell him you're looking for information about scientific methods of rigging gambling devises. I understand the subject inter- ests him."

I had nothing better to suggest, so I said, "All right. I'll search Dantzil's office despite the fact that the police have just done so. Naturally I won't find anything. Then I'll talk with Professor Quilley."

"After you follow up on your search."

"Yes. Of course. Certainly. I'll first investigate my non-findings with my usual ingenuity. Then I'll see Professor Quilley."

Joel Eckling's secretary was expecting me. Her name was Theda Iaconelli, and her black eyes would have looked sultry to any man with a few free moments to gaze into them. She was much younger and far better looking than Leda Rauchman. She added a whole new dimension of attractive ornamentation to Joel Eckling's office, which needed it, but — since gambling is legal in Nevada — I would have bet a substantial part of my hundred-dollar ration that she also was far less competent than Leda.

I had no complaint about the competence with which she handed me the key to Harley Dantzil's office, however, nor about the efficiency with which she gave me instructions for locating it.

Of all the jobs I don't care for, searching a place that has already been searched is the one I most emphatically despise. It is like having to eat food someone else has chewed. I had to do it because the boss said so, but I was under no obligation to enjoy it. This didn't mean that my performance would be slipshod. The contrary. Raina Lambert's psychic hunches were sometimes miles off target and sometimes dead on, and it was dangerous to decide in advance which was likely to be which.

I never proceed on the assumption that police are nincompoops. Most police officers are professionals, they are competent, they are conscientious, and they do capable work. If they have a failing, it is that they are carefully trained to follow a routine. The more meticulous they are with their routine, the less likely they are to go beyond it. Lambert and Associates has achieved spectacular results by going beyond routines in a way no police department would spare the time for. It also cultivates coin-flipping, clairvoyance, and diabolical inspiration when more prosaic methods fail.

Dantzil's office was an oversized closet on the same floor as Eckling's but located down a side hallway beyond the janitor's sink room and another closet where office supplies were stored. There was a hall tree for him to hang his hat on; a rather battered two-drawer filing cabinet that was empty

125

except for an unopened pack of new folders plus four empty used folders labeled with dates from the 1970s; a small secretary's desk that had drawers on one side only; and a very worn, armless, secretary's chair. Behind the chair was a small window with a scenic view of nearby roofs.

Two photographs hung on the wall facing the desk. These were eight by ten color enlargements of snapshots. One showed a boy of about two years old and the other a girl of about four. I sat in the desk chair, tilted back, and tried to see the photos with Harley Dantzil's eyes. The Stevens-Dantzils had no children. Who were these kids?

He thought enough of them to want them there on the wall facing him whenever he looked up. I couldn't put myself in his place without knowing who they were, so I took them to Joel Eckling's secretary. She had never seen them before, but she knew about them because the police officer who searched the room had already inquired. She had asked Mr. Eckling, who said Dantzil once brought the photos to his office and showed them to him. The kids were Harley's niece and nephew, children of his only surviving relative, a sister.

"Has the sister been told about his death?" I asked.

The secretary murmured, "Surely Mrs. Stevens-Dantzil . . ."

I shook my head. "If Harley had a sister who meant something to him, you people should make certain she's been informed. I suggest that Mr. Eckling take care of it personally. Have him call her now, please. After he has extended his condolences, I'd like to talk with her. I'll take the call in Harley's office."

The secretary nodded dumbly. People who work for large organizations are so accustomed to a nebulous atmosphere where no one knows what's going on and everyone is waiting for someone else to decide what to do next that an outsider who gives instructions concisely and firmly can get what he wants four times out of five.

I returned to my search of Harley Dantzil's office.

I first went about the chore of looking into each of the filing folders, just in case. Then I removed the drawers, turned the filing cabinet upside down, examined its interior and exterior meticulously, and reassembled it.

I next gave the same meticulous attention to the desk. The upper drawer contained a few sheets of Diamond D's stationery; an appointment book for the current year with no entries; a memo pad with the cryptic note "Gro." on the top sheet; an assortment of old ball point pens, some with advertising logos of various local businesses; and, inside a small glass jar with a lid, eleven postage stamps ranging in denomination from one cent to twenty-five cents.

The much-deeper lower drawer offered a more

varied assortment — a dried-up rubber stamp pad (but no rubber stamps); a scattering of paper clips; an unopened plastic package of rubber bands in various sizes; three medium-sized Band-Aids in paper wrappers; a tattered pocket dictionary without covers; a plastic lapel button that read "Hazen Days"; a paper punch that reproduced a four-leaf clover; several unused memo pads; a three-year-old Las Vegas telephone directory; two used typewriter ribbons; an empty plastic box that once had contained staples; a 1981 pocket calendar with an advertising message from the Wild Card Cleaners; one used shoelace; and a pocket calculator that didn't work. Invisible at the back and bottom, and buried under all of that miscellaneous junk, was an ornamented box of the kind banks use for mailing reorders of personalized checks. It was filled with cancelled checks. They were neatly arranged by number, and the most recent was four years old. Obviously nothing had been touched in that drawer for months if not years until the detective searching it had stirred the contents around a bit.

I closed the drawer and leaned back, trying again to imagine Harley Dantzil seated where I was sitting. What did he do here? What could he have done? No one had mentioned office duties for him. Did he twiddle his thumbs while waiting for a phone call from someone asking him to run an errand? Did he come here to conceal the humiliation he felt because he was a mere supernumerary? Did he hide out here while putting in extra hours in an attempt to create the illusion that his job kept him furiously occupied? Was he pathetically attempting to give himself a feeling of importance when he pretended to be involved in casino security and tried to send the out-of-town detective chasing all over Las Vegas? I could see no reason why he hadn't borrowed an extra chair and invited me to come directly to his office.

Those who knew Dantzil described him as an uncomplicated, rather simple little man. I didn't believe a word of it. I had already encountered too many things about him that were far from simple. His obsession with being tailed, for example. His renting an apartment in a slum neighborhood. And his getting himself murdered.

I explored the desk with the same thorough technique I had used on the filing cabinet. It harbored no guilty secrets. I went over the room carefully and found no loose floorboards or concealed wall panels. The photos were enlarged from ordinary snapshots, but they had been framed professionally — the backs were stamped with the firm's logo — and no one had tampered with them in order to conceal missing wills or fortunes in bonds.

I returned to the desk, got out the box of cancelled checks, and resignedly set about sorting them. Harley Dantzil had been a check writer. He paid for everything by check. He shopped regularly at a number of local stores, and two-thirds of the checks were made out to Smiths, Lucky, Safeway, K-Mart, Wonder World, and Alpha-Beta. Most of the other checks were for small amounts. Only occasionally did one exceed twenty-five dollars. He wrote a check for ninety-four dollars to Stoffelheim's Garage for auto repairs. That was understandable. He also paid his barber by check, which was not. I wondered whether he had an aversion to carrying money.

The phone rang. Theda Iaconelli's voice said, "Mrs. George Ehler will speak with you now. She lives in Portland, Oregon, and it took a while to locate her. This is Mr. Pletcher, Mrs. Ehler."

A strange voice said, "Hello?"

"Mrs. Ehler?"

"Yes."

"Have you been given the sad news about your brother?"

"Yes. It's a shock, though I hadn't heard from him for years."

"He must have remembered you with genuine affection. He has your children's photographs on the wall of his office. I'm looking at them now."

"I'm pleased to hear that. I couldn't get along with his wife, you see. She's an impossible woman. So we simply drifted apart. But — you say he had my children's photos? I wonder where he got them."

"These are photos of young children. I suppose

they're grown up, now."

"They certainly are!"

"Would you give me their names and ages, please?"

"George is — I have to count back! — twenty-seven, Bill is twenty-six, and Dick is twenty-two."

"No girls?"

"None. I was lucky. I wouldn't want to be raising girls these days."

"Thank you. You've been very helpful. Do you mind my calling you if I need more information about Harley?"

"No. Of course not. Though I doubt that I know anything that would help. It's been so many years since I saw him."

"You've helped already, and one never knows when something out of a person's past will become important."

I hung up and leaned back to look at the photographs. They had been taken in someone's living room — the end of a sofa loomed prominently in the background. Identifying the subjects might require prolonged investigation, and the result almost certainly wouldn't be worth the effort. Were they a coworker's children who had caught his fancy? But no — if they belonged to anyone working at Diamond D's, he wouldn't have tried to pass them off as his own niece and nephew.

Harley Dantzil was becoming more complicated with each new fact I uncovered.

I returned my attention to the cancelled checks. Scattered among the remittances to business firms were occasional checks written to individuals for small sums. There were several for ten dollars, two for twenty, one for twenty-five. I reached for an unused memo pad and made a list of the names. Charles Harbon appeared twice, ten dollars each time. All of the other names appeared once: Faith Kennalt, Ed Vanlie, Mark Gilmin, Linda Bartkowiak, Sue Evard, Frank Jorlanson. Toward the bottom of the stack, I encountered a check to a Betty Varnko for a hundred dollars.

I sat looking at that one for a long time with my lips shaping a silent whistle. The amount seemed completely out of character. Was Betty Varnko a co-worker caught in a financial crisis who turned to Harley for assistance? He was said to be pathetically eager to help people. I knew that Linda Bartkowiak was a keno writer. Mildred Comptom had pointed her out to me.

I started for the door with my memo pad, intending to ask Theda Iaconelli whether any of the others worked for Diamond D's. Then I had a much better idea. I returned to the desk and used the telephone. Miss Iaconelli would conscientiously check payroll and personnel records, and she would find the names if they were there, but names weren't what I wanted. I was interested in people. I asked the switchboard operator whether Mildred Comptom was in the casino. She hadn't come in yet, so the operator obligingly rang her home telephone number for me.

A sleepy voice answered. For all I knew, she had been at the casino all night. "Pletcher," I told her. "Are you wide awake?"

"No," she said resignedly. "What is it now?"

"A list of names taken from some of Harley Dantzil's cancelled checks. They're four or five years old, but in a murder case, one never knows what might be important. See if you can identify them. Charles Harbon."

She snorted. "That deadbeat. He borrowed money from everyone and never paid anyone back. How many times did Harley make loans to him?"

"In this batch of checks, twice. Ten dollars each time. Was he an employee of Diamond D's?"

"He was on the payroll, but I never noticed that he did any work. Mr. Eckling hates to fire people. He finally gave me the job of firing Charles Harbon, and I did it with pleasure. Who else?"

"Faith Kennalt, twenty-five dollars."

"Another employee. That's interesting. It must have been about the time she had her abortion."

She was astonishing. Not only did she know every person on the list, but she also knew what had necessitated several of the loans. Finally I reached the last name. "Betty Varnko, a hundred dollars."

"I've never heard that one. How is it spelled?"

"V-A-R-N-K-O," I told her.

"No. I've never heard it. The hundred suggests a prostitute, but they don't accept checks unless it's from a regular customer, and I'd never believe that about Harley. His wife emasculated him years ago. Sorry. I can't help you with Betty Varnko."

"You've been enormously helpful," I said. "Now I have only one name to identify. You can go back to sleep."

"It's much too late for that," she said.

I hung up and turned to the old telephone directory. There was only one Varnko listed, a Brian Varnko on DeSoto Street. I was reaching for the telephone when I remembered that the book was three years old. I went back to Joel Eckling's office and consulted the current directory. It contained the same listing, Brian Varnko on DeSoto. I copied the information into my notebook.

I returned to Dantzil's office, tilted back in his worn chair, and pondered what I should do next. The check was four years old, and probably there was an absurdly simple explanation for it that didn't have the remotest connection with either the keno scam or Dantzil's murder. It was equally probable that the Brian Varnko in the telephone directory would know nothing at all about Betty. I envisioned her as a sales clerk or a waitress who had told Dantzil her troubles and borrowed money.

It had to be checked out. McCarney should have been able to find out in three minutes whether a Betty Varnko lived at the DeSoto Street address, but I had no intention of asking him. "I'm a man of action," I told myself. "I'm tired of sitting in keno lounges. Thus far I've done nothing at all except discover a corpse. Just for a change, I would like to catch something that's trying to get away. Besides, the boss told me to follow up on anything I found."

I sorted Harley Dantzil's checks back into their numerical order, repacked them, and returned the box to the drawer. On my way out, I stopped at Joel Eckling's office to politely thank Theda Iaconelli for her invaluable assistance. Probably it was my imagination that her eyes looked even blacker and more sultry when she heard I was leaving. I caught a cab and gave the driver the DeSoto Street address.

It was in a new subdivision east of Boulder Highway, which is an extension of Fremont Street. It was a pleasant middle class neighborhood with moderately sized stucco houses on small lots. Its newness was certified by the fact that all of the trees were small and there were few lawns.

I had assumed that the street was named De-Soto for historical allusions. Hernando de Soto came no farther west than the present state of Oklahoma, but the matter of a couple of intervening states wouldn't have discouraged a Las Vegas housing developer. I was wrong. This developer had an unfortunate penchant for automobile names, both current and obsolete, and we passed Dodge,

Chrysler, Edsel, and Buick streets before we reached DeSoto.

I knew immediately that I had come to the right address. Children were playing on the sidewalk, and I recognized two of them, though they were a couple of years older than their photographs. I told the cab to wait, walked up to the door, and rang the bell.

The young woman who opened it was in her early twenties and looked younger. She was an attractive blonde, slender, neatly dressed, a glowing example of the ideal American housewife.

"Betty Varnko?" I asked.

She admitted it.

I apologized for disturbing her. "I'm employed by the estate of Mr. Harley Dantzil," I said. "You may have heard that he was killed recently. Among his effects, I found an old cancelled check in the amount of one hundred dollars that was made out to you. I wonder if you could tell me the circumstances."

She was astonished. "A cancelled check made out to me? I've never even heard of — what did you say his name was?"

"Harley Dantzil. A check for a hundred dollars."

She shook her head bewilderedly. "I just don't remember . . ."

No one would have mistaken her for an intellectual masquerading as a housewife. She had probably quit high school and married the first man to

136

come along who had a decent-paying job and could offer her security.

After a pause, she said slowly, "Maybe I do remember. Please come in."

I followed her through a short entrance hall and into a small living room. The place was meticulously clean and so neat and orderly that it could have been used as a model home display. The furniture was of good quality and well cared for. I saw at a glance that the children hadn't performed indoor gymnastics on it. She offered me the sofa, which I recognized from the photographs, and seated herself in an overstuffed chair across the room.

"That must have been years ago," she said.

"About four years," I told her.

"Yes. I do remember, now. I was expecting a C.O.D. package, and I didn't have any money in the house. My husband is an investigator, too — he free-lances and does very well at it. So I know how that is. You have to chase down every little thing. Where was I? My husband telephoned. He often does when he's out on a case and has a little free time. I told him I was flat broke. He hadn't been home for several days, and I didn't even have money for groceries. He said a man owed him a hundred dollars, and he'd ask him to write a check to me and send it out. A messenger brought it, and I went right over to the branch bank we use and cashed it. I didn't pay any attention to the name of the person who wrote it, and I don't think my husband mentioned it. He just said it was a man who owed him money. You say it was — Dantzil? And he was killed?"

"Yes. The name was Harley Dantzil. You're right, we have to chase down every little thing, but usually it turns out to be something unimportant. I'm sorry I had to bother you." I got to my feet. I had been staring across the room at a large framed photograph that stood on an end table beside her chair.

"What a lovely family you have," I said. "I saw your children outside. Is this your husband?"

"Brian," she said with a nod and a smile. "He's a wonderful person. I'm very lucky."

"You certainly are to have a fine family like that."

I thanked her for the information, exchanged some very small talk with the children as I went down the walk, and climbed back into my cab. "Las Vegas City Hall," I told the driver. "Police headquarters."

He turned quickly and stared at me. Then he shrugged and drove off.

I hunched down in the rear seat and lost myself in thought. Harley Dantzil, the pathetic little man everyone laughed at, had handed me another surprise, and this one was a shocker. Harley Dantzil was also Brian Varnko, and he had fashioned a homey refuge from the formidable Florence Stevens-Dantzil where he kept an attractive little bigamous wife and two illegitimate children.

Normally I don't condone bigamy, but I had a grudging admiration for Dantzil. There was an astonishing boldness to his masquerade. He had maintained his phony identity openly, with a respectable address and an entry in the telephone directory. Anyone performing the most perfunctory investigation would have found him out, but why would anyone have bothered to investigate the innocuous Harley Dantzil?

I didn't know how he had managed all of the problems attendant on maintaining two identities — income taxes, for example, and remembering to carry the correct identification when he switched from one to the other — but obviously he had handled them with a rare competence and perhaps even with a flair. If he hadn't been murdered, he might never have been caught.

8

LIEUTENANT McCARNEY WAS ASTONISHED, but he also was extremely puzzled as to how I had come up with this information so quickly. None of the reports on Dantzil's death had mentioned a Betty Varnko. When I described my identification of the names found on Dantzil's cancelled checks, his face took on a grim look that boded no good for the young detective who had been put off by a collection of junk in a lower desk drawer.

"The woman should be informed that her 'husband' is dead," I said. "That means she'll also have to be told she wasn't married to him. It's a sticky situation all around. She can't even bury him — legally he belongs to Florence. He may have made some attempt to provide for her, though. They seem to have been happy together, and a man who hangs his children's pictures on the wall of his office at the risk of having something like that found out must think highly of them. Everyone concerned will be badly hurt if this isn't handled carefully. My instinct is to keep the press out of it, and I'm certain Florence Stevens-Dantzil will agree with me."

McCarney nodded. "I'll talk to Betty Varnko myself. I wonder if they actually went through a marriage ceremony — not that it matters. I agree that nothing would be gained by publicizing this. What does it do to your case?"

"Everything that happens seems to take me further away from it. I'm going back to the casino and start over."

"I'll hand you one thing," McCarney said. "Dantzil had been tailed for some time, by a number of people, which explains his concern about your being tailed. Last week he asked one of the detectives if anything could be done about it. The detective wasn't encouraging, so Dantzil asked him how to ditch a tail, and the detective gave him some advice. I'm checking to find out whether someone hired a local agency to keep an eye on him."

"What about the missing weapon?" I asked.

"The murderer brought it, and the murderer took it away. The doctor agrees with you — it was a piece of pipe. He makes it an *old* piece of pipe. There were rust particles in the wounds."

We went back to Diamond D's together, and Lieutenant McCarney smuggled the children's photographs out of Dantzil's office in a briefcase. He had decided to return them to Betty before a reporter got his hands on them. He went bravely to his ordeal of announcing Dantzil's death to a second widow, and I remained behind to think up more requests for Joel Eckling's secretary. This was not a hardship. I admired the small ringlets of hair that delicately framed her face, and I might have progressed to the point of calling her Theda had it not been for one unfortunate defect. She had no personality. She was a lovely blank face with a smile attached. She smiled perpetually except when she suspected me of telling a joke. Then she went completely deadpan.

I told her I was stationing myself in Dantzil's office, and I wanted to interview every employee who'd had any contact with him.

"That's everyone," she protested.

"Then I'll have to interview everyone, starting with you. How well did you know him?"

"Not well at all. I still don't understand what his job was. He was someone who passed through the office now and then, usually on his way to see Mr. Eckling. He was always friendly and polite, and he made a point of saying something nice, even if it was only a remark about the weather." She raised her hands. "That's all."

"I didn't know residents of Las Vegas ever mentioned the weather. Did he talk to you about himself?"

She shook her head.

"Or ask you anything personal — questions about your family, or your boy friends, or anything like that?"

She shook her head again.

"What did the other employees think of him?"

"They made jokes about him, especially those working in the casino. Down there, he tried to pretend he was someone important. He wasn't like that at all when he came up here."

"Was there anyone who disliked him?"

"I never heard anyone in the office say anything bad about him."

I spent the remainder of the afternoon in Dantzil's office interviewing employees. None of them knew much about him except that he always spoke pleasantly and caused no problems. I watched to see whether any of them noticed that the photographs were missing. None did. Probably none of them had ever been in his office.

Several people for whom Dantzil had written checks four years before were still working at Diamond D's. Others had borrowed from him more recently. Their stories were similar. They had run short, and Dantzil had been sympathetic and helpful.

Sue Evard, a small, shy-looking woman, said sadly, "I liked the little guy. He was friendly. He didn't have an unkind word for anyone. I must have borrowed from him a dozen times, and never once did he ask for his money back. Several times I was really broke and had to let it ride for a couple of paydays. He never said a thing about it, but I always looked him up and apologized for not being able to pay him."

In everyday life, testimonials are valuable, but they can clutter up a murder investigation.

At six o'clock, the phone on Dantzil's desk rang. McCarney said, "This is going through Diamond D's switchboard. Do you want to phone me?"

"Give me five minutes," I told him.

I went downstairs to the hotel lobby and called him back. He had talked with Betty Varnko and also with the family attorney. "They bought a license and were married in a church," he said. "You'll be interested to know that Dantzil set up a trust fund for this extracurricular family. It has more than four hundred thousand dollars in it. He also had ten decreasing term life insurance policies in his own name — meaning Harley Dantzil — with Betty and the children as named beneficiaries. The attorney has custody of the policies. The initial face amounts were a hundred thousand each, totaling a million dollars. The coverage drops each year, but the current value is more than nine hundred thousand."

"Is Florence Stevens-Dantzil a generous rich wife?" I asked.

"She never gave him a cent. He had his room and his den, but according to the maid, he rarely used them. When he ate a meal there, it was always in the kitchen with the servants. That was some marriage. I'd have felt like committing bigamy myself."

144

"How did Betty Varnko take it?"

"Hard. I called her doctor and also her brother. The brother seems to be very close to his sister. He said he wasn't pleased about her marrying an older man, but he'd been wrong. Dantzil was a good husband and father, the kids adored him, and it was a happy marriage. He liked Dantzil. He was pretty broken up about it himself. It was he who told me about the attorney."

"I suppose you've noted the fact that Dantzil's death makes Betty Varnko an extremely rich widow."

"I have. I asked her where she was night before last, and she was astonished. She was home with the children, of course. She'd never trust a sitter to look after them. I believe it. I'll leave her as a last resort."

"What's the chance that Florence Stevens-Dantzil expressed her opinion of Harley's bigamy by denting his skull?"

"How would she have found out? She ignored her husband totally. Anyway, I simply cannot imagine a Stevens-Dantzil doing something that would cause talk, not to mention headlines. Can you visualize a woman with her icy poise raging at her husband with a length of pipe?"

"Easily. She raged at me for at least five minutes though without the pipe. You say you can't imagine it, but I'm sure you inquired anyway. Where was she the night Harley was murdered?"

"Attending a charity ball at the Union Plaza. Her chauffeur drove her there, and waited for her, and drove her home. She spent the evening closely observed by a couple of thousand people — including my wife and myself. We were there. She was a co-hostess and sat at the head table."

I thanked him for the information and promised to be in touch again the moment I had another revelation for him. As I hung up, I belatedly remembered the professor of physics. It was too late to telephone him at the university, so I called him at home. He sounded politely mystified, but he readily made an appointment to see me the next morning.

I also telephoned Raina Lambert, but her phone rang unanswered.

I gave myself an early dinner, not at Diamond D's, and then I went to see Mildred Comptom. "How many of Diamond D's employees were aware that the wealthy and well-publicized Florence Stevens-Dantzil was the wife of obscure little Harley?" I asked.

She had no idea. She couldn't recall hearing anyone mention it.

"Everyone remarks about how friendly and helpful Harley was. He sounds almost too good to be true. Wasn't there anyone he didn't get along with?"

"Yes," she said. "A year ago, Harley seemed to have it in for Ron Tallus, one of the blackjack dealers. He kept complaining about him to Mr. Eckling — Ron was getting too friendly with the customers, he was rude to players who didn't toke, he picked up the cards so quickly people thought he was trying to put something over on them — Harley had compiled a list."

"Were any of those things true?"

She smiled. "Yes — if you want to insist on perfection in everyone, all the time. The man's wife was seriously ill. He has young children, and he was extremely worried. I prefer to handle that sort of thing with sympathy and a friendly reminder now and then, not a complaint to the boss. It really wasn't like Harley to be bad-mouthing another employee, but I suppose he desperately wanted to show Mr. Eckling he was doing something valuable for the casino. If I hadn't smoothed it over, he might have got Ron fired. Actually, Ron is a very good dealer."

"Did Ron try to retaliate?"

"No, but he probably entertained murderous thoughts about Harley at the time. I'm sure he's forgotten all about it by now."

I was certain he hadn't. "Anyone else?" I asked.

"Audrey Narling, our day shift Diamond Dee, disliked Harley thoroughly. She thought he hid in corners and spied on her. But then — she has a complex about men. She thinks all of them are trying to seduce her."

"Aren't they?" I asked politely.

"Of course they are, but it's her job to have men looking at her, and there are always a few boors who can't keep their hands off a woman. She's acting a part in the same way that an actress on the stage acts a part, and she has to keep her personal self separate from it and realize that the reaction of men to the seductress she impersonates isn't their reaction to her. Most hostesses quickly learn to deal with that, and they become indifferent about it. She still takes it personally. She complained about Harley, but he really hadn't done anything."

"Anyone else?"

She thought for a moment, frowning. "Lately I noticed something between Harley and Clyde Goodler, but I have no idea what it was. Harley was friendly with most people, but he and Clyde avoided each other. Once in a while it was deliberate and very obvious. One of them would go out of his way to shun the other."

"Did either of them say anything about it?"

"No. As far as I know, there was never any trouble between them. But quarrels do happen in a large business firm — for trivial reasons or for no reason at all. Sometimes a person simply takes a dislike to a fellow employee. It can become so destructive that one of them has to be fired. In the case of Harley and Clyde, their jobs rarely brought them into contact with each other, so there were no problems."

I made a list of the swing shift employees. Then I borrowed Mildred Comptom's office and told her I would leave the keno staff for later but I wanted to talk with the other employees one at a time as their jobs permitted.

They were as vague about Harley Dantzil as the office employees had been. They had seen him at work almost daily, but when I asked them what his job was, they would answer with a surprised, "Security, I suppose," as though they had never thought about it before. Between interviews I stood in the open doorway, watched the gambling, pondered ways to rig the keno game, and tried to ignore the noise. Several times I took a short walk through the casino, and on one of these strolls I saw Wes Zerin seated in the keno lounge. There was an empty chair beside him, and I took it.

He still looked like a high school student — in fact, like a clean-cut, All-American boy. I hoped he would turn out better than my All-American girl selection.

"Can you really put yourself through college gambling?" I asked.

"I'm doing it," he said with a shrug. "I don't live in luxury, there's a lot of hand-to-mouth about it, but I keep afloat. A few bucks here, a few bucks there, it adds up."

"Then you don't bet eight and catch eight."

He gave me a scornful look. "That's waiting for lightning to strike. I plan my keno bets very carefully and use way tickets. If I clear fifteen or twenty bucks, that's a good start for the evening. Fifty or a hundred is a bonanza. Then I do something else. If my luck is good, I can pick up a little money at blackjack — not with a machine, in a live game. If my luck isn't good, I don't play long. Usually I can win a little at video poker, but if I don't win right away, I quit. Sometimes I make a few passes at slot machines. I know where the loose ones are. Like I said, a few bucks here, a few bucks there, I keep afloat."

"What do you do when your luck is all bad?"

"Go home. Once in a while I lose all my seed money and have to borrow from myself, but that doesn't happen often."

"Tell me about Harley Dantzil," I said.

"I heard someone say you're a detective. I still find it hard to believe Harley was murdered. He helped people and wouldn't have hurt a fly. So why him? Maybe you know. I suppose catching murderers is like putting a jigsaw puzzle together."

"Not quite," I said. "To investigate a murder, you must first dig up the pieces, and there always are a number of them that can't be found. Those you do find are mixed in with pieces from other puzzles. Before you can use them, you have to decide which belong to the puzzle you're working on. A jigsaw puzzle wouldn't be much fun under those circumstances, and neither is a murder investigation. What sort of a person was Harley?"

"The kind that missed out on life. He used to join me on my break when I worked the swing shift here. We'd go over to the Sports Book and watch football whenever any was on, and I'd try to explain the game to him. Sports was one of the things he'd missed out on, and he was trying to educate himself, but he couldn't quite grasp the finer points. He was that way about so many things. I liked him, and I felt sorry for him."

I felt sorrier for him because I knew the reason for his belated interest in sports. He had a son of his own growing up, and he wanted to be able to share something with him. "Ever borrow money from him?" I asked.

"No, but a lot of people did. Some took advantage of him. He wanted everyone to like him."

"Then you have no idea why anyone would have murdered him?"

He was silent for a time. The next game was called, and he went to collect his winnings and place more bets. He returned counting his money. "Seventeen ahead," he said. "It's almost worth the trouble. Where were we?"

"Why would anyone murder Harley?"

"Yes. Well — something odd did happen week before last. I was getting ready to leave, and he asked a favor of me. He thought someone was following him, and he was trying to find out who it was. He wanted me to walk behind him for a few blocks and try to get a good description of the

151

person. So I did. He walked north to Fremont and then along Fremont for a couple of blocks, and I walked behind him on the other side of the street and watched as carefully as I could, but I didn't see anyone. It's difficult at night."

"It is," I agreed. "He never asked you to do it again?"

"I don't think I ever saw him again. I don't do much betting at Diamond D's. I just drop in now and then to pass a little time and see some friends."

I thanked him and returned to my post. The next time I gave myself a break, I pondered the strategies of slot machine gambling. Some gamblers thought success lay in the technique of pulling the handle. They jerked it, or they eased it forward, or they pulled firmly and held on until the wheels stopped spinning. None of that made the slightest difference, of course — all the handle does is release a spring that spins the wheels.

Some gamblers grimly played the same machine for hours, convinced that a gigantic jackpot lurked somewhere within and all they had to do was persist long enough to win it. Others tried one machine after another, moving on in disgust if they didn't win immediately. One gambler stood around watching the others, and the moment someone gave up on a machine, he quickly claimed it for a few plays.

The problem with all of these techniques is that

slot machines are not created equal. Payback rates are set at the factory according to the buyer's specifications. Casino owners know that the higher the payback, the more money gambled, and the more they — the casino owners — make. A casino whose machines have an eighty percent payback will show far greater profits than one whose machines return fifty percent. The best of all possible worlds for the greedy casino owner would be one in which his customers enthusiastically keep feeding coins to zero packback machines because they hear illusory jackpots raining down all around them and think their turn will come next. Casinos achieve a deception very like this by intermixing machines with different payback rates. The audio stimulation of jackpots from the high payback machines is intended to psych customers into continued play on the low payback machines. When casinos advertise "Up to 101% payback on slots," you can be certain there is at least one machine in the casino that pays off at the 101% rate — one machine hidden among those hundreds of low-payback machines. Try and find it.

Further, not all of the jackpots you hear rattling down are being won by the proverbial tourist from Oshkosh. Casinos may hire special employees — shills — who play the slots in shifts to create the illusion of action and who have a special supervisor to make certain they don't pocket their winnings. The management would be less than human if it

153

didn't place the shills in front of machines with the highest payback rates — an additional problem for those who would like to play one of those generous machines themselves. That 101% machine may always be in use. Even if you succeed in finding it, you still have to contend with a problem few gamblers think about. In order for that overly generous machine to pay out a thousand dollar jackpot, another gambler, such as yourself, has to lose nine hundred and ninety dollars. Make no mistake about this — it's a jungle in there.

It was eleven o'clock when I finished with the last person on my list, a girl who worked in the snack bar. I thanked her politely, closed my notebook, and went to the restaurant to have a sandwich and coffee while I thought about what I was going to do next.

The waitress took me to the table I had occupied the previous night. I gave her my order, and then I leaned back with every intention of purging my mind for a few minutes of all references to keno, Harley Dantzil, shift bosses, casinos, and lengths of rusty iron pipe. I might have succeeded if I hadn't chanced to glance across the room at the booth where fat Elmer had sat the previous night.

Seated there with a drink in front of her, and sending surreptitious glances in my direction, was Leda Rauchman, alias Phoebe Wallark. Her purse lay on the table beside her glass. I sincerely hoped she had no thought of dropping it a second time.

Even an amateur like her should have known she couldn't perform that maneuver two nights in a row without looking downright conspicuous.

The waitress brought my sandwich and coffee. As a purely humanitarian gesture — in order to spare Leda the emotional trauma of trying to think of another way to pick me up — I resignedly took them across the room and slid into her booth opposite her.

"Good evening, Leda," I said politely. "I hope you got home safely last night."

She blushed. Then she said quietly, "I suppose Mildred tipped you off. I knew I couldn't fool a genuine detective very long."

"Not very long," I agreed. "I'm willing to forgive you for trying, though. I'll even answer questions if you'll tell me what you expected to accomplish."

She looked away from me. "Joel Eckling is a nice guy, and I'm worried about him. His bitch of a daughter is trying to ruin him."

I said noncommittally, "Mildred said you and Joletta didn't get along."

Her response was vehement. "Joletta's been running like a bitch in heat since she was twelve. She had her first abortion at thirteen. After that, no one kept score. When she took up with her current lover, she suddenly became an ardent patriot. She tried to talk her father into making large donations to Americans All. When he refused, she figured out a way to rob him."

"What is 'Americans All'?" I asked.

"It pretends to be an ultra-patriotic association. Actually, it's a front for a bunch of neo-Nazis."

"I saw her with a guy from outer space."

"That's the one. He's the head of Americans All and also of Nevada 2100. Manfred von Mach, he calls himself, but I'm willing to bet it isn't his real name. I'll also bet he isn't even German. 'Manfred' means 'man of peace,' I looked it up, and isn't that a laugh. I had German ancestors myself, and they were good, solid people — nothing like this von Mach and the slime he associates with."

Her bitterness astonished me. "Were you Joel Eckling's mistress?" I asked.

She gave me a disgusted look. Probably she had expected something better from a real detective. "Don't be absurd. With the number of pretty girls at loose ends in this city — and I do mean loose — desperately looking for the break that a casino and hotel owner can give them, why would he take up with a homely secretary? As long as I did my work efficiently, he never knew I existed."

"But that didn't prevent you from being in love with him."

"Nonsense. He's an old man, he's overweight, he has dandruff in what remains of his hair, he needs his teeth fixed, his table manners are awful, and he drinks too much. Even so, he's always been very kind to me, and the vultures in his daughter's crowd, and in Harley Dantzil's crowd, and in sev-

156

eral other crowds I haven't identified, are trying to tear his guts out."

"Why did he fire you?"

"He has the misfortune to love his daughter. He never had a son, and he desperately wants to be proud of Joletta and have her succeed him and make a much bigger success of Diamond D's than he has. She has brains, but unfortunately she has to filter everything through her glands. For a long time he tried to give her anything she wanted. All he got in return was the privilege of paying for her abortions and for keeping her wilder flings out of the papers. Now she wants to sell him out and turn over every penny to the ruggedly handsome Manfred, and I told him so. Joletta heard about it and kicked up such a fuss that he had to fire me. Where do you come into this?"

"This situation is so confused I'm not even sure what case I'm working on, but I can guarantee this much: It's Joel Eckling that I'm working *for*. He hired my firm to send an operative here, and he's the one who'll pay the bill. If he's broken the law, he'd be well advised to get himself the best lawyer he can afford, because law isn't my department. Most other forms of trouble I can do something about, including people who are trying to tear his guts out. For dealing with them, I'm an expert. Since we're on the same side, why don't you stop playing detective and tell a real detective what you know. It might turn out to be important."

157

Her eyes had widened. "Mr. Eckling hired you?"

"Of course. Who else connected with Diamond D's would have money to squander on an Investigative Consultant?"

"I thought it was Joletta or Harley and you went to work for them without knowing what they were up to."

"It wasn't. Eckling hired my firm by telephone, but the arrangements for meeting me when I arrived here were Harley's responsibility. I still don't know why he obfuscated things so dramatically, but I expect to find out before I'm finished."

She desperately needed someone to talk to, and she was relaxing visibly. "I had no idea Mr. Eckling hired you. Harley said nothing about that when he telephoned you."

It was my turn to stare at her. "How did you find out what Harley said?"

She smiled. "A friend of mine works on the switchboard. She's been helping me."

"By listening in?"

"On Harley's and Joletta's calls."

I took a deep breath. "My boss will be pleased to hear that. It justifies the phobia she has about switchboards."

She raised her eyebrows. "You have a woman boss?"

"What's unusual about that? My boss is the best detective I've ever met. A lot of people think fe-

158

male operatives are only useful for following female suspects into ladies' rooms, and it's not true."

Her face clouded. "That was a dirty trick you pulled in the Plaza."

"It's a dirty profession. Tell me what you've been doing."

"Diamond D's keno game is being robbed. No one knows how it's done, but over a period of time the casino has lost a huge amount of money — maybe several hundred thousand dollars. But you know about that."

"Not even Diamond D's auditor knows the exact amount," I said. "Some of the winners must have been legitimate. But I know about the problem."

"Joletta is involved in it — she's turning the money over to her lover's neo-Nazi group. Harley Dantzil was involved in it, too, but I don't know exactly how. I've been following one or the other whenever I could. They met three times at a tavern out on Charleston. Once she brought her lover, and he really told Harley off. He never raised his voice, but he was furious, and Harley's face went white. Harley tried to argue, but muscle-man wouldn't listen. He said his piece, and then he grabbed Joletta's arm and stormed out, dragging her after him."

"Did you tell Eckling about this?"

"I tried to tell him about a lot of things. There's a conspiracy to ruin him, one big chunk of cash at a time, and his daughter is the moving spirit behind it. He didn't want to listen to me, but I kept trying to tell him anyway. Joletta found out, and she stormed in and told me I was fired and she'd call the police if I wasn't out in ten minutes." She sighed. "I told her I was Mr. Eckling's secretary, and he was the only person who could fire me. Finally he had to come and do it. He hated it — he was so embarrassed. I'd been his private secretary for years. He really is a nice person. It's so sad to see an old man done in by his own flesh and blood."

"How long have you been trying to keep an eye on Harley and Joletta?"

"Joletta off and on for three or four months. Harley for the last couple of months. I didn't suspect him until I followed Joletta one night and she met him."

"The keno thing probably has been going on for a couple of years."

"I only found out about it a few months ago. I overheard a conversation Mr. Eckling was having with an accountant. I suspected Joletta immediately, so I started following her when I could, and I asked my friend to listen in on her telephone calls for clues. When I saw her meet Harley, I began following him when I could."

"Did you happen to notice anyone else following Harley?"

She shook her head.

"Did you see Harley meet with anyone except

Joletta and her lover?"

"Yes. He met with one man twice, and there were two other men he met with once each. Until I was fired, I mostly tried to follow Harley on his breaks when he was at the casino in the evening. I only followed him a few times when he got off work. I couldn't hang around very late — I had to be at work the next morning. I followed Joletta when she left work, but mostly she met her lover and they went directly to her apartment or his." She added apologetically, "I did the best I could."

"You did very well. In fact, incredibly well. Has anyone been following you?"

She looked at me blankly.

"You weren't the only one who was following Harley," I said. "You may not have noticed anyone else, but if the other party was a professional, he certainly noticed you. His next step would have been to follow you and find out who you were and what you were up to. You were followed last night when you left here."

"How exciting." She sounded very tired. She had been under a considerable strain with a problem she didn't know how to handle.

"We'll find out whether he's still following you when we leave," I said.

She gave me a wry smile. "Does that mean we're going to have the next drinks at my place?"

"It means you've made yourself a central figure in a murder case, and you need looking after. As

161

far as I know, you're the only person who's had a glimpse of the odd associates that Harley Dantzil was cultivating, and you're also the only person who can connect him with Joletta. When his murderer is brought to trial, you may be the most important witness. Your life has been in danger for weeks. Don't smile — I couldn't possibly be more serious. You've given a thoroughly nasty crowd of people ample reason to want you dead."

We got to our feet. She said, "What a disappointment. I was living dangerously and didn't even know it. I never had a chance to enjoy it."

"Now that you know," I said, "you may find it a lot less fun than you'd thought."

9

WE PAUSED AT THE CASINO'S EXIT WHILE I made certain there was a cab waiting at the stand outside. Then I grabbed her arm, and we ran for it.

I called "Sahara!" to the driver — speaking loudly enough to be overheard at least thirty feet away — pushed Leda in ahead of me, and slammed the door. As we began to move, I reached for her.

She shoved back at me with startling strength. "Leave the cave man stuff to Joletta's muscleman," she said indignantly.

"It's just an act for whoever is following us."

"Don't give me that . . ." She broke off and twisted to face me. "Are you serious?"

I recited Pletcher's uncopyrighted Third Law, "Being Tailed at Night." Even when you have identified the tail, it is devilishly hard to lose him because it is so difficult to keep track of where he is. The best technique is to set him up for it. If you keep checking to see if you can spot him, and make sudden moves to trap him into giving himself away, he quickly becomes wary. He starts planning his own moves in anticipation of yours, and when you make your break, he'll be ready for you.

What you must do is act as natural as possible, convince him you don't know you are being followed and anyway couldn't care less, telegraph every move so he can drift after you without thinking and devote his mind to matters that seem more important — and suddenly do a well-planned fade. You can have him so mesmerized he will think he is still following you ten minutes after you cut in another direction.

"If a young lady lets herself be picked up in a casino," I told Leda, "makes love to the guy in a taxi, and starts on a highflying tour of the Strip with him, everything she does from that point becomes predictable, and her tail counts on a relaxed evening."

"You *are* serious!" she exclaimed incredulously.

"Absolutely. It'll be a lot easier to shake this guy if he thinks our minds are on other things than being tailed."

"In that case," she said, "it might as well be a good act."

She threw her arms around me and engraved an imprint of her lips on mine.

Diamond D's is located perhaps twenty-five blocks from the Sahara. My explanation took two blocks, and the kiss lasted for the next twenty-three. I finally pushed her away when the cab turned off Las Vegas Boulevard.

We got out, and I paid the driver. She took my arm matter-of-factly and remarked, "I like the detective business. I've been wasting my life. Nothing like that ever happened while I was a secretary."

Strip is Strip, and Casino Center is Casino Center, and the twain are irremediably separated by a drab, two-mile stretch of Las Vegas Boulevard. People staying at downtown hotels may visit the Strip to see the stage shows and admire the sybaritic diversions of Caesar's Palace, or the joviality of Circus Circus, or the Mirage's overpowering illusions, or Excalibur's sham Medievalism, but large numbers of those staying on the Strip never get close enough to Glitter Gulch to make Vegas Vic's acquaintance.

It was my first visit to the Strip since I arrived. For some reason I had anticipated an entirely different atmosphere, but when we strolled through the door at the Sahara, I found myself facing a drearily identical forest of slot machines. The slots, the blackjack and craps tables, the roulette wheels, and all the related paraphernalia, might have been borrowed from the Casino Center for the evening. The keno lounge and its runners, and the young ladies in risqué costumes dispensing drinks, were so similar to what I had been looking at for two days that only the more lavish décor convinced me we had actually left Diamond D's.

I appointed Leda my resident expert and posed a question for her: Apart from superficialities such as the life-sized tableau of Arabs and camels outside the Sahara, or the real circus acts at Circus Circus, or the Mirage's volcano, or the gingerbread turrets that are supposed to make Excalibur look like a castle, how do casinos on the Strip differ from those in the downtown Casino Center?

"A casino is a casino is a casino," I said. "They all feature the same kinds of slot machines. The craps tables all look alike. The girls passing out free drinks could come to work at the wrong casino and few people would notice. Hotels vary drastically in quality and price in both places. What are the differences — or are there any?"

"Now that you've seen them both, what do you think?"

The most noticeable difference to me was in the noise level. Music played over loud-speakers in the Casino Center tended to be jazzy, blaring, even ear-shattering. The noise volume of live entertainment was devastating. On the Strip, one sometimes heard strings instead of unrelenting brass all the time. Excalibur even played classical music for its gamblers — Vivaldi and Mozart. It should have been easier to concentrate on gambling in the quieter atmosphere, and I wondered why the casinos in the Casino Center hadn't thought of this. Probably they had, but casinos don't want gamblers to concentrate. They want

166

them to lose. The more internal distractions they can offer, the better — hence the scantily clad nymphs dispensing drinks. It is the outside distractions that they strive to protect gamblers from.

Leda disagreed. "Wait until you hear live music on the Strip," she said. "It can blow you right out of the place. And you should never, ever, attend a show in Las Vegas, anywhere, without ear plugs."

But a casino is a casino is a casino, and the customers were a miscellaneous mix in both places. We finally decided that most of the differences were due to managerial mentality. Managements on the Strip thought they had a higher class of customer. They didn't, but because they thought so, they handled atmospheric touches like music and illumination differently.

After a careful look at the Sahara's keno operation, we tried our luck at the slots, and Leda won a hundred and twenty dollars with one pull of a handle. She calmly scooped up the coins and made the shocking announcement that she was quitting. Universally applied, this attitude could sabotage the entire free enterprise system as far as Las Vegas gambling is concerned. People who hit a jackpot are expected to keep playing until they lose it, and most of them do. The slots giveth, and the slots taketh away.

I had been nourishing suspicions about two overdressed tourists who were obviously more interested in us than in the slot machines. I asked

Leda to put her moral scruples aside for one evening and act the part of a restless, finicky gambler. I wanted her to flit about impulsively and try one machine after another, which was certain to tax any tail's ingenuity.

"Moral scruples aren't the problem," she said. "The idea of making charitable donations to casino owners offends my common sense."

We gave our tails a merry chase through the Sahara before we moved on to other casinos. It is only a short jog down Las Vegas Boulevard to Circus Circus, but we tried to make things more interesting for them by taking a cab. By the time we arrived, they had vanished. Then I identified two new tails and began to feel puzzled. We played the slots, we gawked at a circus act, we toured the mezzanine carnival, and finally we slipped out a side exit to angle over to Slots-A-Fun, the slot machine casino next door.

The tails who had drifted after us through Circus Circus didn't try to follow. Instead, a new set picked us up outside the door and kept on our heels through Slots-A-Fun. When we left that casino by the front door, the characters from the Sahara were waiting, and they followed us through Westward Ho! and finally relinquished us to another pair when we crossed the street to the Riviera. And so it went, either by foot or by cab. At least eight men were following us, and they must have had three cars with drivers backing them. Only Lieutenant McCarney should have been able to mount an operation like that, and I was certain that these characters weren't police officers.

To tour the Las Vegas Strip is to plunge from one incongruity to another. Where else would you find a perpetual circus in your hotel lobby? Or a nightclub in the desert that has a real, floating boat for a stage? Or an oriental bazaar combined with an antique auto show? Or a palace dedicated to the voluptuous pleasures of ancient Rome with Renaissance statuary and a Hindu religious shrine? After a couple of hours of this, the fantastic becomes real, and the real world, where there are wars, and murders, and unhappy love affairs, seems like a surrealistic nightmare. None of the tourists crowding the slot machines and gaming tables acted the least concerned over the fact that every one of these hedonistic extravaganzas had been paid for with someone's gambling losses — past, present, and future.

It occurred to me again that those milling about the casinos were not tourists; they were film extras contending for jobs on these fantastic motion picture sets. Those already hired were being coached to act the part of gamblers nonchalantly flourishing stage money. Pretty script girls in uniform answered their questions and showed them exactly where to stand, and assistant directors hovered nearby to make certain that all went well. Large numbers of these extras were lined up and kept waiting while sets were being prepared for banquet or theater scenes. Some merely wandered about, giving an excellent imitation of dazed tourists watching motion pictures being made.

No other explanation could account for such a preposterous assemblage. Surely no one would build such elaborate sets for any other purpose, and the only people who would spend time in this two-dimensional landscape, and actually throw away money there, were film extras dispensing stage currency. One expected to see, at any moment, a quiet, attractive girl acting the part of a sales clerk from Boise who had saved her money for a vacation and would turn out to be the heroine; and the freshly scrubbed farm boy from Iowa who would heroically rescue her from the grisly fate an unimaginative scriptwriter was at this moment trying to invent in a canvas-walled cubicle behind the props.

One expected to see them, but what one mostly saw were clusters of plump, successful, middle-aged tourists with money; or graying, elderly, retired tourists with time.

At the Excalibur we encountered a forlorn secretary from Walla Walla or Hartford who was having difficulty understanding how a keno ticket should be filled out. Several males were giving her their most sympathetic undivided attention. And why not? In a homespun way, the confused little redhead was a genuine beauty. A Hollywood director, backed by an artful make-up man, could have transformed her into a dazzling seductress in three easy lessons.

It was Raina Lambert, and one of the males demonstrating an unrestrained eagerness to educate her in keno and other things was wearing the now familiar space uniform from Nevada 2100. I was tempted to slip a message to her about the army tailing us, but there was no way I could do that without queering her act, and she never would have forgiven me.

I was becoming concerned. We were subjects of a Grand Slam, a massive tailing operation that shouldn't have been wasted on anyone less important than a serial murderer or a depraved evangelist. I had now counted ten operatives and decided there must be four cars involved. We made no serious effort to ditch them except for a couple of seemingly innocent experiments — such as sending Leda to the ladies' room while I slipped out a side entrance, got a cab, and waited for her; or pretending to have a tiff. She dashed outside and found her own cab, and I chased after her in another cab for an affectionate reconciliation. The men following us weren't even inconvenienced. A casino should be a fairly easy place to lose a tail, but with so many men in reserve, there was someone waiting for us outside no matter what exit we used. I began to feel worried when I noticed that several of them carried radios.

By 2:00 A.M., my research had finally turned up a significant difference between the Strip casinos and those in the Casino Center. Many of the keno payoffs in games on the Strip were substantially lower than those in the Casino Center. For example, where Diamond D's paid $20,000 for $2 on the bet seven, catch seven game, Strip casinos usually paid much less — from $16,000 down to around $10,000. I asked Leda if she could tell me in one word why, in the game that gave casinos their highest win percentage, and with the odds so formidably against the customers winning anything at all, the most plush casinos were the most parsimonious in their payoffs.

She was still loyal to Diamond D's. "Try 'greed,'" she said.

I had been wracking my brain for more than an hour trying to think of a way we could extricate ourselves from the noose someone had adroitly placed around us. Eventually I would have to take Leda home, and I didn't want four carloads of unknown quantities following closely when we left lights and people behind.

Coming out of Excalibur, I decided to confide in a cab driver. "We're being followed. We need help."

I passed him a hundred-dollar bill. He looked at it twice and then glanced back at us. "Okay," he said. "I'll play. But first let me give you a piece of absolutely free advice. It's a lot cheaper to wait

172

until her husband is out of town."

He very carefully explained what he wanted us to do. Then he made a loop through the Mirage parking lot, ostensibly to give us a close look at the erupting volcano, and another loop through the curving drive at Caesar's Palace. There were at least two carloads of familiar faces right behind us when he let us out at the entrance to one of the long, overhead, slow-moving sidewalks that extend from Las Vegas Boulevard to the casino's front door, gave us a good-luck wave, and drove off.

It was an ideal place for spotting a tail, so of course no one followed us there, but several men were waiting for us when we reached the casino.

Caesar's Palace does have its own distinctive atmosphere. An opulent hush seems to mute the casino clamor, and in the hotel lobby, one receives an overwhelming impression that even the rustle of paper money would sound vulgar.

We followed the driver's instructions, separating to use the rest rooms and finally leaving through the hotel. Not only were we tailed all the way, but two men were waiting for us at the exit. When the cab drove off, a procession followed. I explained the situation in detail to the driver while he wheeled onto Dunes Road. He took the entrance ramp to the Highway 15 expressway and exited on Sahara Avenue. The procession was still following.

"Are they locals?" the driver asked.

I didn't know.

"We'll soon find out," he said with a grin.

Anyone who believes the Las Vegas Strip is real should have a look at its reverse side. Just behind it on the west, and running parallel to it, is Industrial Road, a gruesome slum of junk yards, of wrecked car storage, of condemned buildings, of shoddy repair shops, of rusting industrial equipment. The cab's headlights picked out one repulsive scene after another, but looming just beyond was the brilliant glow of the Strip and all of its thinly encrusted glitter.

The driver gave us a ride to remember. We bounced over unpaved streets, drove stretches with lights out, took sharp turns that tossed us from one side of the cab to the other, and finally swerved through a truck and bus park to emerge headed in the opposite direction.

One of the cars tailing us tried to cut us off. Our own driver, who must have known the area from babyhood, jumped a curb, roared through the parking lot of a boarded-up building, and got away cleanly. He took the next corner on two wheels and flipped his lights off. A moment later he swung in behind a run-down factory building and coasted to a stop, carefully avoiding touching his brake pedal, which would have lit up that dingy yard like the famous red flower on the Flamingo Hilton.

Leda, who had been clinging to me throughout our wild ride, now clung tighter. She was shivering with delight. "I never had so much fun," she exclaimed.

We had lost one of the cars somewhere along the way. The remaining three prowled the area for all of twenty minutes before they finally began to spread out. Eventually they gave up.

The driver turned to Leda. "With a husband like yours, I don't blame you for playing around — but I still think you should wait until he's out of town."

We took Highway 15 north, switched to 515, and exited just beyond the downtown Casino Center. Avoiding Glitter Gulch, we headed south, and I gave the driver the address of Leda's apartment on Gottford Street.

"You didn't ask me for that," she said reproachfully.

"I got it when I saw you home last night."

"You saw me home last night?"

"Of course. A girl like you needs a permanent bodyguard."

"Imagine that. Me with a body that needs guarding."

When we reached her apartment building, I rewarded the driver lavishly and made one additional request. He was to wait until I signaled. If the signal didn't come within five minutes, he was to radio for the police.

He looked at Leda again and shook his head regretfully. "So that's the way it is. Your husband is some character. Did you ever consider divorcing him?"

I hurried her up the walk to the building. We climbed to the second floor, and I took the key from her, placed her as far as possible from the door, and opened it with my automatic ready. I reached inside and found a light switch. After locking the door behind us, I left Leda in the small entrance hallway while I quickly went through her apartment. It was a pleasant place for a single woman, with one bedroom, a large kitchen with a dining nook at one end, a small but comfortable living room, and a bathroom. The furniture was stylishly practical, and she was a gem of a housekeeper: everything neat, appliances sparkling, kitchen and bathroom floors looking freshly waxed, a white carpet in the living room that didn't have a smudge.

When I was satisfied there was no reception committee, I flicked the living room light on and off and went to the window to wave at our cab driver. He flicked his own lights and drove away. I returned to Leda.

There were no ashtrays in the apartment, and she hadn't touched a cigarette in all of the hours I had spent with her, but I asked anyway. "Do you smoke?"

She shook her head.

"Have you had an invited guest today who smoked?"

She shook her head again.

"Then you've had an uninvited guest who did,"

I said. "Probably he was a pipe smoker. He didn't drop any ashes, and the smoke has a faintly jazzed up aroma." I escorted her into the kitchen and placed a chair for her. "Wait here while I figure out what he was up to."

She sat with a puzzled look on her face, periodically taking deep sniffs, while I prowled from one room to another.

"I can't smell anything at all," she said when I returned. "Are you sure?"

I was sure. That is the one advantage to being allergic. I can detect extremely faint odors of tobacco smoke. Occasionally this turns out to be useful.

I slipped off my shoes, climbed onto a chair, and inspected the ceiling fixture. "This light is going off for a moment," I warned her. "Turn on the one over the counter, will you?"

Using my handkerchief, I unscrewed the bulb. Then I unscrewed an oddly shaped object that fitted neatly into the fixture and had its own bulb socket. When the bulb was in place, the object was almost unnoticeable. I found what could have been a switch on its under side and pushed it. Then I climbed down and showed it to her, holding it in my handkerchief with the lightbulb.

"Have you ever seen anything like this before?"

"Never," she said. "What is it?"

"I think it's a bug. If it has a battery — which it must have, or it would only work when the light is on — it'll be designed to recharge automatically. That's quite an order for such a small contraption. In fact, this thing is a genuine eye opener, and your apartment is a strange address for it. It didn't come from K-Mart or even from Radio Shack. It's the sort of gadget one would expect to find in top-secret places like foreign embassies when someone with unlimited resources has an overpowering curiosity about any little thing that might happen. Your kitchen doesn't qualify. Neither does your living room, but it's bugged, too. You don't happen to have any heroin hidden in your refrigerator, do you? Or marijuana in that candy dish?"

"Certainly not!"

"Or any dark secrets you'd prefer to keep unofficial? The police are about to go over this apartment with a thoroughness that's rare even for them."

I removed the bug from a lamp in the living room and turned it off. Then I slipped my shoes on and went to the telephone.

Lieutenant McCarney was emerging as my favorite kind of unflappable policeman. Asked to produce technical experts at three in the morning, he calmly estimated that it might take as long as forty-five minutes. Asked to put an informal cordon on the block before the experts arrived — just in case there was someone watching the building who would vamoose the moment he caught sight of the police — he amended the delay to an hour. Asked

178

whether there would be a man available to keep an eye on an important witness, he said, "Of course." Then he added, "See you," and hung up.

While we were waiting, I asked Leda whether anyone had been snooping through her property. I showed her how to open and close drawers without touching the handle, and she enthusiastically opened and closed every drawer in the apartment. She thought someone had been in her desk, though he had carefully tried to put things back the way he found them. She was less certain about the dresser drawers. The kitchen hadn't been touched.

I next questioned her about the men she had seen meeting Harley Dantzil. She was positive she could identify the one who met Dantzil twice, and she thought she could recognize the other two. I made her wrack her memory and describe them to me as well as she could.

"The one I saw twice was an elderly dandy," she said. "A former lady killer who thinks he still is if he wants to work at it."

"How old?" I asked.

"How old is a woman who's been thirty-nine for years? He'll never see sixty again, and he's going on forty. Dyes his hair — if it's really his. Wears a sporty checkered suit with a conservative tie just to show he has taste. Gives the ladies a treat by taking mincing steps when he walks. Those places are poorly lighted, but once he went right past my table, and I got a good look at him. I didn't see him standing beside Harley, so I can't judge his height very well. Call him short, slender, and very, very proud of his waistline."

"The police could use you to write their 'wanted' notices. What about the others?"

"One was Dandy's opposite — a hayseed in overalls. Call him a slob. He slouched. He had thick, bushy, brown hair, probably with straw in it, but the room was too dim for me to see that. He needed a haircut."

"A custodian at a casino?" I suggested. "Someone who'd have access to a keno machine?"

"Not at Diamond D's, or I'd have recognized him. Maybe a custodian at one of the other casinos."

"How old was he?"

She hesitated. "Middle-aged or a little beyond. He wasn't trying to look younger, like Dandy. He gave the impression of not giving a damn about his appearance — age, clothes, anything."

"The third one?"

"A former football star, but not the handsome halfback. A rugged defensive back whose face got run over regularly for several years."

"Anything special about his clothes?"

"Nothing." She shrugged. "Touristy, I suppose, except that he was wearing a touristy sport shirt at night in chilly weather, and most tourists have better sense than that. He might have got himself up for the part. I'll know Dandy again no matter what he's wearing. I might not know the other two if I saw them dressed differently. On the other hand, I might. The slob's hair and the football star's run-over face were memorable."

"You," I said, "are the prize witness of all time — I think. I'll know for certain when you point to one of those characters on the street."

I was waiting at the downstairs door when Mc-Carney arrived with four officers who carried equipment.

"Let's keep it as quiet as we can," I suggested. He agreed, and the six of us tiptoed back up the stairs. I introduced the electronics men to the gadgets I'd found. They reacted with joyful mutterings, but the fingerprint man had first claim and made them wait until he'd done his dusting. There were no prints. McCarney, Leda, and I took seats around the table in the dining nook and we let the experts work while I explained the situation.

He interrupted me only once. *"Four* cars?"

"Four," I said firmly.

When I finished, McCarney turned to Leda. "Who murdered Harley Dantzil?"

"Joletta," she said instantly. "Or her lover. Most likely the lover. I don't mean he did it himself. He has an army of muscle-men at his disposal, and their version of law and order says whatever der Führer orders is law."

"Why would either Joletta or her lover want Harley Dantzil dead?"

"He knew about their plot to get her father's money. He may have been obstructing them in some way."

McCarney turned to me. "Is any of that possible?"

"You know Joletta better than I do. My first impression of her was highly favorable. Since then I've received nothing but nasty revelations. Do *you* think it's possible?"

"She's been wild ever since she was a kid, but murder doesn't seem like her kind of game."

"I don't know what her game is, but I'm certain she didn't know Harley was dead until we found his body. Possibly her playmates murdered him without her knowledge, but I'd need to know a lot more about Americans All before I put that in a public statement."

"We all need to know a lot more about Americans All," McCarney said sourly. "I hope you aren't thinking a pretty girl is incapable of murder. I could cite numerous examples . . ."

"So could I. I'm thinking about the telephone call Harley was supposed to have made when he'd been dead for more than twelve hours. If Joletta had known about the murder, she certainly wouldn't have mentioned it."

"She told me the voice on the phone sounded a bit odd to her, but she was too busy at the moment to think much about it. It said, 'This is Harley. I can't meet Pletcher. You'll have to do it.'

182

She started to protest, and it said, 'Sorry, I can't meet him,' and hung up. I don't believe her. I don't think there was a phone call.'

"She could have been instructed to meet me by someone who knew Harley was dead but didn't bother to tell her. If he'd known I would immediately traipse over to the secret apartment with Joletta in tow and discover the body, he would have kept her out of it. I was supposed to return to my hotel and wait for instructions — in which case Harley wouldn't have been found until someone in the building complained about an unpleasant odor."

"It could have happened that way," McCarney conceded.

"There also was the young man who gave me the telephone number to call, and I don't believe he knew Harley was dead, either. He was trying to get me away from that corner before Harley arrived."

There had been no sign of a stake-out on the apartment, but McCarney agreed on the wisdom of a guard for Leda, and we discussed where to put him. If he sat outside in a car, everyone in the neighborhood would be talking about him by breakfast time. Leda finally agreed to let him sleep on the living room sofa and accompany her whenever she went out. Hopefully the case wouldn't last long enough for her to be seriously inconvenienced.

We waited until the technical experts had finished. McCarney left with them after asking me to please make no more discoveries before dawn.

Leda saw me to the door. I gave her a light kiss in parting, and then a much firmer one. I have been pursued many times, but I never enjoyed a chase more, and I told her so. She was in fact a perfect companion for detective heroics. She had done exactly what I asked and done it quickly and well, she had shut up when she had nothing to contribute, she hadn't screamed or giggled once, and I still liked the way her face crinkled when she smiled.

But now she wasn't smiling. She said bitterly, "A great development this is. How is a girl to have any love life with a policeman in the living room? Why can't you guard me yourself?"

"I have a hard day's work ahead of me, and how much sleep would I get on your living room sofa?" I asked her blandly.

"Probably none," she said. She smiled. "Everyone says I'm a frightfully loud snorer." She closed the door.

10

THE NEXT DAY, THURSDAY, WAS ONLY MY third day in Las Vegas, and I felt as though I had been there for weeks. I also felt as though I should return to bed for another six hours of sleep. After breakfast, I took a short walk to clear my head and scrutinize the weather. The sky was promising another monotonously perfect, sunny day.

At nine-thirty my taxi pulled into the driveway of Dr. Harold Quilley's residence. It was a sub-stantially-sized ranch home — a single-family, stucco house in a neighborhood of single-family stucco houses — located in a new subdivision in the same general northwest area as the Stevens-Dantzil mock castle but much farther out. I had by this time identified stucco as a favorite building material in Las Vegas. All of these houses were distortedly similar, and all of them looked as though the builders had just left. There were no trees, and the owners hadn't had time to nurture lawns into being over the caliche, the desert's hard, rock-like undersoil, so the small, brick-walled yards consisted of bare dirt. The subdivision's newness was also evidenced by the huge air conditioners on the roofs of the houses. Thus the march of progress in southern Nevada: Older houses had smaller air conditioners on their roofs. The oldest had tiny air conditioners in their windows.

I was met at the door by Mrs. Quilley, a shapely brunette wearing shorts despite the morning's coolness. She was outgoing and poised but very young-looking, from which I deduced that the professor had married one of his students. A detective makes such deductions automatically whether they are relevant or not. I handed her my card, and she invited me into a well-arranged and tastefully furnished living room.

Her husband, a lank man in his mid-forties, arrived a moment later. He was informally at home and wearing long trousers and a sweat shirt. She passed my card to him, and he gave her a wink and a nod and escorted me to his study, a room where every centimeter of available wall space was lined with book shelves except for one four-by-four area that contained a blackboard. Not all of the shelves held books. The professor was a gadgeteer, and the *disjecta membra* of discarded scientific experiments were scattered about.

I have met enough university professors, in enough places, to know that there are no generic specifications for one, so Dr. Harold Quilley offered no surprises. He wore a beard, but he kept it neatly trimmed and didn't make an issue of it.

"Please sit down," he said, pointing at the one extra chair in the room. His own chair, which faced the broad table he used for a desk and a computer stand, was a monstrous structure, a super reclining chair with a high back and plush fabric upholstering. It seemed inappropriate for anyone below the rank of university president. He settled into it with the air of having spent endless hours there, tilted back and meditating. He pivoted to face me and studied me for a moment before he turned his attention to my card.

"J. Pletcher?"

"The 'J' stands for 'Jagoda,'" I said.

"Really? You look Anglo-Saxon to me. I know an English professor who would love to have one of your cards. I'll give him this one. He'll quote 'Investigative Consultants' as an example of contemporary linguistic degeneration. What can I do for you?"

He was extremely soft-spoken, and he had the disconcerting habit of looking away from the person he was talking to. This conveyed the impression that his thoughts were winging to the sound of another drummer, which I hoped was not the case.

"Didn't anyone tell you what the problem is?" I asked.

He shook his head, smiling. "Yesterday morning, I was informed by the president's office that a man named Pletcher was going to call on me. The president himself urgently requested that I assist you in any way possible. I was surprised. People who can exercise political clout on that level rarely have an interest in scientific matters."

"Just blame it on my not knowing the protocol. You must have caught the news report about a man found murdered day before yesterday. That murder was connected with a scam to defraud casinos on their keno games. The investigation isn't likely to make much headway until we figure out how the scam was worked. How would a scientist go about rigging a keno game?"

He looked away with a frown and asked, "Have you observed the mechanisms casinos use for their keno games?"

"According to Sherlock Holmes, there's an emphatic difference between seeing and observing. I've *seen* the keno mechanisms, but I can't claim that I observed very much. I have no idea how one would go about cheating on a game of keno. I suppose there'd have to be some method by which preselected numbers would come up instead of a random selection."

"Yes. With one type of mechanism you have a mixing chamber with a blower to agitate the balls; with another you have the revolving wire cage. Of course you already know there are eighty balls, each bearing a different number from 1 through 80, and after they've been thoroughly mixed, the twenty winning numbers are drawn from the bowl or cage one at a time. The entire operation is untouched by human hands. You mark your favorite numbers on a keno ticket and turn it in before the drawing, and if enough of them appear, you receive a substantial reward. You don't have to catch all of your choices to win, of course. If you mark the maximum twenty numbers . . ." He paused. "I don't remember exactly how the payoffs run, but I'm sure you could do very well for yourself by catching sixty or seventy percent of them. That would be twelve to fourteen numbers."

I had Diamond D's keno card in my pocket, and I pulled it out. "On a five dollar bet, twelve numbers would win a thousand dollars. That jumps to five thousand for thirteen numbers and to twelve thousand five hundred for fourteen."

"That's a fantastic return on such a small bet," he said. "All you would have to do is to find a way to tilt the game a little in your favor. It isn't necessary to win the big jackpot — just alter the odds enough to give yourself a slight advantage over the house. If you can keep playing that way, you'll win a fortune. In a game that offers a fifty-thousand-dollar jackpot, a mere thousand seems piddling, but if you could win it three times a week, you'd have a hundred and fifty thousand dollars a year, and the casinos don't even require identification and tax forms on a thousand dollars. If once in a great while you accidentally hit it big, that would be a nice bonus, but it really isn't necessary. Even without tampering with the game, you should be able to catch eight or nine numbers once in a great while, but eight or nine only pay — what?"

"Ten dollars for eight and twenty-five for nine."

"Next to nothing," he said with a disparaging wave. "Your objective is to tilt the game just enough so that instead of now and then catching eight or nine, as would normally happen, you will catch twelve or fourteen. It doesn't matter if this works only one time out of fifty or even one time out of a hundred. Forty-nine losses only cost you two hundred and forty-five dollars. Do you have an idea for accomplishing this?"

"I was wondering whether some form of magnetism might be involved."

He pivoted slowly and turned his attention to the most remote corner of the ceiling. "Ping-Pong balls aren't affected by magnetism," he said. "They're non-metallic. I suppose it might be possible to paint the numbers on them with a metallic or even a magnetic paint, but it would take an extremely powerful magnetic field to produce the effect you have in mind."

He thought for a moment. Then he went to the door and opened it. "Edna!" he called. "Would you see if you can find a Ping-Pong ball anywhere in the neighborhood? Try the Savard kids — they have a table in their rec room."

"Will do," she called back.

"They should have a few extras. Try to abstract one without breaking up their game."

He returned to his chair. "One basic truth about human nature stands out vividly whenever this kind of problem comes up. There's virtually no limit to the time and effort people will invest in trying to figure out ways to defraud gambling casinos. The amount of money they're willing to spend on it equals the sum of their bank accounts and their credit. The bite of the EMB, the Easy Money Bug, is as dangerous as the bite of a flea infected with bubonic plague. It can consume a person's life. Sometimes one visit to a casino, and a glimpse of all that money floating about, is instantly infectious. I'm only a professor of physics. You'd have to see a psychologist or a psychiatrist for a medical explanation."

"I'm something of an expert in the disease myself," I said. "Its victims don't restrict their activity to casinos. They operate everywhere, and they keep a lot of detectives gainfully employed."

He nodded. "Yes. Of course. I find the disease incomprehensible. Perhaps that's because I'm immune to it. I can walk through a casino and experience amusement, or curiosity, or amazement, or disgust — but no greed and very little compassion for those afflicted.

"Every way I could think of to rig a keno game poses enormous scientific and technological difficulties, and there also would be the casino's security measures to overcome — but that doesn't mean it couldn't be done. It merely means that anyone doing it would have to have considerable ability and be willing to invest the necessary time and money. Look at the people who develop card-counting techniques to win at blackjack. They have to cultivate their skill for months or years, and even after they become successful, they must practice daily in order to keep themselves sharp. All of this seems unbelievable to a normal person. Normal people wouldn't go to such lengths to win at a game of cards.

"If a scientific genius with a knack for gadgetry were to drop everything else and work for years on a keno scam, he certainly would find ways to overcome many of the difficulties. If he were lucky, he might overcome all of them — but he still could be tripped up by casino security or something even simpler.

"There's a book that describes the experiences of a group of very bright young people who dedicated themselves to producing a tiny computer that could be smuggled into a casino and fed information by way of special keys that they could operate with their toes. It gave them performance analyses of roulette wheels so they'd know what numbers to bet. Their technique worked — after a fashion — but the returns were pathetically small compared with the years of time they invested and the money they spent. Of course the pursuit of that goal

192

forced them to deal with complicated scientific problems and ways to express them on a computer. They had to develop special mathematical algorithms and perfect their own unique technology, so perhaps their adventure had an educational value that was beyond price.

"What I'm saying is that people who are extremely bright and really have the urge can overcome enormously complicated problems. In the end, though, whatever apparatus they devise has to operate undetected in the chaotic environment of a casino, and that alone is enough to defeat most efforts."

"I'm assuming a casino employee is involved," I said.

He raised his eyebrows. "That certainly ought to make it easier."

Edna bobbed into the room and handed him a Ping-Pong ball.

"Thanks, dear," he said. "Did you have to disrupt their game?"

Edna grinned. "Nope. But I had to look for it — it was lost behind the washing machine." She bobbed out again.

"I did hear the Savard kids talking about that," Quilley said. "Perhaps it has a bearing on your problem. According to them, these balls have the mysterious property of always ending up in the most difficult place to find them, which in their house is behind the washing machine."

He carefully placed the Ping-Pong ball on his desk, twice prevented it from rolling away, and finally, when it remained motionless, contemplated it for a moment. Then he took a comb from his pocket, rubbed it energetically on his sleeve, and slowly moved it toward the Ping-Pong ball. As the distance diminished, the ball began to quiver. Closer, and the ball moved — but Quilley moved the comb away, and the ball rolled after it.

"Electrostatics," he said. "Know anything about it?"

"Next to nothing. I can remember doing simple experiments in school with tiny balls of paper."

He rubbed the comb again and repeated the experiment. "Some substances work better than others, and this comb would pick up a greater charge if I had wool to rub it on." He jumped up and strode to the blackboard, where he scribbled a formula:

$$\mathbf{F}_{12} = k\frac{q_1 q_2}{r^2}\ \mathbf{n}$$

"Coulomb's Law," he announced. "If anyone has found a way to use electrostatics to rig a keno game, he had to start with that. The force between two isolated small bodies varies inversely with the square of the distance separating them and directly according to the magnitude of the charge. So said Coulomb in 1785; so says any physicist today."

I asked politely, "What does it mean?"

He returned to his chair, rubbed the comb, and

extended it toward the Ping-Pong ball. "The force with which the ball is attracted depends directly on how much charge I can put on the comb by rubbing it and inversely according to how far it is from the ball. In simple terms, I must keep moving the comb closer to the ball until the amount of the charge is able to overcome the distance between them. A larger charge would affect the ball from a greater distance; with an extremely small charge, I might have to move the comb so close that it virtually touches the ball. As for applying this to a keno game . . ."

He gestured toward the blackboard. "If they're using electrostatics, they've had to find ways around the square of the distance problem and also the problem of developing an adequate electrical charge without producing a static discharge, which could cause sparks and also embarrassing and sometimes dangerous electrical shocks."

He tilted back in his massive chair, pivoted until he was facing a side wall, and fingered his beard with one hand while he thought for a moment. "There's very little that's new about the theory of electrostatics but there are new developments all the time in its application. Neanderthal Man may have been the first electrical scientist. If he had any kind of furry pet, he knew that at certain times the fur became charged when he stroked it. In the dark, there would be sparks. As long ago as ancient Greece, Thales of Miletus learned that rubbing a piece of amber gave it a mysterious property that enabled it to attract small objects.

"Nothing much was done with this knowledge until Otto von Guericke built the first electrostatic generator, the friction machine, about 1660. During the next century, research into electrostatics became extremely popular. Experiments were used as a kind of parlor game that anyone could play. Benjamin Franklin made enormously important contributions. Not only did he fly his famous kite and prove that lightning was a form of electricity, but he also identified two types of electricity, which he called 'positive' and 'negative,' and he actually built an electrostatic motor that would work. About the same time, Coulomb's Law gave electrostatics a scientific basis.

"In the nineteenth century, however, electrical research turned in another direction. Faraday discovered electromagnetic induction. Volta invented the wet cell, or battery, and for the first time scientists had a source for electrical current. The research these two things made possible revolutionized civilization. Electrostatics was almost forgotten. By 1900, those who thought about it at all were trying to find ways to avoid it. Its sparks caused explosions. Flour mills, for example, had to be eternally wary of electrostatics because flour dust could explode with disastrous results. Sparks during surgery could actually kill the patient and sometimes did — they caused ether in the patient's lungs to explode. People became aware of the undesirable things that could be blamed on electrostatics such as dust and dirt sticking to walls, electricity-charged yarns acting up in knitting mills, and so on.

"But new applications were developed. A man named Cottrell invented the Cottrell precipitors that used electrostatics to remove ash from the waste products of smelters and cement mills and eventually from coal-burning power plants. That practical application of electrostatics keeps millions of tons of ash from the atmosphere. As the century advanced, more and more uses were found. Electrostatics separated materials in mining, it made it possible to spray paint, it was used in applying dry coatings to paper or fabrics in the making of such products as sandpaper and emery cloth. It simplified many manufacturing processes. More recently, electrostatics has provided a foundation for the photocopying that has revolutionized modern business. Some non-impact or dot matrix printers utilize electrostatic principles. The ion-drive rocket propulsion system makes use of electrostatic fields to accelerate charged particles. One form of electron microscope has electrostatic lenses. Electrostatic speakers are valuable in stereo systems for their accurate reproduction of high frequencies.

"Important as electrostatics has become, we haven't lost sight of its bad qualities. For example, natural electrostatics is still a prominent field of research. Scientists continue to look for ways to protect airplanes and helicopters from atmospheric electricity." He smiled. "In other words, from lightning."

I waited patiently until he had finished. A fondness for lecturing is an occupational disease among university professors, and when you go to a genuine expert, you must be prepared to be told more than you want to know. "Then you think electrostatics could be used to rig a keno game?" I asked.

"That seems possible to me. Of course the problems would be enormous, but as I've already suggested, if a talented person were to direct his attention at them for several years, who can say what he might accomplish? The mixing chamber with a blower would seem to be far more vulnerable than the revolving cage. That cage is open on all sides, and the wires could prevent the penetration of an electrostatic field. The mixing chamber sets on a wood base with the blower underneath. The apparatus that catches the balls is at the center of the chamber. The blower keeps the balls in motion, and now and then one is caught.

"If the wood base were treated with a conductive substance — a fluid containing a copper compound, for example, that could be applied like furniture polish — and then connected to a source of electricity, this might result in the keno machine setting in an electrostatic field that would negate the distance problem defined in Coulomb's Law. A simple modification to the blower could provide the electrostatic charge needed. An invisible fluid could be developed through experimentation to enhance the balls' response to the charge. If someone were to operate an air purifier nearby, that would provide a stream of negative ions for the air blower to pick up, which might heighten the scheme's effectiveness. Probably there are a number of such things that could be utilized.

"This certainly would affect the operation of the keno apparatus. *How* it would affect it, or how to make the most effective use of electrostatics, would have to be determined experimentally. With the electrostatic field *under* the mixing chamber, balls sensitive to it would be pulled back on their upward flight and accelerated on their way down. If the attraction produced an apogee, with the treated balls moving slowly in the vicinity of the mechanism, they certainly would be more likely to be caught. The erratic flight of a number of balls might look peculiar, but that could be offset with an intermittent switch that turned the electrostatic field on and off. Other balls could be given a different coating — say with an anti-static fluid that would minimize the electrostatic attraction on them. Because electrostatic charges can either attract or repel — opposite charges attract and like charges repel — the scientist has two ways to apply his ideas. Hundreds of trials may have been necessary to find the arrangement that best places the preselected numbers in a position for the mechanism to catch them. Whatever the technique, it would fall far short of a hundred percent effectiveness, but that wouldn't matter. Once in a while — one time out of fifty, one time out of a hundred — your conspirators are going to catch eight or nine numbers anyway. If they can increase that to fifteen, how much do they win?"

"Twenty-five thousand dollars," I said.

"You see — all they need to do is exert enough influence on the system to catch a few more numbers. They can win a fortune without ever hitting the big jackpot. Like you, I'm assuming an employee is involved. After the winning ticket is cashed, the employee will turn off the electrostatic charge, and the balls will behave normally on the next play. When they're removed for cleaning, which the casino must do regularly, the employee can replace them with a set in which the two fluids have been applied to different numbers, and the conspirators will be ready to run the scheme again whenever the employee turns on the electrostatic charge.

"I like this. Even if it only works occasionally, it still will be an enormously profitable operation. But remember — the technology is nothing like as simple as I'm describing it. It may be fantastically complicated. Someone performed an endless series of experiments, trying hundreds and hundreds of different coatings to find the best formulae for the balls, trying hundreds and hundreds of different solutions to find the one that best produces an electrostatic field with a wood base, running experiment after experiment. I have no idea whether the technique I just described would actually work. In order to find out, I'd have to perform some of that research and experimentation myself — with no guarantee that the answer I found would be the right one. Have the casinos lost much money?"

"One of them has lost a great deal, and we have to assume that a scam that worked in one casino would be tried in others."

"Wouldn't that increase their risk?"

"It's another application of your Easy Money Bug principle. Most appetites have built-in regulators. One can eat only so much food at one sitting. The body automatically punishes those who overindulge. But there is no regulator on greed. If someone has found a way to rig one keno game, he'll try to apply it to all the keno games in the universe."

"I suppose so." The professor was gazing absently at the ceiling as though he had already lost interest. "There's not much more I could tell you without researching the matter myself," he said after a pause.

"You've given me something to work on," I said. I got to my feet. "How would we go about checking the apparatus to find out whether it's been rigged?

Would a fluid applied to the balls be easy to detect?"

"You could test the balls for traces of conductive or anti-conductive chemicals. The simplest electrostatic meter is your own hand — you can feel the presence of an electrostatic field when the hairs respond to it. Or you might rig a meter with a little gold leaf."

"It would have to be something that could be done secretly," I said. "If the culprits see someone snooping around the keno machine with a meter, or performing chemical tests on the balls, they'll put their scam in a deepfreeze and wait for the investigation to go away. They may already have done so because of the murder. We don't want to frighten them — we want to catch them in the act."

"Yes. Yes, I can understand that. If you don't proceed carefully, they'll lay low until you give up looking for them, and then they'll start over again. There is one point that should be helpful. A person with the ability to apply electrostatics to a keno game has a level of scientific or mechanical skill that would be difficult to keep hidden. He may have other inventions to his credit. I'd suggest that you look around for them."

"We've already found one," I said, "but it won't help us unless we're able to figure out where it came from."

11

Two minions in space uniform sat near me at lunch. While I ate, I tried to think of a way to swipe one of their laser guns. I wanted to take it to Professor Quilley and have him test it for electrostatic effects. Nevada 2100 had an ostentatious scientific aura, but whether the science was high-tech, or pseudo high-tech, or merely comic-strip high-tech, I had no idea.

At noon I telephoned Raina Lambert and brought her up to date. She listened without interruption and offered no criticism. When I'm in an optimistic mood, I interpret this as a compliment. Reporting to her is like keying information into a computer. Her tart questions and comments are the error messages. She then sorts and saves the data and eventually plays it back to me in surprising new combinations.

She had spent the morning perusing various records, including those of keno payouts made by each shift of employees at Diamond D's. This gave her the interesting information that Clyde

Goodler's swing shift wasn't the only one taking a beating on its win percentage. The day shift, which had a boss named Karl Wollen, also had lost money spectacularly. From this I deduced that both shift bosses were involved. I had checked with Mildred Comptom and learned that cleaning the balls was one of their regular chores. It would have been a simple matter for them to apply the anti-conductive or conductive fluids during the cleaning operation.

"I've been trying to get descriptions of the people who played the rigged numbers and collected all that money," Raina said. "As far as anyone can remember, they were disgustingly nondescript — male and female, various ages and races. They spoke with Western drawls, or Southern accents, or New England twangs, or whatever. The few distinctive physical features, such as an oversized nose, or facial warts, or tattoos, easily could have been cosmetical. The one severe limp could have been faked. One person was on crutches, which means nothing at all. It's a devilishly difficult problem because we don't know which of these winners were genuine and which weren't."

"Even so, it sounds like an unexpectedly large gang," I mused.

"Do you think so? To me, it sounds like a gang with an extremely able make-up man. It also has a forger to supply it with bogus Social Security cards and driver's licenses. I telephoned some of the winners — or tried to. I had interesting conversations with a couple of them about their great Las Vegas vacations. The local phone companies had never heard of the others. Checking all of them will be an enormous job. I'll put the L.A. and the New York offices onto it."

"Do you have anything new on Joletta Eckling?" I asked.

"I followed her and von Mach last evening. They drove out to Nevada 2100, where some kind of meeting was in progress. People were waiting for them, and they were applauded when they walked in."

One reason I enjoy working for Raina is that she takes on the really tough assignments herself as a matter of course. "I talked with Joletta's father about her," she went on. "He disapproves of von Mach, as almost any father would. He says he can't stand the man. Unfortunately, he's disapproved of every male friend Joletta's ever had, which probably contributed to her problems and certainly is a basic factor in his."

At least it explained why von Mach let Joletta out two blocks from her place of employment. Normally this would have been none of our business, but a family quarrel always makes an investigation difficult. Joletta may have been trying to ruin her father because he disapproved of the men in her life, but Joel Eckling certainly wouldn't appreciate our handing that to him as a solution to his keno problem.

"Her father knows she wants to donate his money to Americans All," Raina said. "He's already taken legal steps to prevent that."

I mentioned my suspicions about Nevada 2100's obvious high-tech connection. She said the organization performed ingenious scientific stunts to entertain tourists, but she didn't know how deep its interest went.

"I'm dating a spaceman," she said. "I've represented myself as a mousy little heiress who needs strong direction in her life and a gentle but strict master to manage her inheritance for her. Americans All and Nevada 2100 — which for our purposes are one and the same — have squads of virile, passably good-looking young men who are waiting for a call like that. Unfortunately, none of them want to talk about high-tech matters. All they're interested in is politics, ultra-right-wing variety, and I foresee difficulties in trying to work questions about electrostatics into one of their political discussions."

Her next item sounded more promising. "Edwin Morabin, the retired professor who called on the widow yesterday, is a mechanical engineer with an international reputation. He has a number of inventions to his credit, and several of his patents are said to be highly profitable."

"I like him much better than Wes Zerin, who is only an engineering student," I said. "Obviously he's an old friend of Florence's, so he must have been acquainted with Harley. If he was itching to try out a new theory about the effect of electrostatics on keno, what better way to do it than to make use of Harley's casino connections? This definitely is worth looking into."

Raina had no interest at all in my sensational news about Harley Dantzil's double life. "He was a pathetic character," she said. "I've arranged for you to search his bedroom and den. His wife has been informed by a high official that a police officer, accompanied by a special investigator named J. Pletcher, will call at two o'clock. The officer will pick you up at Diamond D's at one-thirty."

She wouldn't tell me the name of the high official.

I next telephoned Lieutenant McCarney and asked, "Any progress?"

Probably I sounded more cheerful than I felt. He said disgustedly, "Look — it was after four this morning when I saw you last. What progress could you reasonably expect between then and now?"

"What about my bugs? You must have some kind of report on them."

"Your bugs are an ingenious exercise in microengineering, to quote a phrase that was tossed at me not for quotation. They're also damned complicated, to quote another. The experts have dissected one, and they're preparing a blueprint, but they haven't begun to figure it out. It not only picks up sound, but it also transmits it, which means that somewhere in the neighborhood there may be another ingenious exercise in micro-engineering in the form of a receiving unit with a tape recorder that operates when the bug broadcasts. I sent some men out to look for it, but they won't find it. A proper search would have to include every apartment in the building and all the nearby houses, which would cause an uproar, and we couldn't get search warrants on the evidence we have. I figure it's been removed by now anyway."

"I spent the morning talking with a physics professor," I said. "He taught me how to cheat at keno — maybe. It's complicated. He didn't say so, but it wouldn't surprise me in the least if the keno scam also represents an ingenious exercise in micro-engineering. Isn't it a peculiar coincidence that we have two high-tech aspects to this case?"

"Not according to my definition of 'coincidence.' Do you have anything else?"

"You're greedy," I complained. "Look what I've given you since Tuesday evening, and all you can say is, 'Do you have anything else?'"

"Thank you very, very much for what you've given me since Tuesday evening. I'm humbly grateful. Do you have anything else?"

I hung up.

The mock castle looked different on my second visit. There was a large black wreath on the door, and the Mercedes and the Toyota were not in evidence. Instead, there was a flaming red Corvette parked by the garage doors. The elderly handyman who had been washing cars on my previous visit was on a ladder doing something to one of the shutters.

I expected the grumpy widow to erect obstacles regardless of the high official who had made the arrangement, but — after the doorbell had instructed us to make deliveries in the rear and take our soliciting elsewhere — the young maid, whose name was Selena, admitted us without even asking for our credentials. She escorted us to the suite Harley Dantzil had occupied, which was located in the most remote part of the house, the rear of the upstairs area above the garage. Before we entered it, I asked her, "Is there any way to keep these rooms locked?"

She looked at me blankly. "Why would anyone want to lock them? No one ever comes here except to clean, and there wasn't much of that because Mr. Dantzil wasn't home much."

"How often was he home?"

"Just now and then. He had some kind of traveling job."

"How often?" I persisted. When she hesitated, I said, "Once a week? Twice a week?"

"I never kept track. He just came now and then."

"How long have you been working here?"

"About three months," she said.

"Do you have to clean this big house all by

yourself?"

She giggled. "Mrs. Gabble helps. She's cook and housekeeper. And a part-time maid comes in when she's wanted."

I let her go and turned my attention to the rooms.

Officer Sanding, my escort, was a good-looking, pleasant young black man in a brand-new uniform that he was very proud of. His only function was to make what I did look official, which required neither skill nor experience, so headquarters had assigned the man most easily spared. Sanding was a recent graduate of whatever the Las Vegas Metropolitan Police used as a cadet school.

"Did they give you any orders?" I asked him.

"Yes, sir. My commanding officer told me to watch you carefully. He said you're an expert, and I might learn something."

I decided not to ask him whether his commanding officer also told him to make certain I didn't snitch anything. "There's one problem with searches that I've never been able to overcome," I said. "No matter how carefully I look, and no matter how energetically and resourcefully I work, I still can't find something that isn't there. When there's nothing to find, inevitably I find nothing."

A casual outsider would have said Florence Stevens-Dantzil had done well by her husband. The suite consisted of two rooms with a private bath, and it was pleasantly decorated in masculine tones of brown and cream. The furnishings — single bed and an elaborately carved bureau in the bedroom; desk, bookshelves, TV center, and a comfortable recliner chair in the small den — had been selected by someone with a firm notion of what a man ought to like. I had no doubt that Dantzil had hated them. Because he hated them, he put as little of himself into these rooms as possible.

Before the police were admitted on Tuesday night, Florence Stevens-Dantzil certainly had removed any embarrassing secrets she was able to find on short notice, and that could have been her first visit to this part of the house since she bought it. The single bed told its own story.

Except for the suite's remote location, there was nothing about it to suggest that Florence had anything but the highest regard for her husband. The paneling in the den and the ornate molding in the bedroom spelled luxury. The den's revolving TV stand and the bookshelves — empty except for a twenty-year-old *Encyclopaedia Britannica* that looked as though the volumes had never been opened — had been custom-built with an ingenious sliding panel that made it possible to watch the TV from the bed in the next room.

I pointed out this latter touch to Officer Sanding as a lesson in snob economics. Probably Florence's suite had a similar arrangement. It would have cost far less to buy a second TV set for the bedroom.

"The problem," I told Officer Sanding, "is that

211

Harley Dantzil never actually lived here."

"Why do you say that?" Sanding asked.

"First, because he had two other addresses plus a place of employment where he certainly spent most of his time. Second, because these rooms were furnished without any consideration of the man who was supposed to occupy them. They contain things he never would have put here himself. Those ashtrays, for example. What are ashtrays doing in the rooms of an emphysema-plagued man who didn't smoke?"

"Perhaps they were for visitors," Officer Sanding suggested.

"Harley never entertained even one visitor here," I said. "He wouldn't have dared. It's possible, though, that Florence Stevens-Dantzil knew so little about her husband that she wasn't aware of his emphysema."

The ashtrays were another lesson in snob economics. They were monstrosities of machined metal, eight inches high and conical in shape with the top truncated to form a receptacle for butts and ashes. They swallowed both at the touch of a button. Except for the fact that they had no ornamental value, they belonged to the family of expensive but totally impractical gadgets one sees displayed in jewelry stores or posh gift shops. Like the *Encyclopaedia Britannica* and the silver toiletry set in the bathroom, they probably had never been used.

An old suit and a pair of old trousers hung in the closet. The bureau contained little more than a change of underwear and socks. There were no extra shoes and no slippers; no robe and no pajamas; not even a razor. I asked Officer Sanding, "What did Harley Dantzil do here? What did he wear?"

Sanding was scrutinizing my every move and waiting for me to produce a rabbit from some unlikely hiding place. He shook his head. "Maybe he brought an overnight bag."

"For a visit home?"

Despite the fact that Florence and the police had already searched the place, we meticulously explored drawers and turned furniture over so that no surface or crevice went uninspected. We flipped all of the pages of all of the volumes of the encyclopedia. We measured partitions looking for secret hiding places or hidden stairways. We checked for loose floorboards. We invested two hours, which was far more time than the situation merited. When we finished, I seated myself in the den's plush reclining chair, tilted back, contemplated the *Encyclopaedia Britannica*, and thought about Harley Dantzil sitting there.

"No," I announced finally. "If Dantzil owned anything at all that he considered personal, or confidential, or that he was merely fond of, he wouldn't have kept it in this house."

I got to my feet and went to the window. It

looked out onto the Stevens-Dantzil rolling acres, a park-like expanse behind the house. There were palms, shrubs, dormant flower beds, graveled walks. I opened the window and leaned out.

A high-pitched giggle floated up from somewhere below. Looking down, I saw a small swimming pool. The sun had brought the temperature into the sixties — still a mite chilly for swimming attire — but the two figures sprawling beside the pool were not being troubled by the temperature. Neither were they inconvenienced by the narrowness of the chaise longue they occupied. One was a blond youth in his early twenties. He was almost wearing swimming trunks. The other was Florence Stevens-Dantzil, who was almost attired in a dress designer's preliminary sketch for a bikini. After I'd scrutinized the scene for all of thirty seconds, I still didn't believe it. She grabbed her companion, kissed him, and giggled again.

I beckoned to Officer Sanding. He watched for several minutes while I retreated to the reclining chair and lost myself in thought.

Finally he shook his head and quietly closed the window. "Isn't that something?"

"I must be completely out of touch," I said. "Could she possibly have attractions I'm not able to appreciate?"

"You have to understand Las Vegas. A lot of folks come here and lose all their money. Some of the cars you see on the used car lots were sold

214

for bus fare by people who didn't have enough money left to buy gas for the trip home. You've noticed the pawn shops, I'm sure. When a casino employee wears flashy jewelry, you can bet it was bought cheap from a tourist who needed money in a hurry. Some people even have to find jobs and go to work in order to get out of town. That's all your Romeo is doing — he's earning money for his trip home. He probably figures this job has better hours and working conditions than anything else he could find. How old is she? Fifty?"

"I'd guess fifty-five. This must be a great city for a rich, middle-aged woman with a fondness for young men. When she tires of one, she can buy him a bus ticket and find herself another. Even so, there's something highly peculiar about this. It doesn't go with Florence Stevens-Dantzil's social position."

Sanding said blankly, "Say — could this have something to do with the murder?"

"Her husband had an attractive young woman and two kids. Why would he care what Florence did? And after what you just saw, do you suppose Florence cared what he did? So we'll file it. Maybe we'll find a use for it before we're done. When you write your report, describe exactly what you saw and leave that bit about Romeo earning his fare home for your superiors to think up. They may know Florence personally, in which case they'll prefer to interpret the situation themselves."

When we were leaving, Selena intercepted us at the front door. "Mrs. Stevens-Dantzil wants to ask you something," she told me.

The funeral was scheduled for the next afternoon. In normal circumstances, one would expect the widow to be at the funeral home greeting family and friends instead of amusing herself at home with unconventional playthings. But few of her friends had been acquainted with her husband, and probably none of her husband's friends had ever met her. She had been wise to let the mourners, if there were any, work things out for themselves.

She kept me waiting while she put on something more suitable for receiving a detective than the outré bikini. When she finally appeared, her dress was beyond reproach. She was attired simply and tastefully in a plain black gown, but her face was as red as I remembered it.

She had another surprise in store for me. She was escorted by a man about forty, passably good-looking but with an unfortunate knack for making an expensive suit look sloppy. There was a familiar manner about him that I couldn't place. I had the feeling that in New York City I would have recognized it instantly. In Las Vegas, it eluded me.

She introduced him. "This is my nephew, Darnell Condellor."

I didn't believe it. I wondered whether her young men were awarded a provisional relative status, like the temporary commissions given to

216

military officers in wartime.

Condellor shook my hand, and the three of us sat down.

"Mr. Pletcher, my friends on the police force tell me you're a highly regarded investigator," the widow said. "I'd like your advice about something."

"If you'll describe the problem, I'll be glad to give you any suggestions that occur to me."

"I've been thinking about Harley. He wasn't much of a husband. He wasn't even much of a man, but he certainly didn't deserve to be murdered. Would it help if I offered a reward?"

I said cautiously, "It wouldn't do any harm. Whether it would help or not could only be determined by offering it."

"How large should it be?"

"That's entirely up to you."

She hesitated. Then she blurted, "Is a thousand dollars enough?"

"You have the reputation of being an extremely wealthy woman. Are you?"

"I don't know that it's any business of yours, but — yes. I am."

"It's my business only because I'm trying to help you. If an extremely wealthy woman were to offer a thousand-dollar reward for information leading to the arrest of the person who murdered her husband, public reaction would be highly derogatory. People would consider it the gesture of a tightwad, and they'd also view it as an indication

217

of how little her husband meant to her. You should discuss this with your attorney. He'll be able to advise you concerning the possible effectiveness of a reward and also the probable public reaction to it."

"A thousand dollars isn't enough?"

"Not nearly enough."

Condellor spoke for the first time. He had a rich baritone voice. "He's right, Florence. I never thought of that, and I should have." He turned to me. "I'm in advertising. A reward is a form of advertisement. Chintzy advertising from a wealthy firm never goes well. How much would you suggest?"

That was why he looked familiar to me. If he came to Las Vegas from New York, his dossier certainly read, "Failed Madison Avenue." He couldn't possibly have succeeded there wearing his suits the way he did.

I tried to make my voice sound as rich as his and much more sincere. "A hundred thousand dollars."

Florence Stevens-Dantzil said bitterly, "You'd like that, wouldn't you? You'd like to be able to claim it yourself."

"The firm I work for, Lambert and Associates, prohibits its employees from accepting rewards."

"I see," she said. "You think a hundred thousand dollars . . ."

"If you offer any reward at all, it should be at

least a hundred thousand dollars. That's my advice. Discuss it with your attorney."

"I'll do that," she said. "Thank you."

"This may seem impertinent under the circumstances, but — could I ask you one or two questions?"

She hesitated. Then she said, "You've already been impertinent, so I don't suppose a few questions will matter."

"Your husband seemed like such a harmless creature. Contemptible, perhaps, but harmless. I'm trying to understand why anyone would want to kill him. Do you have any suggestions?"

She shook her head. "I rarely saw him or even thought about him. I know more about the private lives of almost any of my friends than I did about his. I meant him no ill — I simply had no feeling about him at all. He must have enjoyed whatever it was he was doing with his life. If he hadn't liked it, he easily could have done something else. He had plenty of money, you know. He earned a fairly good salary and spent it as he chose. He lived here as much as he wanted to, and he never contributed a penny to this home or to its upkeep."

"Do you have any idea how frequently he used the rooms we searched?"

She shook her head. "I paid no attention. The servants must have known, but they also knew I didn't want my husband mentioned."

"Thank you." I got to my feet, bowed to her,

shook Condellor's hand again, and left.

Officer Sanding was waiting patiently in a room that would have been called the library if Florence Stevens-Dantzil had owned any books. When Selena came to show us out, I asked her, "When Mr. Dantzil stayed here, what time did he arrive, and what time did he leave?"

"He mostly came late — long after dark — and he must have left real early. He'd be gone when I got up."

I thanked her, and we took our leave of the mock castle.

Since neither of us had eaten much for lunch, I suggested a stop at Lon's 24-Hour-Cafe for a snack. I explained the connection with Dantzil's murder while we waited for the waitress. Sanding looked the place over critically.

"It doesn't fit, does it?" he asked with a frown. "Living in that mansion, and working in a hotel and casino — and eating here? He must have had a very common appetite."

"That was my thought, too."

Food arrived for our own common appetites, and Sanding ate hungrily. I left my sandwich untouched while I leaned back and thought about how one would go about organizing a highly successful keno scam.

If the gang won a modest jackpot twice a week, with an occasional larger payoff, from each of six casinos, it might be raking in two or three hundred thousand a month. If it was hitting twelve casinos, double everything. The Las Vegas illusion of free-flowing money had been made a reality.

Six casinos would mean at least six casino employees. Add Dantzil, four or five people to collect the winnings, and two or three for high-tech expertise, and you had perhaps fifteen people, each of them receiving fifteen or twenty thousand a month — or more. Of course the split might not be in equal shares, but there didn't have to be that many people involved, either. Probably the scam could operate smoothly with as few as ten, which would make the monthly take per person twenty to thirty thousand.

I backed up and revised my figures. There had to be at least two employees for each casino and probably more — one working on each shift at the keno desk to turn the device on and off and doctor the balls, and a maintenance technician of some kind who did a sleight-of-hand installation of the device in the first place and kept it concealed and operating. However the money was sliced, we were still talking about a lot of it. Even if the conspirators received only ten thousand a month, that was a hundred and twenty thousand tax-free dollars a year.

Dantzil's function seemed obvious. His so-called job at Diamond D's imposed no schedule on him. He spent his days — or nights — wandering about, talking with people, pretending to be busy.

He was in an ideal position to look after the house-keeping on a scam aimed at defrauding his employer. The fact that he ran errands for all and sundry and could come and go at odd times gave him leeway to look after other casinos as well.

He had to be the go-between. Perhaps he also distributed the money — in which case he would be in deep trouble if members of the gang got the idea he was holding out too much for himself. The men Leda Rauchman had seen him with could have been casino employees. They also could have been phony tourists who played the winning numbers and collected the jackpots.

Dantzil's meetings with Joletta and her muscle-man fell into a different category. Von Mach could have been supplying the technical expertise and putting pressure on Dantzil to give him a larger cut. That accounted for everyone except the two out-of-state thugs we had caught watching the apartment building. I couldn't fit them in at all. Certainly they had no connection with von Mach. He was able to supply his own thugs.

I next contemplated the mysterious tails Dantzil thought he had and the beating he certainly had received. The tails had to be connected with the keno scam — why else would anyone be interested in innocuous little Harley Dantzil? — but a beating that long ago could have been another matter entirely.

Was it even remotely possible that Dantzil created the scam himself? I couldn't imagine him performing those hundreds of electrostatic experiments on his own. There was no high-tech element of any kind in his background. He was a man without hobbies. If he had built ships in bottles or done anything at all that by a farfetched stretch of the imagination could have brought him into contact with high-tech professionals or even hobbyists, I might have considered him for a more responsible role, but there was nothing. He didn't even work crossword puzzles.

Harley had to be the go-between, making use of his casino contacts to find employees who would cooperate. Of course he'd had to have *some* contact with high-tech people, or they with him, in order to get the scam launched.

"Computers!" I exclaimed aloud.

Officer Sanding looked at me blankly. "How's that?"

"Computers are high-tech, aren't they?"

"I certainly would have thought so."

"I've been wracking what passes for my brain to find a high-tech connection for Dantzil, and his slum apartment is next door to that of a computer programmer. Do you suppose . . ."

There were several things about that coincidence that were worth supposing, and I proceeded to do so.

Officer Sanding, leaning back with a full stomach, uttered a small sigh of contentment and then exclaimed, "You haven't eaten anything!"

"That's always been a problem with me," I said. "I'm not able to eat and think at the same time. It's like walking and chewing gum. Some people can do it, and some can't. Come on!"

I paid both of our checks, absently picked up a book of matches labeled *Lon's 24-Hour-Cafe*, and hurried Sanding away.

At a pay telephone, I called McCarney. "Is the Swoboda Street apartment still sealed?" I asked.

"Of course."

"While I have this capable young officer with me, I'd like to search it."

"Do you figure we missed something?"

"I figure *I* missed something. I didn't look for it at the time because I didn't know it existed. Now I know what should have been there, and I'd like to look again."

"I'll meet you there," he said.

We drove to Swoboda Street, swung to the curb where the green Volkswagen had been parked when Dantzil's body was discovered, and waited. Lieutenant McCarney arrived five minutes later. We climbed the outside stairway in a solemn procession, and McCarney broke the seal on Dantzil's apartment and opened the door.

I walked directly to the massive table lamp I remembered, glanced inside its elongated shade, and pointed. The bug was identical to the ones I had found in Leda Rauchman's apartment.

McCarney swore volubly. Then he turned and stared at me. "How the devil did you know?"

"They're very hard to see when you aren't looking for them," I explained.

"So how come you find them so easily?"

"I don't unless I'm looking for them."

I carefully removed the bug and handed it to him in my handkerchief.

He was about to summon his technicians to do the apartment over again, but I persuaded him to let Officer Sanding and me have a crack at it first. We went to work with the same thorough technique we had used on Dantzil's room and den, and we achieved the same empty result. It was another exercise in the futility of searching for something that wasn't there, and I reminded Sanding of this when we finished.

McCarney sat and watched us. By the time we finally gave up, he had decided there was no point in having the apartment searched a third time.

"I can tell you one thing for certain," I said. "It wasn't one of the high-tech people who murdered Dantzil."

McCarney looked at me blankly.

"The high-tech people were suspicious of him, which is why they planted this bug. They may have been tailing him. But they didn't murder him. If they had, they'd have had the good sense to remove the bug when they left."

"Thanks," McCarney growled. "That saves me

the trouble of trying to figure out why high-tech people would commit such a low-tech murder."

"You're missing the point," I said irritably. "If that bug has been broadcasting to a nearby tape recorder, the tape should contain a dramatic real life recording of a murder taking place. I'd very much like to hear it."

McCarney stared at me for a full ten seconds. Then he telephoned an order for his own high-tech people to pick up the bug and search for a tape recorder with a wireless receiver.

He settled himself to wait for them. "Rauchman is at police headquarters looking at pictures," he said.

"Was there any attempt to tail her there?"

He shook his head.

"Has she recognized anyone?"

"She was just getting started when I left, but probably she won't. Our mug shots are of people with records, and this is the kind of scam that amateur crooks think up."

"They were professional enough in the ways that counted," I said.

I told him about Florence Stevens-Dantzil's poolside activities and the alleged nephew. He was flabbergasted. "There's never been any kind of a scandal about her," he said. "No rumors at all. Not a whisper. Are you saying this is a motive for murder?"

"I don't see how it could be. Harley wasn't

interfering with her extramarital romps. He was fully occupied with his own romps. And she certainly didn't eliminate him in order to marry one of her gigolos. That would ruin her socially."

"She probably thought she was being extremely discreet," McCarney said. "Those houses have large lots and plenty of shrubbery, and if she only plays in her own backyard, I can understand why there haven't been any rumors. You wouldn't have suspected a thing if you hadn't chanced to look out of that particular window at that particular moment."

"And she still has an absolutely unbreakable alibi," I said, grinning.

"Right. I know exactly where she was at the moment Harley was murdered because I saw her there myself. If I got her indicted, her attorney would subpoena me as one of her witnesses."

12

MCCARNEY REMAINED AT SWOBODA STREET to direct the search there. Officer Sanding dropped me at police headquarters on his way home. I wanted to read the most recent reports on the Dantzil investigation, but first I had a telephone call to make. I looked up the phone number of Edwin Morabin, noting that he had an office telephone listed at his home address.

Because of the late hour, I called his home number. I sparred first with a maid and then with Mrs. Morabin; the mention of Florence Stevens-Dantzil's name finally got me through to the professor.

He said, "This is Edwin Morabin. What is it about Florence?"

I introduced myself and explained. I wanted to call on him to find out anything he could tell me that might advance my investigation into the murder of Florence Stevens-Dantzil's husband, Harley Dantzil.

"There must be some misunderstanding," he

said. "I know nothing about Harley Dantzil."

"I understood that you and Mrs. Stevens-Dantzil are old friends."

"We are indeed. My wife and I have known Florence for many years. We play bridge with her once a week, but I've never met her husband. To the best of my knowledge, I've never laid eyes on him. My wife met him just once. She was attending a party of Florence's when Mr. Dantzil arrived home unexpectedly. She said he was an odd little man, terribly shy and completely out-of-place, but Florence brought the whole thing off with a great deal of aplomb — as she would, of course. And that's as much as I can tell you. I know nothing whatsoever about him except what I read in the obituaries."

It could have been true. It also could have been the best line to take if he was involved in the keno scam. I thanked him for his cooperation and hung up. He was the type who took dead aim at a subject and never swerved from it. It would be extremely difficult to investigate him while pretending to be doing something else. One would have to confront him head on.

Leda Rauchman was somewhere in the police dungeons going through stacks of photos. I left a message for her at the desk, asking her to look in on me when she finished. Then I turned my attention to the police reports. After I read them, I leaned back and passed my day's work in review.

I had accumulated huge amounts of information — I even knew that Otto von Guericke built the first electrostatic generator about 1660 — but none of it seemed to take me anywhere.

The police investigation also seemed to be going nowhere. Two points that should have been receiving diligent attention weren't even mentioned: the thugs who had been watching Dantzil's apartment house, and the tails he complained about. It was easy to understand why. No possible connection with the case had been suggested for the thugs, and they weren't volunteering any; and a belated check of Dantzil's complaint would have been difficult. Anyone following him would have instantly taken cover when he was murdered.

At times he had been leading a parade. In addition to Leda Rauchman, who had followed him only intermittently, we knew the high-tech crowd was after him, since it had bugged his apartment. So was the Nevada 2100 crowd, which may or may not have been the same thing. So were the two Frisco thugs we had caught at it. There may have been others, outsiders wanting a piece of the action and insiders who suspected Dantzil because he was the go-between.

In the day's one positive development, the police had identified the owner of most of the legible fingerprints left in Dantzil's apartment. They belonged to a woman who came in twice a week to clean for him. Otherwise, the only thing I learned from reading the reports was information about Las Vegas police procedures.

When Leda emerged — discouraged because she hadn't recognized a single face in the stacks of mug shots the police had inflicted on her — I offered her a slum dinner.

"*Slum* dinner?" she echoed. "Couldn't we have something a bit more nourishing than that?"

" 'Slum' refers to the surroundings. The food will be adequate. Of course there won't be any parsley on the mashed potatoes, but working detectives have to put up with hardships like that."

"You're taking me along as a working detective?"

"Of course."

"I see. I wasn't aware that I'd been promoted, but I suppose anyone who makes out with a detective in a taxicab has to expect some kind of contamination. I'd have to know in advance what I'm committing myself to."

"Have dinner. Enjoy your meal — if you can. Keep your eyes open and see if you recognize any of your fellow diners."

"Is it all right if I bring my own parsley?"

Her police guard was waiting to take her home. I offered him a receipt for her along with a couple of hours off, and Leda and I took a cab down Las Vegas Boulevard toward Lon's 24-Hour-Cafe. We got out at Cone Street and walked the last half-block in order to check for tails. There were none.

I was holding Lon's door open for Leda — she had stepped back to look the place over distastefully — when my attention was caught by a car parked farther along the street.

I released the door. "Come on," I said.

She had to hurry to catch up with me. "So that's a slum dinner. Was I supposed to acquire nourishment by inhaling deeply, or do we keep making passes at the door until we get our courage up?"

"Walking is good for the appetite, and appetite definitely is an asset when you eat at Lon's. Try thinking like a detective."

"I'm trying. What am I supposed to think about?"

"That green Volkswagen. It's a detective's sight for sore eyes." I knew it was the car I had seen parked on Swoboda Street before I saw the license number. Vintage-model, apple-green Volkswagens are not that common.

I explained why it interested me.

"How'd you know it would be here?" Leda demanded.

I told her about the matches and my feeling that if I kept checking Lon's, eventually it would connect itself with Dantzil's murder.

"You don't really know the thugs eat here," she pointed out. "They may be visiting the hardware store next door."

"That'd be stretching coincidence to the breaking point, but we'll soon find out."

We returned to the cafe. The thugs were indeed eating there. Leda and I found a booth for ourselves on the opposite side of the room, and I got out my map of Las Vegas and checked their addresses. They lived only three blocks away, so it was perfectly natural for them to be eating at Lon's. Probably it was inevitable. I gave myself a mental kick for not having thought of it.

Leda had never seen them before. "If I had, I'd remember them," she said. "I never saw two guys who so aptly illustrate the word 'thug.'"

I passed a menu to her. She glanced at it and made a face. I said, "Cheer up. It's Thursday."

"So?"

"So at least we're not surrounded by orders and odors of fish and chips, which I know without looking will be Friday's special."

We settled for ham dinners. The ham was appetizing; the French fries were done perfectly, crisp without being burned; the peas — from a can — were soggy. The food was much better than Leda had expected, and she enjoyed it. I ate slowly while I thought my way through a parade of suspects — the high-tech group; the casino workers; the gamblers who'd collected the winnings — and wondered how many of them would be likely to eat at Lon's.

The thugs left. Leda watched them out the door, and then she turned to me and shook her head. "Definitely not. I'm sure I'd recognize them."

I agreed with her. They were well over six feet tall, but it was their bulk that made them memorable. They were huge.

They had to have *some* connection with Dantzil, or they wouldn't have been watching his apartment building. Further, they ate at Lon's, from which the book of matches came.

"Here we go round the mulberry bush," I murmured and began to eat quickly. Leda watched me with a perplexed expression on her face.

"Do you still think you could recognize those characters Dantzil met?" I asked her finally.

"One of them, certainly. The other two, probably."

"Do you think you could recognize them from across the street?"

"Same answer as before. One certainly; two probably."

"You may have to do it at night, under street lights and neon signs, but this is a bright street, and I can provide binoculars. I'm sure you'll manage. Finish your meal. I want to make a phone call."

Outside, I paused to scrutinize the empty repair shop across the street. When we found a telephone that met my privacy standards, I called Lieutenant McCarney at home. He wanted to talk about the bugs. I told him they were his problem, and he was welcome.

"My orbit right now is Lon's 24-Hour-Cafe, and I have a bright idea." I described it.

"Now wait a moment!" he protested. "Just because the Frisco thugs eat at Lon's doesn't necessarily mean . . ."

"I know what it doesn't necessarily mean."

"You're old enough to have heard the one about the needle in the haystack, aren't you?"

"Of course," I said with accents of wounded dignity. "I also know about not crossing my bridges before they hatch, but I'm likewise fully up-to-date on the latest scoop about making hay while the sun shines and striking while the iron is hot. Miss Rauchman and I will be performing the labor. All I'm asking is the loan of some equipment and a little help in getting access to that empty repair shop. I'll even buy the film myself."

"But you'll expect me to develop it for you."

"Only if there's a photo of someone Leda recognizes. Of course if you really aren't interested in Dantzil's cohorts, I wouldn't dream of taking up your time showing you pictures of them."

"Just tell me one thing," he said bitterly. "Why do you get all of your bright ideas after hours?"

"Because I have no hours. My devotion to duty is timeless."

"Mine isn't. Call me in the morning — after nine o'clock — and I'll see what I can do for you."

"Nope," I said. "The characters we're after may be addicted to breakfast. Lon's is a 24-hour cafe, as its slogan suggests, and I want to be photographing its customers at the stroke of dawn. You're a lieutenant. Can't you call up a sergeant and order him to do some work? Or would you rather I asked Miss Lambert to telephone a captain?"

He decided to do it himself, and a couple of hours later everything was set. He still thought we were bucking formidable odds. I maintained that in Las Vegas, of all places, the police should be willing to gamble occasionally, but I understood his reluctance. The Dantzil investigation was only two days old, and my bright idea — wild hunch, actually — was the kind of project police prefer to save as a last resort.

Friday morning, facing the cold light of dawn in the unheated former repair shop's barren and dusty upstairs, I looked down at the bleak entrance of Lon's 24-Hour-Cafe and wondered if perhaps I should go back to bed and start the day over again. Leda stood beside me, shivering. Her police guard was muttering complaints from somewhere behind us.

"Last night," I announced, "when I was persuading Lieutenant McCarney to let me try this, it seemed like a brilliant idea. I wonder why."

"You should have consulted me," Leda said bitterly. "I don't like being a working detective. I'm resigning. I've been slammed into cars. I've been taken on wild chases through all the back alleys of

Las Vegas. My diet has been tampered with. Now I'm being frozen. Next I suppose you'll be lighting matches under my toes to make me confess. Why don't you do that now and keep my feet warm?"

Our observation post was a second-floor room that had served as the repair shop's office. It was totally bare and — at that hour of a January morning — frigid. There was a rest room, but the plumbing wasn't working. I had scrounged a comfortable chair for Leda and boxes for the detective and me to sit on. Leda was positioned by the window where she could look down at Lon's through a powerful pair of binoculars mounted on a tripod. Beside her, a camera with a telescopic lens was focused on Lon's entrance.

She was to study Lon's customers, giving priority attention to those who would be facing her as they left the restaurant. She also was to photograph them. There was a backup camera to use while we were changing film. Whether she recognized anyone or not, we would have a photographic record of every customer to study later. If she did recognize someone, I would abandon my philosophical meditations and follow him.

The previous evening, this had seemed like an idea whose time had come. The longer I stood in that empty, unheated room staring down at Lon's deteriorating facade, the sillier it became.

Needle-in-the-haystack projects are not uncommon in police work. "Thou shalt be patient; thou

237

shalt persist," are numbers one and two in the detective's list of commandments. There was a notable murder case in England where the police undertook to fingerprint the entire male population of a community. More than 46,000 sets of prints were taken before one finally matched those of the murderer. In different circumstances, I'm confident Lieutenant McCarney would have committed his men to far more tedious and less promising projects. With an investigation that had only begun, my wild hunch seemed like an unnecessary distraction. He thought "needle in the haystack" a flattering appraisal of our chances. There was no certainty that any of Dantzil's elusive cohorts ate at Lon's and no guarantee that Leda would recognize them if they did.

It was mid-morning when Leda said wearily, "I suppose the characters I'm looking for only come here for midnight snacks."

"Perhaps on some days they don't come at all," I said. "That means we'll have to do this for at least a week."

Her reply wasn't ladylike.

"Cheer up," I said. "Look at all the photographic experience you're getting." The police officer added his own rude comment, and I told him to be grateful that Lon's didn't have a rear entrance. The only way to cope with that would have been to put him down in the alley with a camera.

During our breaks, we visited Lon's for refreshment and the use of the rest rooms. I did the photographing while Leda and the officer were gone; she was to return in a rush if one of her elusive suspects showed up while she was at the restaurant. On my first break I bought two large thermos bottles and some styrofoam cups from the hardware store and had the restaurant fill the bottles with coffee. This took some of the chill off the morning.

When I became curious about what was happening in the rest of the world, I used the pay telephone across the street to call Raina Lambert. "Harley Dantzil's funeral is this afternoon," I said. "I'd intended to go, but it looks as though I'll be tied up here for the day if not for an entire week."

"Don't worry. The police will have it covered."

"My motive was sociological. Florence has no relatives except honorary nephews, and Harley's sister certainly won't come. That leaves only Florence's society friends and Harley's casino friends. I wanted to find out if they'll sit on opposite sides of the chapel, like the bride's and the groom's families at weddings."

"The most interesting action will come after the ceremony," Raina said. "The mourners are being informed that Harley's often expressed desire to be cremated will be honored. The hearse will leave with his body, supposedly bound for a crematorium but actually headed for another funeral home. Along the way he'll become Brian Varnko, whose

239

funeral is tomorrow. After the Varnko funeral, there'll be a procession to the cemetery, and Betty will bury her husband with proper ceremony. Dantzil's attorney arranged it. He must have had a delightful time working that out with Florence. Neither party wanted to publicize the bigamy, and Florence certainly doesn't care what name her husband is buried under, or whether he's buried at all, but she's capable of being stubborn and also spiteful. Did you see the news report on Brian Varnko's auto accident?"

"No, I didn't," I said. "I've had Lon's Cafe on my mind, but I'd like to attend both funerals and shake hands with the attorney."

Early in the afternoon, McCarney stopped by and watched the operation for a few minutes. He complimented Leda on her patience and politely made no reference to the lack of results. We walked down the stairs together and paused on the empty lower level so he could tell me privately about the discussion he'd had with Florence Stevens-Dantzil's attorney concerning the advice I had given her.

"He agrees she'd be a laughing stock if she offered a measly thousand-dollar reward, but he thinks twenty-five grand is sufficiently large to underscore her sincerity without being foolishly extravagant. The problem is this — whose murderer would she be offering a reward for? To put it another way, in what identity was Dantzil murdered?

As Harley Dantzil? In that case, no problem. Florence is willing to pay the twenty-five thousand. But she adamantly refuses to pay a reward for information leading to the arrest of the murderer of either Brian Varnko or John Swailey. Since we probably won't know which of Dantzil's three identities was the murder victim until we find the murderer, and we may not know then, I doubt that any reward will be offered."

He also told me he had been unable to find a local detective agency that admitted to tailing either Dantzil or Leda Rauchman.

"That's too bad," I said sympathetically. "It certainly would have been helpful to know what Dantzil was doing the last week of his life. Without some kind of break like that, you may end up running chapter two of this experiment yourself. You can put Miss Rauchman in the Las Vegas Club at a second-story window overlooking the corner of Fremont and Main and have her photograph everyone who walks past."

Leda's police bodyguard had returned from lunch with an enormous bag of snacks, and we spent the afternoon munching potato and corn chips, and popcorn with various coatings, and a variety of synthetic cheese products. We also took a lot of photographs. It was another sunny January day in Las Vegas, with the afternoon temperature reaching sixty-seven degrees. We were no longer cold, but all three of us were feeling extremely tired.

Lon's business fell off in the afternoon and then picked up dramatically as five o'clock approached. I began meditating how long I should persist with this farce — certainly through the dinner hours. Perhaps to nine or ten o'clock. I wasn't yet ready to face the question of whether we should try again the next day. Darkness settled in. There was plenty of light in front of Lon's, but there also was a subtle play of shadows, and the faces of pass-ersby became just a bit harder to see. There was no problem with those emerging from the restau-rant, however.

Leda had lost track of how many times she had pressed the camera shutter. As she dutifully took one more picture, I suddenly saw a familiar face emerging from Lon's doorway. It was Wes Zerin, Mr. Collegiate Gambler, and I wondered how I had happened to miss him when he went in. Leda didn't know him, and I didn't know where he lived.

"I read somewhere that if one remains in the same place long enough, anywhere in the world, everyone he knows will pass by," I said.

"I don't intend to stay here that long," Leda announced.

It was almost seven, and the police officer had just brought us a pizza, when Leda exclaimed, "There's Dandy!"

I jumped to the window for a look. There was no one there.

"He just went in," she said. "It's the elderly character who met Harley twice."

"Did you take his picture?"

"Certainly not! Did you want the back of his head?"

I gave the suspect twenty minutes before I went down and waited in front of the hardware store. When he finally emerged, Leda's handkerchief signal wasn't necessary. I recognized him at once from her description.

He was a cigarette smoker, which I took as a favorable omen. Another man was with him, but they separated at the first street corner, Ewell, and he turned from brightly lighted Las Vegas Boulevard onto the dim side street. I lengthened my stride and gradually overtook him. He was walking slowly and contentedly, concentrating on nothing more exciting than digesting his dinner, and he certainly had no premonition of being followed. I was only three strides behind him when he met a pedestrian going the other way.

They knew each other. "Evening, Sam," Dandy called.

"Evening, Ford," the other said.

Dandy strolled on.

South of Las Vegas's downtown can be found a strange mélange of new and old, commercial and residential, restoration and deterioration. Towering new office buildings rise abruptly among small residences. What once were large, luxurious homes have been restored for business or professional use. Smaller homes have the grim air of being under siege. Scattered through the area are courts of tiny, stucco houses with old roll-roofing that would have been renewed years ago in any climate where it rained frequently. Among them are single family buildings as well as duplexes with entrances at either end of a dilapidated porch. Walls are cracked; window and door trims are badly in need of painting. A few have deteriorated beyond repair and are boarded up.

There was one such court off Ewell, and Dandy turned in there. He walked all the way to the row of buildings at the rear and entered one of the duplexes. When a light came on at the back of the house in what probably was the bathroom, I hurried up the walk and checked his mailbox with my penlight. The name, neatly printed on a torn strip of masking tape, was "F. Fernard."

On my way back to the vacant repair shop, I detoured to make two phone calls. One was to Raina Lambert. The other was to Lieutenant McCarney.

Leda and her police guard were celebrating when I returned. The officer had bought a bottle of cheap champagne to go with the pizza — as a joke, he thought — and they raised styrofoam cups to toast me as I walked in.

"Did you find out who he is?" Leda demanded.

"Does the name 'Ford Fernard' mean anything

to you?"

Leda shook her head.

"Your boss is on his way," I told the officer. "Pour me some champagne."

McCarney sent our accumulation of exposed film to be processed, and he personally placed a stake-out on the court where Fernard lived. Leda and I considered it unrealistic to expect a second needle to emerge from that particular haystack, so we adjourned to McCarney's office, taking the pizza and champagne with us. We finished both, and then, while we waited to see how the photographs turned out, I occupied myself by checking on Wes Zerin.

It took very little checking. His name and address were in the telephone directory, and he did live near Lon's. "Half the population of Las Vegas lives within a few blocks of Lon's," I complained. "Why, incidentally?"

"There are plenty of rooming and apartment houses around there," the police officer said. "Also, it's on bus route six, the strip to downtown, which makes it one of the few places in Las Vegas with good public transportation."

"How does Zerin get to the university from there?" I asked.

"With difficulty," the police officer said, grinning. "He'd have to go downtown and transfer. Or own a car. Or know someone who owns a car. Or walk, but it'd be a long walk."

The photographs were not of studio quality, but they were adequate. McCarney rushed copies of Fernard's photo to the officers on the stake-out. Leda, exhausted but triumphant, left for home with her bodyguard.

I told McCarney, "Unless the conspirators are idiots, they removed all evidence of the scam as quickly as they could after Dantzil was murdered. If they were using electrostatics, the specially treated Ping-Pong balls were replaced by normal balls. Whatever turned on the electrostatic field couldn't have been very conspicuous, and it certainly is much less so now. You *might* find some trace of their tampering if you went in immediately and disassembled all the keno games in town, but that's by no means certain, and I suppose it would cause an uproar."

"Any earthquake that occurred while it was going on wouldn't be noticed," McCarney said. "But that's the Gaming Control Board's responsibility."

"I'm disappointed to find Fernard living in a dump. I was hoping for signs of recent prosperity."

"Appearances can be misleading."

"In that case, I'm pleased to leave this investigation in such capable hands. I, too, have had a long day, and I'm going home."

I went to bed with the disquieting feeling that I had been eating all day and still managed to miss all of my meals.

I restrained myself until noon the next day,

Saturday, and then I telephoned McCarney. "What about Fernard?" I asked.

"It's a washout," he said wearily. "Sorry, but there's nothing about the man that's even faintly suspicious. He's retired and has to scrape along on a small pension. He's always broke at the end of the month, but he pays his bills faithfully the moment his check arrives. He's highly thought of and considered completely honest. Everyone who knows him seems to like him. A very congenial and entertaining man, they say. That's all."

"That's an extremely thorough report on a suspect you never heard of until dinnertime last night."

"He's the first real suspect we've had. We gave him a good play, but nothing about him fits. Men, and occasionally women, visit his house, but no one remembers seeing him with Dantzil — there or anywhere else. I'm afraid Rauchman made a mistake. A lot of those taverns keep the lights dim for what they consider good and sufficient reason."

"I think you're going at it the wrong way. If Fernard and Dantzil were plotting something, of course no one saw them together. They met at an out-of-the-way tavern to avoid that."

"Perhaps. It'd be easier to believe if there was a shred of evidence connecting Fernard to the scam. We'll keep watching him. If nothing else breaks, we'll pull him in for questioning."

I called Raina Lambert and passed along what

McCarney had just told me about Fernard. "He says it's a washout."

"Nonsense," she said. "This is the best piece of work you've done on the case. It breaks it wide open."

"How do you figure that?"

"Didn't McCarney's detectives think to find out what Fernard is retired *from*? He's a former actor. He appeared on the stage when he was only a child, and he acted all his life."

"Even so, he certainly hasn't worked for years, and that place where he lives reeks of poverty."

"I know you had a tedious day yesterday," she said impatiently, "but that's no excuse for putting your brain in storage. Fernard's been an actor all his life, and he's acting a part now. Remember those descriptions of the keno winners — male and female, various ages, and races, and accents? An accomplished and experienced professional actor could have handled all of those roles easily. I'm saying one did. Fernard is the member of the gang who played the winning numbers and collected the money."

13

SUNDAY MORNING I WOKE UP THINKING about Harley Dantzil. I was wondering again how he had occupied himself in that sterile suite of rooms at the top of the mock castle. How did he manage without proper changes of clothing or pajamas and slippers? Far more perplexing was the question of *why* he managed.

As Brian Varnko, he had a loving wife and the responsibilities of fatherhood. Even as John Swailey, he had an occasional party to attend next door. As the husband of Florence Stevens-Dantzil, all he could do was watch TV or read the *Encyclopaedia Britannica*.

The longer I meditated, the more mysterious it seemed. With the cute Betty Varnko and two lovely children waiting for him in an attractive home of his own in which he must have felt very comfortable, why had he wasted even an occasional night in the barren splendor of Florence's castle?

McCarney quickly turned up information concerning Darnell Condellor, Florence Stevens-

Dantzil's "nephew," but he found out nothing at all about the blond youngster. Condellor had been employed by Preswick and Lyonce, an advertising agency, for four years. He was considered capable but not outstanding. None of his friends seemed aware that he was living with an "aunt"; none of Florence Stevens-Dantzil's friends seemed aware that she had a "nephew" living with her.

Not even the biggest gossips in Las Vegas, McCarney said, adding that there were two and he knew them both, could offer a hint of scandal about her. If she had taken up nymphomania as post-menopausal recreation, she certainly managed it with discretion. No one had seen her at the corner of Fremont and Main — or anywhere else — trying to pick up a young man. McCarney's theory was that Condellor pandered for her — and perhaps for himself as well — but this gave the mock castle sexual undercurrents I preferred not to contemplate.

However bizarre Dantzil's relations with his wife might have been, they seemed to have nothing to do with his murder, but they had a great deal to do with the kind of person he was. I needed to know more about him. The young maid hadn't been there long; the other servants were the cook-housekeeper, whom I hadn't seen, and the elderly handyman. A chauffeur had been mentioned, but the handyman might perform both functions. He was more likely than anyone else in that strange ménage to have functioned on Harley Dantzil's wavelength. I decided to talk with him.

I was tired of taxicabs and the uncertainties of finding one away from the casinos, and they had already cost me far more than I would have paid for a rental car. I took a bus to the airport and acquired my own wheels. Then I drove to Florence Stevens-Dantzil's posh neighborhood and threaded my way through the winding streets, admiring the palm trees and swimming pools. I was approaching the mock castle when I suddenly realized I had made a silly miscalculation.

It was Sunday morning. Very shortly, Florence would be leaving for church. No doubt the handyman would put on a chauffeur's cap and drive her in the Mercedes, in which case he wouldn't be available until he brought her home again.

I parked down the street and waited to see what would happen. Florence left for church at twenty minutes to eleven, as expected, but she drove herself in the Toyota. Before she was out of sight, I was on my way down the long, curving drive. One branch extended toward the garage and the rear of the house; the other made a loop past the front door. I drove to the garage and parked beside the flaming red Corvette, which McCarney had said was Condellor's. My simple intention was to call at the rear door and ask for the handyman. Even if he lived elsewhere, the maid should recognize me as the detective who was there earlier and make no fuss about giving me his address.

I followed a cement walk that led around the side of the house, and to my surprise, I found the garage large enough for four or five cars. Curtained windows suggested living quarters. The rear half of it was in fact the handyman's residence, and when I reached the back, I almost fell over him.

He was kneeling on the cement slab in front of his doorway repairing a power lawn mower. Parts were scattered about. I had only seen him from a distance, and I found him older, balder, and grayer than I remembered, with just a suggestion of a whispy mustache. His badly fitting clothing had patches and rips and grease stains that made him look like a fugitive from a trash heap.

He looked up at me with a scowl while I introduced myself. I reminded him that I had been there earlier investigating Harley's murder.

His hands continued to work. He glanced down at them, glanced up again. "Jay Pletcher, you say?"

"J. The letter 'J.' It stands for 'Jamil.' Could I ask you a few things about Harley?"

He shrugged. "I never had much to do with him, but you can ask." His fingers kept working on the lawn mower. He was reassembling it, and there was a pause when he had to reach for another part.

"How long have you lived here?"

He chuckled. "About as long as Harley did. Florence is my cousin. I came here to live when she bought this place. She gives me a home, and

252

I do odd jobs and help out when I can."

He did vaguely resemble Florence. They had the same sharp nose and penetrating eyes, and their builds were similar, but his was wiry where his cousin's was simply skinny. Otherwise, they were a study in contrasts — his manner relaxed and confident; hers, nervous and impetuous.

"Living in the same house with him all those years, you must have got fairly well acquainted with him," I suggested.

He shook his head. "Harley wasn't all that easy to know. We never had much to talk about. He had his interests, and I had mine."

"But you must have seen him regularly," I persisted.

He was putting the final touches on the mower. When he finished, he fished a clean rag from his pocket and wiped his hands carefully. Then he pulled the cord. On the third try, the motor started with a roar. Conversation was impossible for the next few minutes while he tuned it to his satisfaction, stepped back to watch it run, and finally turned it off.

He nodded toward a cluster of lawn chairs in a delightful, palm-shaded nook. I followed him there, and we sat down side by side. Beyond it was a sweep of grass that must have been perfect for croquet, and beyond that was the swimming pool.

"Sorry — I didn't catch your name," I said.

He took the "makin's" from his pocket, cigarette

papers and a roughly fashioned cloth pouch. The odds and ends of tobacco the pouch contained certainly were not Bull Durham. He expertly dumped a scant ration onto a cigarette paper and rolled a cigarette with one hand. I hadn't seen it done for years. He carefully brushed a few crumbs of tobacco back into the pouch and returned the pouch to his pocket. Then he lit the cigarette and puffed deeply. "I'm Thad Yaegler. About Harley — I never paid much attention to him. Florence told me yesterday he'd been having an affair with some woman. I was surprised. I wouldn't have thought that of him, but I really didn't know him at all. We hardly spoke to each other."

He paused for another long puff on the cigarette. "When we first moved here, this was where he lived. He came home when he was through work. As the years went by, I suppose he came home less and less, but no one thought anything of it. Florence certainly didn't care."

"Did he suddenly start coming home less, or did it happen gradually?"

There was a long pause while he smoked and meditated. "I think it happened gradually, but I couldn't swear to it. Like I said, I never paid much attention. He usually parked his car along the drive where the Corvette is now, but he kept coming later and later and leaving earlier and earlier, and most of the time I wouldn't know he was here."

"Can you think of a reason why anyone would

want to murder him?"

Yaegler shook his head. "I always thought he was as harmless as a man could be. He did irritate people, though. He was fussy. Wanted everything just so. Wanted *little* things just so — things most people wouldn't give a hoot about. Florence is fussy, too. Hard to work for. I never could understand how those two managed to marry each other."

We were interrupted by a youthful shout. "Thad!"

Yaegler got to his feet.

A boy of about eleven was standing by the lawn mower. "Does it work?"

"Works fine."

The boy pulled the cord; the mower started with a roar. His whoops of delight were drowned out by the racket, but he acted them out, leaping and clapping his hands. Then he turned the mower off, waved, and vanished around the edge of the garage with it. Yaegler sat down again.

"Was Harley ever here on weekends?" I asked.

"You can't figure weekends for those that work in casinos," Yaegler said. "Casinos are open seven days, and every employee has to adjust his own week to that and take time off when it's given him."

"Harley must have had a couple of days off each week," I persisted. "What did he do with them? What did he do when he stayed here overnight?"

Yaegler shook his head and pointed at the door

that led to his quarters. "That's where I live —
and work, too, when I'm not doing something for
Florence. I've got a little business that brings in
pocket money. I repair mowers and appliances. I
almost never go in the house unless something
there needs fixing. I have no idea what Harley did
with his free time."

"Did he have any hobbies?"

"I never noticed any."

"Did he go places with Florence?"

"As long as I knew them, I never saw them go
anywhere or do anything together. They never
even talked together. Once in a great while Florence would talk to him, but it was like a judge
lecturing someone he'd just found guilty. She talked
and Harley listened."

"It doesn't sound like much of a marriage," I
observed.

"Most marriages aren't," Yaegler said. "That's
why I never married. It's a pig in a poke proposition. You can't tell what sort of wife a woman will
make until you've made her one, and then it's too
late."

"Or what sort of husband a man will make," I
suggested.

He dropped his habitual expression of gloom
and grinned at me. "Yeah. If I *had* married, some
woman would be telling you right now what a lousy
husband I am and how I never could hold a job and
all the rest of it."

"Would Harley have been better off single?" I asked.

"I think maybe he would. He had an odd sort of job, but he liked it, and he made enough money to live comfortably. I can't see that he got a thing out of being married. Florence was no kind of wife to him, and he was no kind of husband to her. There wasn't any secret about that. Her being rich didn't help any. It just made Florence so snooty that no ordinary husband would have done for her. Whenever she had company, she tried to keep him out of sight. One evening he came home and found the garage closed. He started around to the back door — that was Florence's order, he had to come in through the garage or use the back door — and he walked right into a garden party she was giving. One or two of her friends knew him, so she had to introduce him to everyone. She gave him hell for it afterward." He chuckled. Then he said seriously, "You know, I never thought about that — what Harley did with his free time. I think he had a TV up there. Maybe he watched it."

"Is Florence a tightwad?" I asked him.

He shot a quick glance at me and then looked away. "In some ways I suppose she is. It's never bothered me. I work for my room and board, and I earn my own spending money. I wouldn't take money from a woman anyway." He paused. "I'm pretty sure she never gave Harley any money, if that's what you're aiming at."

We sat there silently for a time while I asked myself again why Harley had spent even one night a week in that barren suite of rooms upstairs, watching TV but otherwise completely cut off from human companionship, when he could have gone home to a loving wife and children.

I couldn't think of any more questions, so I thanked Yaegler, shook hands with him, and left.

I ate my Sunday dinner at Lon's 24-Hour-Cafe. While I was eating, Ford Fernard joined several acquaintances at a large table in the center of the room. There was nothing unusual about that. Lieutenant McCarney had turned up information that the ex-actor ate at Lon's at least once a day and usually two or three times. I had chosen an off day for my photography experiment.

According to Fernard's neighbors, he subsisted on a small pension and was forced to borrow or eat cat food when his money ran out at the end of the month, and it interested me that he should be taking so many of his meals in a restaurant. Granted that Lon's didn't charge gourmet prices, but neither did it give food away, and the regulars at Lon's couldn't recall a day when Fernard had lacked cash for a meal. I noticed he was eating steak, the most expensive item on the menu.

His well-preserved good looks had a strangely feminine quality. He was short — the built-up heels made him no taller than five feet eight — and he looked smaller than he was because of his slender

258

figure. A great actor might have overcome such deficiencies, but Fernard had never been better than mediocre. Throughout his career, he always had been the one member of the cast the critics forgot to mention — he was neither good enough to praise nor bad enough to pan. Such actors often lead bitter lives and think themselves the victims of a massive conspiracy.

He moved gracefully, and he had attractive, slender hands. Making himself up as a woman would have been easy for him. With a woman's shoes, a dress, a padded bra, a wig, and a close shave, he could cut a swath through the male geriatric set.

Character parts would have been the one professional avenue left open to him as he grew older. He could prolong his theatrical career by sharpening his expertise in make-up, dialects, and mannerisms. Now he had come out of retirement to achieve his greatest successes, and for once it wouldn't hurt his feelings if the critics overlooked him completely. I wondered whether he kept a record of the costumes, make-up, and dialects he used so that each big winner would be a totally different person; and whether he rehearsed himself — "Today, I'm a farmer from Kansas!" — before he went public with a character.

Did he take that character to a casino several times before a fraudulent game was scheduled, playing and losing like an ordinary tourist and giving the employees an opportunity to become aware of him before he played the rigged numbers? Probably he did.

Unfortunately, we hadn't turned up a scrap of evidence tying him to the scam. He had met with Dantzil at least twice, he was an ex-actor, and the scam couldn't have worked as smoothly as it did without someone like him, but none of this proved he'd had anything to do with it.

At least Lieutenant McCarney had stopped lecturing me about needles in the haystack, and he was turning Fernard's background inside out and having him followed around the clock. Raina Lambert approved, but she was content to leave that chore to the police. She was trying to link the keno scam to Americans All, Nevada 2100, and Joletta Eckling's lover, and she also was taking a close look at Edwin Morabin. She had managed a conversation with him through the simple expedient of following him to church and introducing herself to him afterward as a university pre-law freshman who was interested in becoming a patent attorney. She asked him whether an engineering degree would be useful to her, and he thought the question so unusual — or the questioner so pretty — that he invited her to call on him.

She told me about it when I telephoned to describe my conversation with Thad Yaegler. "I'll see Morabin tomorrow," she said. "What are your plans?"

I was intrigued by the fact that no one had tried to follow Leda Rauchman, or watch her apartment, since the night of the Grand Slam, but a negative is difficult to investigate. Ford Fernard interested me, but there already were so many detectives at the little court off Ewell Street that they were an impediment to traffic.

Some cases become sharply focused as information and clues accumulate. This one seemed to diffuse. "I think there's more to be learned at Lon's 24-Hour-Cafe," I said. "I also have some experiments I want to try. Leda Rauchman recognized Fernard. I'd like to know if he recognizes her."

"He won't recognize anyone."

"I don't think Dantzil was smart enough to keep things that compartmentalized."

"Someone was," she said. "This scam was well-organized and well-run. But go ahead."

McCarney winced when he heard what I was up to. "That won't help a bit," he said. "What we really need is evidence tying Fernard to the scam. Rauchman wasn't part of the scam."

" 'Little drops of water, little grains of sand,' " I murmured. "Let's not try to add things up until all the numbers are on the board."

The following noon, I took Leda to eat at Lon's when Fernard was there. We occupied a booth at one side; Fernard sat in the center of the room with several friends. I told Leda to walk past his table, suddenly seem to recognize him, and exclaim with casual friendliness, "Why, hello, Ford! How are things?"

Fernard reacted like the veteran actor he was. "Things are going very well," he told her. "No complaints at all. How about yourself?"

"I'm saving my complaints for my old age," Leda told him with a laugh. She walked on. Fernard looked after her with a puzzled frown. Obviously he didn't recognize her.

I discussed this with Raina Lambert the next time I telephoned. "I'm not sure what it proves," I said. "Certainly Harley Dantzil would have recognized Leda if he saw her following him. She was his boss's secretary. Either he didn't notice her — which suggests that in certain circumstances she was much better at tailing than I'm willing to believe — or he did notice her but didn't point her out to Fernard."

"Why would he point her out to Fernard?" Raina demanded. "Dantzil had no reason to tell Fernard anything at all about the scam except the next winning numbers. How the game was rigged, and who did it, and what problems they might be having with insiders or outsiders were none of Fernard's business. Dantzil would tell him what numbers to play, what casino to play them at, and the precise time of day to play them. All Fernard had to do was make himself up for the role he'd decided on, play the numbers, collect the winnings, and then meet Dantzil as agreed to turn the money over to him."

"Do I proceed with this even though I'm not proving anything?"

"Of course. You did prove something. Fernard didn't recognize Rauchman. Now find out whether there's anyone he does recognize."

"What about Professor Morabin?"

"He likes to talk with pretty young ladies," Raina said, "but at heart he's a sour old chauvinist who can't believe any female could be a successful anything. I'll have to think of something else."

Leda and I were looking for needles in a haystack again but not at Lon's. We resumed our casino crawls, and at random times during the day we passed in review as many casino employees as possible in search of the other two men who had met Dantzil. It was a complicated task because there were three shifts to check, and many of the casinos used part-time employees.

Each night we toured the casinos again. I was driving my rental car now, which gave me much more flexibility for dealing with tails, but in that respect, the project also was a flop. Leda had none.

Our sacrifices to the Great God Mammon were even less successful. This is the deity who keeps the Las Vegas roulette wheels turning, the cards flipping, the dice rolling, the keno numbers flashing, and the slot machines beeping. Las Vegas's illusory flow of money was brilliant, but none flowed in our direction. Each night we persisted until both of us felt ready to wilt. When I took her home, her police bodyguard would be in residence and already asleep on the sofa.

I noticed, with considerable pleasure, a subtle change in Leda as the week progressed. She began to dress with more taste. Her police guard couldn't have been much help to her on that score, so I suspected she had shopped for new clothing and found a knowledgeable sales clerk. She even abandoned her nondescript hair style for an attractive upsweep. I admired the results and told her so.

She murmured demurely, "That's very kind of you. I'm sorry I can't return the compliment, but your appearance hasn't improved in the least. I keep trying to imagine surrealistic gravy stains on those bleepy solid-color neckties you're so fond of, but they really don't help."

After the crammed events of the first few days, our case seemed to be bogging down. Preparations for my next experiments took most of the week. One of them was aimed at finding out whether Fernard and Joletta Eckling knew each other. Raina Lambert arranged with Joel Eckling to have one copy of a coupon for a special promotion printed. It entitled the bearer to a free dinner at Diamond D's restaurant. Meal coupons circulate through Las Vegas like a tidal wave, all designed in the hopeful expectation that people will come to eat and stay to gamble, but usually the coupons offer discounts — a dollar or two off or two meals for the price of one. The special coupon, for a free dinner, was unusual, but it had to be presented between six and seven o'clock on Friday evening. Fernard received it in the mail on Wednesday. I made certain Joletta would be in the building at the critical time by asking her for an appointment at six.

I'd had very little contact with her since the day I arrived in Las Vegas. She was as radiantly beautiful as I remembered, but she also seemed extremely worried.

"What did you want to see me about?" she asked.

"I've good reason to believe that Harley was involved in the keno fraud," I told her. "If he wasn't, he may have known who was doing it."

"Was that why he was murdered?"

"It certainly seems likely. I've been trying to identify everyone he was seen with during the month before he died. One man eats dinner regularly in Diamond D's restaurant. If he comes in tonight, I want you to take a careful look at him and tell me whether you've ever seen him in the casino."

She asked uneasily, "Is he there now?"

She was worried that my suspect might turn out to be Manfred von Mach, who did eat at Diamond D's occasionally — perhaps in order to case the place in anticipation of getting his hands on it.

"I have a detective waiting at the entrance," I told her. "He'll call me here if the man comes in this evening."

We waited, and her uneasiness increased.

Finally the phone rang. As I expected, Fernard had been unable to resist a free meal. "Let's go," I told Joletta.

The hostess seated us according to instructions I'd given her earlier. We pretended to study our menus while I directed Joletta's attention to a man across the room, a police detective supplied by McCarney. Of course she'd never seen him before, and she was vastly relieved. She brightened and chatted with me almost amicably.

Ford Fernard was seated at the next table. The two of them looked directly at each other whenever they raised their heads. Fernard's reaction was nothing more than a normal masculine interest in an unusually pretty girl. Joletta showed no interest whatsoever in him. Nearby, in equally strategic locations, were two detectives, male and female, whose only task was to watch Joletta and Fernard for signs that they recognized each other.

There were none. Both detectives were willing to swear that the two had never seen each other before, and I agreed with them.

When I reported this to McCarney, he refused to get excited over one more negative. " 'Little drops of water,' " I told him. "You won't get anywhere if you insist on drinking the whole ocean

266

before you admit it's wet."

The experiment provided an unexpected bonus. At a table in a far corner, Wes Zerin, the gambling collegiate, and Darnell Condellor, Florence Stevens-Dantzil's unlikely nephew, were chatting together as though they had known each other for years. This gave me considerable food for thought during an otherwise uneventful meal. I couldn't imagine a more improbable twosome.

My second experiment concerned Lon's. I had been eating most of my meals there, and I quickly became acquainted with Lon herself and also with Velma, the principal waitress. Lon was the elderly, gray-haired woman at the cash register. She was a widow. Her husband had been the original Lon, and now all the regulars called her Lon. If they hadn't, they would have called her "Mom." She would have made a great bartender. She had a kind word for everyone and was willing to listen to anyone's troubles. She had run the kitchen when her husband was alive, and she knew the business thoroughly.

Velma was a hard-boiled, cynical woman in her late thirties. She was tall and heavyset but surprisingly graceful, and she covered the distance from booth or table to kitchen with enormously long, quick strides. She was an excellent waitress, and I doubted that two ordinary employees could have operated among those cramped tables and booths with comparable speed and efficiency. Unfortunately, her conversation lacked variety. It mostly concerned her sore feet. She rarely smiled.

She smiled at me because I left tips that must have seemed enormous in a restaurant where many of the customers didn't tip at all. I discovered that when she left work at 9:00 PM. — after a fourteen hour day — she stopped at Forrie's Bistro, the bar down the street, sat down in a booth, slipped her shoes off, put her feet up on the seat opposite, and slowly drank two bottles of beer. By Friday, she'd had ample time to warm up to my tips if not to me. After my dinner with Joletta, I followed Velma to Forrie's and walked in with the casual air of an old customer as she was finishing her first bottle.

"Velma!" I exclaimed. "You look like a woman of leisure!"

I sat down opposite her. She moved her feet to make room for me but kept them on the seat.

" 'Woman of leisure' doesn't sound quite decent," she said, "but I'm too tired to care."

I nodded. "You work hard for your money."

"I sure do," she said with feeling.

I waved to the waitress. I pointed at Velma's bottle and held up two fingers, and she brought beer for both of us, carelessly filled our glasses — splashing the table — and thumped the bottles down.

I took a sip, leaned back with a smile, and announced, "That was a crime, wasn't it? A waitress who's that careless should lose her license. I've never seen you spill a drop of anything."

"So don't tip her," Velma said with a shrug. "In this place, people get lousy service and tip anyway. At Lon's, I give everyone good service, and some of those creeps don't know what a tip is."

"Life is unfair," I agreed. "But sometimes it develops a guilty conscience and goes all out to make amends." I slowly unfolded a ten-dollar bill and smoothed it out on the table in front of me. "This is for you," I said. "Maybe. Would you like some easy money?"

"Don't be silly," she said. "I turned down scads of easy money when I was younger, and even now it would take a lot more than ten bucks to tempt me. What kind of a pervert are you?"

I laughed. "The worst kind. All I'm after is information."

"I'm still not tempted, but go ahead and ask."

I passed Fernard's photo across the table — a much better picture than the one taken from the former repair shop. "Of course you know Ford."

"Sure I do. He's been eating at Lon's for years. That's a good shot of him."

I handed her photos of the two Frisco thugs, one at a time. "Know them?"

"Sure. They've been regular the last few weeks. Make that two or three months. Not every day, like Ford, but almost. Say three or four times a week."

I pushed the ten-dollar bill across the table. "See how easy it was?"

"For that?" she demanded incredulously.

"Not quite. I have one more question. I'm giving you the money in advance because I want you to understand that there's no penalty if you don't know the answer. All I ask is that you answer honestly. Did you ever see those three characters together?"

She frowned and closed her eyes. A moment later she opened them and stared at me. Her eyes were grayish-green, and she probably had been attractive before she buried her youth and good looks under cosmetics and the tough cynicism of frustrated middle-age.

She closed her eyes again. "Yes," she said slowly. "But not recently. It was at least a month ago. Maybe longer."

"Excellent. The ten is yours. Would you like another?"

"As long as you're playing Santa Claus, I'll take whatever's offered."

I handed her the second ten. She was still suspicious. She dropped it on the table in front of her. "What's it for?"

"A few more honest answers," I said. "If you have them."

"Ask, and then I'll decide."

"If you prefer it that way. Remember — there's no penalty for not knowing. The ten is for trying

270

— and for answering honestly if you do know."

She picked up the two bills and tucked them into her purse. "All right. Ask."

"Can you remember what they were talking about?"

"They didn't talk at all when I came near the table."

"How would you describe their behavior? Were they good friends joshing each other, were they business associates celebrating a big deal they'd just put over, were the two big guys ganging up on the little guy to get something out of him — how would you describe it?"

She said slowly, "They didn't look like any of those things. They were more . . . sneaky like. They took a booth back in the corner — it's the only time I ever saw Ford eat in a booth instead of at a table. We weren't very busy, and there was no one at all on that side of the room. Ford came in first and stood looking the place over before he went back to the corner. The other two came in a little later and joined him. They talked in low voices with their heads close together."

"And stopped talking when you waited on them?"

"When I went anywhere near them. If I just walked past on my way to the kitchen, they shut up and looked daggers at me like I was trying to snoop." She tossed her head. "As if I care what the likes of them talk about."

"How do they usually treat you?"

"The big guys, so-so. Ford is always nice — polite, anyway — and he always tips though not much."

I picked up the photos and got to my feet. "Painless, wasn't it?" I said with a smile. "This is a bonus. You've helped me enormously." I spread another ten on the table in front of her.

She kept her eyes on me. "Will this get them in trouble?" she asked with a worried frown.

"Not unless they *are* in trouble. And in that case, it's their doing, not yours. Do you understand?"

She nodded and took the money.

I felt elated. I had finally connected the thugs with the keno scam. "Fernard was pressing Dantzil for more money," I told Raina Lambert. "Probably Dantzil explained how complicated the scam was and how many people had to be paid, but the setup looked simple to Fernard. He was handling huge sums of money, and what Dantzil let him keep seemed like very little.

"His complaints got him nowhere, so he tried to put a different kind of pressure on Dantzil. He noticed a couple of thugs eating at Lon's. He hired them to threaten Dantzil — but once the thugs grasped what was going on, calling them off was like putting toothpaste back in the tube. They hung in there, started following Dantzil on their own, and tried to claim a piece of the action for themselves."

"That's possible," Raina said. "It's even likely. But both Fernard and the thugs had a stake in keeping Dantzil alive. The same goes for everyone else who was following him. Why was he murdered?"

"He was attracting too much attention to himself — and at least one person would have been very unhappy about that. I think the scam's Big Boss was having him followed just to see what he was up to."

She said slowly, "You think the Big Boss decided Dantzil had become a liability and eliminated him?"

"Something like that. Maybe he also thought Harley was holding out on him — as he must have been to accumulate that trust fund for his family."

"That's mob mentality you're describing. The ruthless Godfather who doesn't hesitate to wipe out his own people if he thinks they're disloyal. Is the mob back in Las Vegas?"

"Mob or not, it's the scam's boss who murdered Dantzil — or had him murdered — and he certainly is ruthless. No other explanation makes sense."

"There's one small problem."

"Yes," I agreed. "We still have no evidence at all."

14

JOEL ECKLING HAD ONCE BEEN HANDSOME, but his curly hair was thinning and streaked with gray, his waist was accumulating layers of flab, and his sagging jowl had already established the foundation for a formidable double chin. He looked like a worried old man with troubles. Most millionaires are accustomed to solving problems by giving someone an order, and they become severely traumatized when this suddenly doesn't work.

Raina Lambert had requested a conference in his private suite. She insisted on meeting him there rather than at his office because she didn't want to risk having Joletta catch as much as a glimpse of her in her real identity. She asked me to stand by in case I was needed, and when Eckling said he wanted to meet me, she telephoned me in my room and invited me up.

She introduced me, and we shook hands. "Lieutenant McCarney speaks highly of you," he said.

"Lieutenant McCarney has been most helpful and cooperative," I murmured.

Raina had called the meeting because she believed millionaires were entitled to their money's worth like anyone else. There had been no major keno winners since Dantzil was murdered. The win percentage was back where it belonged. If Eckling was satisfied with that, she thought we were ethically bound to let him quit. A complete unraveling of this case might cost a fortune.

But he wanted us to continue. "He understands that it may take a prolonged investigation to settle both the murder and the keno scam," Raina told me. "He also understands that if we succeed, and if Joletta is involved, she'll be swept up with the other guilty ones."

Eckling was nodding. "She's a bad girl," he said brokenly. "She's so beautiful that everyone gives her a second chance, and then another second chance, and she does something worse." He paused to blow his nose loudly. "It's time she accepted responsibility for her actions. I've given her every opportunity — given her everything — but when she starts plotting to ruin her father, and stealing from him . . ." His voice broke. "That's too much."

This resolution was no less courageous because he had arrived at it belatedly.

There was nothing more to say, so we left him and went to my room. Raina dropped into my one chair and announced, "He took the bit about his employees pretty hard. He wants them to be one big happy family reminiscent of the old days when the mob ran the casinos. Some owners make it a condition of employment that their employees sign a consent to take a lie detector test on request. Eckling scorns things like that — he thinks loyalty should be a two-way street. At first he refused to believe his employees could be involved, but the longer he thought about it, the angrier he became. Now he wants them all caught and punished.

"He tries to foster an unusual kind of hospitality at Diamond D's. This place is just far enough from Fremont Street to miss out on the regular flow of tourist traffic, and it owes its survival to tourists who discover it by accident and keep coming back and to locals who enjoy a casino that really makes them feel welcome. The Miss Diamond Dee ploy may look corny, but the hostesses work hard to create an atmosphere of genuine hospitality for both old and new customers. Eckling wants Diamond D's thought of as Las Vegas's most friendly casino."

"Will he hold to that fine resolution about Joletta when he sees her in manacles?" I asked.

"No jury is going to convict Joletta of anything. Not only is she beautiful, but it's obvious that she's being used."

"The question is whether we're going to convict any of these people. We still have a small problem with the evidence. We haven't got any."

"This case has spread out so much that we've

276

lost the focus on what we were doing. We need a change of direction. Let's have no more midnight carousing from one end of the strip to the other."

"That's unfair. I don't carouse when I work, and I don't confine my investigations to the Strip. Not only do I give Glitter Gulch equal time, but I've even hit remote casinos like Showboat, and Palace Station, and Sam's Town. What do you have in mind?"

"We'll start over. I want you to concentrate on Harley Dantzil."

"That's a change of direction? The police have been concentrating on him for almost two weeks. They actively resent having an unsolved murder on their hands."

"Either they're interviewing the wrong people, or they're asking the wrong questions."

"Very well. I'll look for the right people and ask them the right questions. What about the casino employees Harley was meeting?"

"We don't know they were casino employees. Leave it for later."

"What will you be working on?"

"I haven't finished with Nevada 2100. I can't decide whether Joletta and von Mach were insiders demanding a bigger cut or outsiders trying to take over."

"Fernard brought in the Frisco thugs to help him pry more money out of Dantzil. Something similar may have happened with Joletta and von

Mach. Someone brought them into it and then couldn't get rid of them."

"That's possible," she said, "but it's also possible that Nevada 2100 is the elusive high-tech element. Or that members of Americans All masqueraded as tourists and helped Fernard collect the money. I'd like to know." She got to her feet. "When you decide what you're going to do, call me."

She left. I dropped into the chair, put my feet on the bed, and commanded myself to think.

Lieutenant McCarney didn't sound friendly when I telephoned an hour later to tell him I needed help with another experiment, but when he heard what it was, he agreed immediately. I packed and checked out of Diamond D's, and by noon I was officially installed as the new tenant of 212A in the L D Apartments. I paid a week's rent. Chris Olsen, the elderly manager, was delighted. The police had refused to let him rent the apartment, and he was losing money.

Harley Dantzil's body was gone, but his ghost seemed vibrantly present in the decrepit living room. I wondered whether it would tell me anything. Next door was the larger apartment occupied by Wilbert Kuyper, the computer programmer. The woman who had cleaned for Dantzil lived at the far end of the lower level. None of the other tenants admitted any connection with him.

Because both living room and bedroom were

former motel rooms, each had a door and a large window that looked out on the porch that ran the length of the building. The living room of 212, which was the end apartment, also had a side window that offered a view of the cluttered yard and the alley where Joletta Eckling and I had walked. Beyond were the single-story buildings of the Farnby Street Apartments — new within the last few years. The view wasn't inspiring, but it gave me several things to think about.

The side window also looked down on one of the two stairways that led up to the second-floor porch and apartments. If Harley had been standing at the window on that fateful night, he would have seen the top of the murderer's head ascending — unless the murderer had used the stairs at the other end of the building. The side window of the first-floor apartment offered a more direct view of the stairway. I had noticed that when I climbed up with Joletta.

I reported my arrival to McCarney and to Raina Lambert. Then I telephoned Leda Rauchman, gave her my new telephone number, and told her I was abandoning my casino research.

"You cad," she said. "I suppose you're also abandoning me."

"Certainly not. I now have my own slum apartment. You can come any time, by appointment, and cook a meal for me."

"Would I have to bring this police person along?"

"Of course. That's what you have him for — to protect you from characters like me."

"No, thank you. Cooking for two is fun. Cooking for three isn't, and if the third happens to be a policeman . . ."

"He's a nice policeman. He bought us champagne and a pizza."

"He's been sleeping on my sofa too long, and I want to get rid of him. I complain to Lieutenant McCarney every morning. You said living dangerously would be less fun than I thought, but you didn't tell me it would be a bore."

She hung up, and I went out and bought some groceries to make my new apartment seem more home-like.

I wanted to know more about my next-door neighbor, the computer expert. I thought he might be able to explain the finer points of keno to me, so I left my door slightly ajar, hoping to intercept him either coming or going. Then I continued my meditation.

The woman who cleaned for Dantzil had never seen him here during the day. The parties he attended always took place at night. He must have used the apartment only as a place to meet people. He certainly met Fernard here. The actor couldn't have set the Frisco thugs to watching the building if he hadn't known the address. And of course Fernard — or another habitué of Lon's 24-Hour-Cafe — had dropped the matches.

But I couldn't imagine Fernard bashing Dantzil's skull. If he had, he was as stupidly shortsighted as the man who killed the goose that laid the golden eggs. Other participants in the scam must have come here to meet with Dantzil and receive their orders and perhaps their shares of the money. It seemed ironic to imagine stacks of currency changing hands in this shabby apartment, but Las Vegas was full of such incongruities.

I fixed myself something to eat — from a can — and continued my meditations. Suddenly the afternoon had passed and it was getting dark. The outside light over the stairway was turned on automatically by a photocell, and with the window shade up, it sent a slanting patch of illumination into the room.

There still was no sign of Kuyper. I decided he must be sleeping off one of his celebrations.

Diffused glows from Glitter Gulch and the Strip were becoming visible above the darkening western and southwestern horizons. I couldn't see them from my apartment. Looking out on the dingy scene below, I almost couldn't imagine them. They belonged to a different universe. This was the real Las Vegas I was looking at — one of its many realities — and after the effervescent world of the Strip and Glitter Gulch, it seemed wholly fantastical.

When I turned on the large table lamp that once had contained a bug, I was reminded of something

I first noticed the night we found Dantzil's body. The apartment was very dimly lit. I couldn't remember the last time I had seen a 25-watt bulb, but that is what both the table lamp and the ceiling fixture contained. I thought of demanding larger bulbs from the manager, and then I decided I didn't need light. After I made myself a sandwich, I turned both lights off and ate it in the dark, standing at my favorite window. The seeping darkness was blotting out the grubby back yards and the alley except where the merged glare of outside lights from this building and the next exposed their shabbiness relentlessly. While I watched, a car drove up the alley and turned toward me. I moved to the front window and saw it pull into a space in front of a downstairs apartment. A woman took a large bag of groceries from the trunk. She stood out sharply for a moment in the illumination from a window below and then vanished under the porch. She was middle-aged, she wore no make-up, and her hair needed combing. She looked as though she'd had a long, hard day.

I turned on the table lamp again and opened a thick packet of material that McCarney had given to me. I leafed through a stack of photographs until I found that of Hester Smith, who was the middle-aged woman I had just seen. She worked as a cashier in a convenience store, her husband worked in a casino, and they'd had their apartment for about four months. Neither of them admitted to knowing Harley Dantzil.

The two women who occupied the apartment directly beneath Dantzil's interested me more. They arrived home together, and one of them left again almost immediately. I gave the other time to get comfortably settled for the evening, and then I put McCarney's packet in a briefcase and went downstairs. According to the annotated directory the lieutenant had provided, the women were graduate students at the university, but the term "college girls" would have been a misnomer. They were in their mid-thirties, and they both had full-time clerical jobs. When I knocked, the curtain over the glass in the door was pulled back, and a plump face peered at me nearsightedly through thick glasses.

The door's chain was on, and it opened no more than an inch. I introduced myself and handed my card through the crack. "We're still looking into the murder of the gentleman who lived upstairs," I said.

"Oh, my God!" She clapped her hand to her forehead, but she resignedly took the chain off and let the door swing open. "The police were here I don't know how many times and now you. What are 'Investigative Consultants'?"

"Private detectives. The dead gentleman's employer hired us."

"Come in." She looked me over frankly. "You're better looking than the police, but I can't tell you anything I haven't already told them. If I'd known you were coming, I would have saved something for you."

She was short and plump with extremely large breasts. She was wearing blue jeans, and her baggy sweat shirt was embossed with a typical Las Vegas sweat shirt graffito: IT'S ALL I'VE GOT/SO I'M GLAD THERE'S A LOT. Her hair was in curlers — indication that she had counted on a relaxed evening at home with no visitors.

"Memory is a tricky commodity," I told her. "If we ask the same questions in different ways, sometimes we get different answers."

The apartment was newly painted — probably the women had done it themselves — and both it and the furniture were in good condition. She gathered up an armful of newspapers from the sofa and said, "Make yourself comfortable. Go ahead and ask. But I'll warn you — this is the time of day my memory insists on putting its feet up and relaxing."

"Let's see — you're Sally."

"Sally Barchor, the short, fat one. My roommate is Violet Matovski, the tall, skinny one. Violet should be back in a few minutes."

"I'll try not to waste your time," I said. "What I would like to do first is look out of your side window."

She gestured indifferently. "Be my guest."

Dantzil's murder had shocked the two women into elaborate efforts to secure their apartment.

Not only was there a heavy new chain and a new lock on the entrance door, but the windows were covered with a metal mesh that was firmly screwed into place.

Sally raised the shade over the side window and stepped aside. Under the powerful outside lights, there was a good view of the stairs and the yard beyond despite the mesh.

"*If* the shade is up, and *if* we happen to be looking out, we can see everyone using the stairs — and didn't the police make a big thing of it," Sally said. "As though we have nothing better to occupy ourselves with than to stand at the window waiting for someone to climb up."

"Right," I said sympathetically. In the police report, they had sounded like a couple of amiable snoops who just might have done that. "If the shade had been up, and if you'd chanced to look out at the right moment, and if the murderer had used the stairs at this end of the building, you certainly would have seen him."

"If dishes were horses, this kitchen would be a mess. That's what my mother used to say. You police certainly do a lot of iffing."

"Would you do me a favor?"

"Glad to — I think."

"Go outside to the alley and then walk back toward the building and climb the stairs as far as the landing."

"I'll do anything reasonable to get the police off

our backs."

She slipped on a jacket and went out the door — which she hadn't bothered to lock again after she let me in — marched across the yard to the alley, and then turned, waved a signal, walked back toward the building, and climbed the stairs. While that was going on, I heard a car pull up outside. I paid no attention; nor did I move when the door opened behind me. Sally Barchor had reached the stairway, and I wanted to see the end of my experiment.

When I did turn, I heard a gasp and then a scream. "Who the hell are you?"

It was Violet Matovski, and she was an inverted image of Sally. She also wore blue jeans and a baggy sweat shirt — without a motto — and her hair was in curlers, but she was extremely tall and thin. She stood white-faced, clutching a bag of groceries and staring at me.

"Sorry to give you a start," I said. "Sally is outside — here she is."

The laughing Sally hurried in and introduced us.

"Sorry to give *you* a start," Violet Matovski said, "but after what happened upstairs, we haven't been feeling very secure about this place."

"I don't blame you. But it may make you feel better to know that Mr. Dantzil probably was done in by one of his associates. The address had nothing to do with it. He brought his troubles with him."

"And took them away with him — I hope," Violet said fervently. She set the bag of groceries on a kitchen cabinet, fished out three cans of frozen juice, and put them in the refrigerator's freezing compartment.

"Mr. Pletcher wants to jog our memories by asking the same questions in different ways," Sally said. "I've already told him it won't work."

"No," Violet said. She shook her head. "I talked with at least six police officers, and I told each of them exactly what I saw that night and when I saw it. I cannot describe what I didn't see."

"I know what you told the police. Let's sit down and talk about it."

The three of us took chairs around a drop leaf kitchen table. Sally obligingly raised one of the leaves for me to put my papers on.

"They kept asking me if I saw any strangers that night," Violet Matovski said. "And I didn't. I can tell you that emphatically. I saw several people use that stairway between the time I came home, about six, and the time I went to bed, which was about eleven-thirty. And I recognized all of them. I didn't know them by name, but I knew they were tenants I'd seen coming and going repeatedly."

"And I saw the same people she did," Sally Barchor said. "We were moving around getting supper, and then we were doing the dishes, and later she decided to have a snack before she went to bed. She can have snacks," the fat Sally went

on bitterly. "She leaves the refrigerator full of de-
serts and dares me to touch them. Ice cream,
chocolate mousse — with whipped-cream topping
— malted milk, pastries. It never shows on her.
She decided to have a snack, and I was tempted,
and then I decided not to. But we were up and
around together, and we saw the same people."

"Then the shade must have been up."

"We weren't so careful then," Sally said. "We
didn't see any need to be, because people using
the stairs really can't see in unless they jump or
stand on something, but we can look right down
on them."

"Let's go through this one more time, and then
maybe you'll be finished with it. According to the
police report, you normally aren't home weekday
evenings because you take classes at the university, but the university is closed in January."

"It closes each year just before Christmas and
opens again about the first of February," Violet
said. "Mini-courses are offered in January, but we
enjoy having a little time off."

"When you have classes, what time do you get
home?"

"That depends on when the class lets out and
what we do afterward. Never before ten. Often it's
eleven or later."

I took a summary of their testimony from my
briefcase. "Since it was January, you came directly
home from work that night instead of going to

class. You got here shortly after six and started to prepare your evening meal. While you were at it, you saw Mr. Kuyper arrive."

"We saw one of the tenants."

I showed them Kuyper's photograph, and they both nodded. "He's lived here longer than we have," Sally said.

"Then Mrs. Smith arrived. You saw her through the front window." I passed them her photograph. They both nodded. The police had it right — the women were amiable snoops and a detective's favorite kind of witness, but they had kept their natural instincts too severely under control. It hadn't occurred to them to step outside or climb the stairs themselves to see which apartments these people were entering.

I took them through their evening program: what they did, whom they saw. Lieutenant McCarney had it down on paper, every *i* dotted, every *t* crossed, and they confirmed all of it. After doing the supper dishes, they had watched TV until almost ten o'clock when Violet began thinking about her snack. She got up and took a dish of chocolate mousse from the refrigerator.

"She smacks her lips when she eats it," Sally said bitterly.

The sight, sound, and smell of the mousse being devoured worked powerfully on Sally. She got up to get her own snack. Then her self-control reasserted itself, and she sat down again without one.

It was while she was up, poking around, that she saw Mr. Roffer arrive, though at that time she had never heard his name. She'd seen him frequently, either returning home from work or on weekends. He was wearing overalls — he always wore overalls to work — and he went up the stairs quickly.

About the same time, Violet had taken her dish to the sink, and she also caught a glimpse of Mr. Roffer. I passed them his photo, conveniently posed in overalls, and they both nodded.

The police, again dotting the last *i* and crossing the last *t*, had included Mr. Roffer's own version of his arrival home. The time was correct; so were the overalls. He had climbed the stairs in a hurry and passed Harley Dantzil's apartment without paying the slightest attention to it. He couldn't even recall whether there had been a light on. He seemed straightforward enough to the police, and they saw no reason to suspect him of stopping off to smash Harley Dantzil's skull between the time Sally and Violet had seen him going up the stairs and the time his wife said he arrived home. Neither did I.

That was the sum of it. The women had been over that ground so many times that they no longer recalled their testimony. They recited it. Their stories *were* their memories, and it was much too late for a routine interrogation. Jogging a memory is exactly like searching a room. You can't find what isn't there, and if a search has already been made, you have to pick your way through whatever clutter it left behind.

"One more question," I said. "Please think carefully. Did you see or hear anything at all that night that seemed odd, or unusual, or peculiar?"

"Odd how?" Sally demanded. "It was just people coming home from work or shopping or whatever. What could have been odd about that?"

Violet was silent for so long that we both turned to look at her. "There was one thing I wondered about at the time," she said finally. "I'd forgotten it. Mr. Roffer was carrying an umbrella. That seemed odd to me. I mean — it'd been a lovely day, and it was January, and why an umbrella?"

"I didn't see any umbrella," Sally said.

"I did, and I wondered about it. We hadn't had any rain for weeks. Sometimes in the summer you see people using umbrellas like parasols to keep the sun off, but — after dark, in January?"

"I'm sure he wasn't carrying an umbrella," Sally said. "He had groceries in both arms."

Violet turned and stared at her. "Now just a moment — he wasn't carrying anything at all except the umbrella."

"Let's start over," I suggested. "Think back to that night. Violet is smacking her lips over her mousse. Sally gets up to find her own snack, looks out, and sees Mr. Roffer." I gave her the photo. "Did you actually see his face?" I asked.

She hesitated.

"Exactly where was he on the stairway?"

"Just below the window."

"Many people look straight ahead or down when they're climbing stairs. Are you sure you saw his face?"

Questioned, she wasn't sure. She knew him because she had seen him on other occasions, and she was positive he'd had a bag of groceries in each arm and wasn't carrying anything else, especially not an umbrella.

I turned to Violet. "This is important. Sally is looking around for a snack. In the process, she looks out and sees Mr. Roffer. Then she decides to forgo the snack and returns to her chair. You take your mousse dish to the sink, and you also see Mr. Roffer. Where is he on the stairs?"

"Why — just below the window."

"Wearing overalls and carrying an umbrella?"

She nodded. "I'm positive about that. And no bags of groceries."

"How long was it between the time Sally looked out the window and the time you looked out the window?"

Both of them were silent.

"Think carefully," I said, "because what you just described is impossible. Sally looked out and saw Mr. Roffer climbing the stairs. Then Violet looked out and also saw him climbing the stairs — *and both of you saw him in exactly the same place.* After Sally looked, how long was it before Violet got to the window?"

They exchanged glances. "I never thought about that," Violet said. "It seemed as though I looked right after she did, but it could have been two or three minutes later."

"Or even five or six," Sally said. "Or more."

I passed Mr. Roffer's photograph to Violet. "Are you certain, now, that this is the person you saw with the umbrella? Did you actually see his face?"

"No," she said slowly. "I only saw the top of his head. And his overalls, of course. And his umbrella as he went on up the stairs."

"What sort of an umbrella was it?"

"It was cloth with some kind of pattern — plaid, I think. Probably I didn't see it very well."

"How did he carry it?"

"By the handle, hanging down at his side. It was perfectly visible, if that's what you're getting at, but with it folded up, not much of the pattern showed."

"Did he wear his hair like this? You'll have to imagine yourself above him and looking down."

She thought for a moment. "His hair was bushier than that," she said finally.

"Brown and bushy?"

She nodded.

"A person with brown, bushy hair who wears overalls. Have you ever seen such a person before — with or without the umbrella?"

"Yes," she said slowly. "I have seen him before, and I remember thinking he looked like a farm hand."

"A real hayseed, in fact."

She nodded. "I guess it was his long hair that made him look that way."

"How many times did you see him?"

"I don't know. Two or three. I assumed he was a new tenant."

I turned to Sally. "Can you remember seeing this other person? Overalls; brown, bushy hair; needs a haircut; looks like a hayseed?"

She had the answer ready. "Yes. I've seen him late at night at least twice. Like Violet, I thought he was a new tenant. But it wasn't him I saw the night of the murder. I'm certain about that."

"No. You saw Mr. Roffer. Violet looked out a few minutes later and saw this other character. It was the coincidence of their arriving close together and both wearing overalls that caused the confusion. It must be difficult to keep track of who actually lives in this place. Anyone who visits here regularly could easily be mistaken for a tenant."

"You're so right," Sally said. "There's a big turnover in places that rent by the week, and the rent here is steep considering the poor condition some of the apartments are in. People only stay until they can find something better."

I got to my feet. "Suddenly both of you are extremely important witnesses. The police will want you to tell this story again in a sworn statement, and they'll probably ask you to help a police artist draw a picture of this bushy-haired character."

"My God! Tonight?"

"I'm sure they'll make every effort to do it at your convenience. I thank both of you very much."

I went back upstairs and telephoned McCarney at home.

"Not another experiment, I hope," he said testily.

"I have a description of Dantzil's murderer. If you'd rather wait until morning . . ."

"Let's have it.

"It was one of the characters Leda Rauchman saw him with — the hayseed with overalls and bushy hair. He climbed the stairs to Dantzil's apartment the night of the murder, and Violet Matovski saw him. Her description tallies with Rauchman's with one significant difference. She saw him carrying an umbrella."

"Just a moment." The muffled sounds suggested that McCarney had suddenly decided to sit down. "Did you say an umbrella? He called on Dantzil that night carrying an umbrella?"

"And *that* is how the piece of pipe got on the scene. It was concealed in the umbrella. Violet Matovski is my new favorite witness. I'm thinking of taking her on a casino crawl to see what else she can observe. The number one question now is whether we've finally tagged the Big Boss, or whether Hayseed was only another go-between, a link to Harley Dantzil, who was a link to Fernard and the casino workers."

McCarney said slowly, "That's a rather good number one question."

15

WHEN I DESCRIBED THIS SENSATIONAL DE-velopment to Raina Lambert, her shrug — over the telephone — was almost audible. "The police were already looking for Hayseed. Now they'll look harder — but they won't find him."

"Don't malign my favorite police force," I told her sternly. "Until tonight, all the guy had done was meet Dantzil in a tavern, which is not illegal. His priority on the 'wanted' list was slightly below that of people suspected of using slugs in slot machines. Now they'll really go after him."

"They still won't find him."

"Why not?"

"Because he doesn't exist. That bushy hair has got to be a wig. If he removes it and puts on a suit, he may look like a casino pit boss or even a politician."

"I still think I'm onto something here."

"Then keep after it."

I hung up and went to the side window. Seen from the air at night, Las Vegas is a brilliantly lit city with fascinating lines and patterns in contrasting colors. Seen from the ground, the light functions like electrostatics in Coulomb's Law. It varies inversely with the square of the distance from the nearest major thoroughfare. The stairways of the L D Apartments had the brightest illumination in the area. Outside lights at the Farnby Apartments were dim by comparison. Street lights were too remote to be noticed. Along the alley a few yard lights threw shallow patches; otherwise, it was a dark night out there.

Probably no one cared. Supper had been eaten, dishes were done, and in the Farnby apartments visible to me, every living room seemed to be lighted for TV viewing. The complex consisted of two long, narrow buildings across the front, facing Farnby Street, and four identical buildings placed perpendicular to them on the alley side. The end window of one rear building was directly opposite my side window. According to the layout of the other units, this should have been a living room, but it was dark.

I continued to ponder the use Harley Dantzil might have made of this apartment. The fact that he had been attending Kuyper's parties for more than a year could mean only one thing. He'd had another refuge somewhere nearby before he rented this one.

McCarney telephoned to tell me a police artist would work with Leda Rauchman, Violet Matovski, and Sally Barchor the next morning to see if he could come up with a portrait of Hayseed that satisfied them. I mentioned my tenuous notion that Kuyper, the computer expert, might be Dantzil's high-tech connection. The lieutenant snorted.

Then he said, "Excuse me. For all I know, that may be true. But starting last Monday, I indulged my own morbid curiosity and tried to have the guy tailed, and my officers almost died of boredom. When he's working, he doesn't go anywhere. He doesn't meet anyone — except now and then a pizza delivery man. When he finishes a job, he goes shopping, buys stuff for a party just like he said, has himself a binge, sleeps it off — and starts work on his next job. I can tell you positively he wasn't a connection for anything at all during the time I had him watched."

Police reports had been so uneventful of late that I had stopped reading them, so I missed that one. I thanked the lieutenant and went for another look out of my side window. The end room across the alley was still dark. I checked it several more times before I went to bed. It remained dark.

I was up early the next morning. Returning from a walk through the neighborhood, I saw a police car picking up Sally Barchor and Violet Matovski. I hurried over to apologize for disrupting their weekend, and Sally said brightly, "Oh, well. We haven't had this much attention from men in years."

They returned shortly before noon, and their driver kindly brought me photocopies of two drawings the artist had made from facial characteristics they and Leda Rauchman were able to agree on. One showed the head only. The other showed head and shoulders, including the overalls.

I folded the copies carefully, tucked them into a pocket, and set about tracking down the original in my own fumbling fashion. I first walked up and down the alley, which had an unusual amount of traffic considering the location. Tenants of both the L D Apartments and the newer apartment complex were able to avoid the delay of a major traffic intersection or two on Fremont Street by coming home the back way.

I walked through the Farnby Apartments complex, pausing to discreetly peek into the window of number 30, the apartment I had observed the night before. It seemed to be vacant. At the manager's office, which was located in one of the front buildings facing Farnby Street, a plump, motherly looking woman named Mrs. Junnilla had no objection to showing vacant apartments on Sunday morning. She had two units immediately available. I mentioned number 30, and she nodded and went to her desk for the keys.

"It's in lovely condition," she said as we walked along. "The last tenant had it for less than a month. She really took good care of it. I was sorry she had to leave, but her mother died suddenly, and she went home to look after her father."

I kidded Mrs. Junnilla into describing this woman, who had been a middle-aged blonde, probably of the synthetic variety, with an exceptionally good figure but a face that had been around the track a few times. She had been quiet and pleasant, paid two months in advance, took good care of her apartment, caused no problems, and never bothered anyone. Mrs. Junnilla thought the person who got the apartment next could consider himself lucky.

"Did she have any visitors?" I asked.

Mrs. Junnilla made it clear that spying on her tenants wasn't her job.

"Of course not, but it's your duty to keep track of strangers hanging around the apartments. What sort of visitors were they?"

She lacked the natural inquisitiveness of a Sally Barchor or a Violet Matovski, but several times she had noticed a man calling on Win Upway, which was the tenant's name. A series of men would have been a horse of a different color, she added quickly, but this was not a college dormitory, and no fuss was made if a female tenant received visits from a male friend as long as they didn't disturb anyone. He usually came in late in the evening, and Mrs. Junnilla had a really good look at him only once.

When I asked her to describe the gentleman, she said, "I guess he wasn't exactly a gentleman, but he seemed quiet and very polite."

I unfolded one of the police drawings of Hayseed, and she nodded excitedly. "That's him! That's him exactly!"

By that time she had me labeled "police," and she was relieved to find out I was only an Investigative Consultant. She waited outside the apartment while I walked through it quickly and stood for a moment at the end window, looking across the alley at Harley Dantzil's end window. Then we relocked the apartment and returned to her office, and I telephoned Lieutenant McCarney.

I questioned Mrs. Junnilla further while we waited. She really did pay very little attention to her tenants — if they didn't bother her, she didn't bother them — but a few times she had seen Win Upway arriving at her apartment late in the evening, on foot, by way of the alley, which seemed odd to her.

I explained the situation to McCarney and left him to make what he could of it. I returned to Dantzil's apartment. Half an hour later, leaving his technicians at work in what was certain to be a futile search for evidence, McCarney strolled across the alley to see me.

"First Saturday night and now Sunday morning," he said plaintively. "Don't you ever discover anything on Monday afternoon?"

"I told you — the calendar has no meaning for a tireless worker like me."

We stood together at the side window, looking

302

across the alley. "I hope you don't mind my asking," McCarney said, "but I've never experienced such a difficult time in making sense out of evidence. Where'd you get the notion that particular apartment was connected with this one?"

"Whenever I stood here looking out, that window looked back at me. Last night I waited for a light to be turned on there, and none was. I was wondering why Dantzil rented this particular apartment, and obviously it's an excellent place for spying on that window. Then I turned the proposition around. That window is perfectly placed for spying on this apartment — or, if the occupants were in cahoots, the lights in either place could have been used to signal with. As soon as my copies of the drawings arrived, I went to see the manager. There are other units that have windows facing in this direction, but that's the one that happened to be available when Win Upway came shopping for an apartment."

"Then you played a hunch."

"I always do. If I'm wrong, the only time wasted is my own. Your routine would have accomplished the same thing as soon as you started canvassing the neighborhood with those drawings of Hayseed. All I did was speed things up a little. Obviously Hayseed visited his blonde and waited there until Dantzil signaled to him."

"Is she part of the gang, or was Hayseed making use of her because she had such a convenient apartment?"

"If he was using her, it was with her consent and cooperation. She rented the apartment on the same day Dantzil rented this one. She looked at it, slipped Mrs. Junnilla twenty to hold it until the next morning, and then came back later that day and rented it."

McCarney scratched his head fretfully. "Then she's part of the gang. She didn't want to commit herself until she was certain Dantzil had got this apartment."

"I'll give you something else. Somewhere in this neighborhood, you'll find another pair of apartments Dantzil and Upway rented before they moved here. We know Dantzil had a place nearby because he attended Kuyper's parties."

"I have a hard time fitting him into those parties. Even Kuyper thought he seemed out of place. Why do you suppose he went?"

"Because he had time to kill. Diamond D's got concerned if he hung around there after hours — they called it overtime — but when he had a late appointment, he didn't want to go home and then have to come back again. So he came here — to this apartment or the former one — with several hours to wait, and one thing he'd never learned how to do was nothing. For example, there wasn't a scrap of reading material here. When a neighbor mentioned a party to him, he went along. That must have been how he found this apartment. He noticed it was vacant when he came to one of Kuyper's parties, and it seemed like a better setup than the one he had, so he sent Win Upway to see what was available across the alley."

"We already canvassed the neighborhood with his photo," McCarney said.

"Then someone didn't want to get involved. Try again with the drawing of Hayseed. You also should get the best description possible of Win Upway and look for the previous place she rented."

He went back to see what his technicians had turned up. I phoned another report to Raina Lambert. This time she was interested. She made me run through Win Upway's description twice.

"It'll be a couple of days before I can look into that," she said. "I have loose ends of my own to deal with."

"I've exhausted my luck here. It'll take police routine to find any more nuggets. Do you want me to carry on anyway?"

"No. I have something else for you. There are interesting sightseeing tours for Las Vegas and vicinity. Have you noticed?"

"I've seen the advertisements," I said guardedly.

"There's a tour of the Valley of Fire that also includes Nevada 2100. I want you to take it tomorrow."

"All right. I'll invite Leda for protective coloration, and we'll pretend we're supercilious tourists.

What am I looking for?"

"Anything that seems out of place in a tourist attraction."

"We still haven't nailed down Dantzil's high-tech connection. Is that what you have in mind?"

"I'm trying to bring something to a boil without being caught stirring the pot. Just be your own resourceful self and don't get involved in any laser gun duels."

"Right," I said.

"By the way — Joel Eckling just telephoned. Florence Stevens-Dantzil called at Diamond D's today — probably right after church. She was very polite, but she insisted on seeing him. She wanted to know why Harley's belongings hadn't been returned to her. Eckling protested that as far as he knew, Harley hadn't kept anything there. A police detective, and also a private investigator, had searched his office, and neither of them mentioned finding personal property. If she wanted to look herself, she was welcome.

"She did. She took one look and threw a tantrum. The mere idea of the husband of a Stevens-Dantzil working in a cramped and shoddy place like that was an insult. She wanted to know what he did, and of course Eckling had difficulty describing it. The longer they talked, the angrier she got, and the more embarrassed he got."

"It's been almost two weeks," I said. "If she had any real concern about his property, wouldn't

306

she have thought of it earlier?"

"His property has nothing to do with it. She's playing the role of a grieving widow. Society imposes it on her, so she's making the most of it. Probably she found an etiquette book that had the steps written out for her. Today was number seven, 'Call at husband's place of employment and create a scene.' I wonder what number eight will be."

I telephoned to reserve two places on the following day's tour of the Valley of Fire — a state park with spectacular desert topography — and Nevada 2100. Since tourists are picked up at their hotels, I promised we would be waiting at Diamond D's. Then I telephoned Leda Rauchman.

"How would you like to be a tourist?" I asked her.

"I've never been one, but I've always envied them except for the snooty kind. Would I have to be snooty?"

"That requires experience. Beginners are excused. Your police guard can drop you off at Diamond D's shortly before eight-thirty tomorrow morning, and I'll meet you there. We'll be tourists for the day."

"Are you sure you want to be seen there in daylight with a disgraced former employee?"

"I am not Joletta Eckling. Anyone I date, I display proudly. I'll see you tomorrow morning. By the way . . ."

I wondered if she were having financial problems. She had lost her job, and she had been too occupied playing detective to look for another. She might be running short of money. This is not a subject that is easy to work into a casual conversation, so I made a joke of it. "It's your police guard I'm concerned about," I said. "It'd be a severe jolt to him if your landlord evicted you. He'd have to find another sofa. If you need help . . ."

"Don't be silly," she said. "I own the apartment building. I inherited it from my mother."

I took the time to glance at a Sunday paper. Prominently featured on the first society page was Florence Stevens-Dantzil, impeccably attired in black and presenting a check for five thousand dollars to the President of the University of Nevada, Las Vegas to establish a Harley Dantzil Scholarship Fund. Raina Lambert had delineated her perfectly. This was number six of the grieving widow's schedule, and it had happened the day before. For number seven, she had just visited Diamond D's. Like Raina, I wondered what number eight would be.

Late in the afternoon, McCarney returned. "Miss Lambert asked me to meet her here," he said. "She has something she wants to show us. You were right about the other apartment. For more than a year, a blonde resembling Win Upway — but using a different name — rented one of those converted garages down the alley toward

Cutler Street. She moved out the same week Win Upway rented the apartment."

"What about Hayseed?" I asked.

"I'm assuming that he and the blonde worked things the same way. He could come and go in relative privacy by way of the alley. Dantzil must have had a place nearby, probably in one of those houses that's been mutilated into apartments, but no one admits to recognizing his photo."

"Unless you can persuade someone to talk, that's as much as you'll ever find out. Look — tomorrow morning I'm taking Leda Rauchman on a sightseeing tour. The Valley of Fire and Nevada 2100. She's to be dropped off at Diamond D's shortly before eight-thirty. Then her bodyguard can have the day off."

"What are you looking for at Nevada 2100?"

"My boss thinks there's something queer about the place. I'm taking Leda because a snooping couple are less likely to arouse suspicion than a man snooping by himself. Would you like to come along as support gun?"

"There's no way I could convince my superiors that a sight-seeing tour constitutes work. Did Miss Lambert give you any clue as to what she means by 'queer'?"

"None. That's the way we operate. If I'm able to see it myself, that'll give her the confirmation she wants. If I don't see it, I'll be confirming her frequently stated opinion that men are stupid."

"Why do you think you need a support gun?"

"Because I have a 'Daniel' feeling about this expedition. I'm being thrown to the lions."

"You'll be traveling with a coachload of tourists. What in the world could happen to you?"

"No idea. At least Leda will be along, so I'll have a witness. Did you find anything in that apartment?"

"The place was wiped clean. And I do mean clean. I've never seen a furnished apartment left in such a tidy condition."

"That's too bad," I said. "I have a dream of someday finding myself in one of those detective story cases where the murderer leaves fingerprints all over everything. Or just one fingerprint that's clear enough to use."

Raina Lambert arrived a few minutes later wearing a babushka and no make-up at all and looking as though she had just performed a hard day's work. She brought company with her — a junior edition of the thugs from Frisco. He was tall and beefy but with less height and more flab. She introduced him to me. His name was Al Olindon, and he acted as shy as a juvenile summoned to the principal's office.

McCarney already knew him. He was Betty Varnko's brother, and the lieutenant had met him when he called on Betty to tell her that her supposed husband was dead.

"We have a number of loose ends to dispose

of," Raina Lambert said. "I've been talking with Al, and since one of them concerns him, I decided to bring him along. Al says Harley Dantzil was his best friend. Will you tell us about that, Al?"

"He *was* my best friend," the young giant said in an incongruously piping voice, "but I never called him Harley Dantzil. He was Brian Varnko. A year ago, when I was out of work and having a really rough time, he didn't just lend me money, he gave it to me. He got me straightened out and made me move in with him and Betty until I found a job. He was like that. Our mother died when Betty was sixteen, and everything fell apart. I didn't know how to go about looking after her. When she married Brian, we were a family again. I *belonged* somewhere."

He had tears in his eyes.

"But you didn't feel that way at first," Raina Lambert prompted him.

"Well — he was an older man, and Betty was young and inexperienced, and I worried about her. I thought he was bad news for her in every way. I tried to get him to leave her alone."

He broke off. Raina prompted him again. "You didn't have much success reasoning with him, so one night in front of Diamond D's you used a different form of persuasion."

"Yeah. I guess I beat him up pretty bad. He didn't hold it against me, though. He kept saying he was as concerned about Betty as I was, and

311

eventually I had to believe him."

McCarney's face had turned pink on its way to becoming red. I wondered how many hours the police had squandered on the investigation of Dantzil's beating. "Why didn't you tell me about that when I talked with you?" he demanded.

Olindon shrugged. "It happened years ago. I forgot all about it until Miss Lambert started asking questions. When I talked with you, Betty had just heard about Brian, and she was in hysterics, and I was mostly thinking about what would happen to her and the kids."

"As it turned out, you were right. He was bad news for her. Now she has the responsibility of a family, and legally she's not even a widow."

"I don't see it that way," Olindon said. "They were real happy together. She had some wonderful years with him. The kids are darling, and she's got them. Brian left her the house paid for and a good income. There'll be money to send the kids to college. She's a lot better off than she would have been without him."

We thanked him and shook his hand, and he shuffled out.

"I wanted to exorcise that ghost just in case either of you had a lurking suspicion that the beating might have been connected with Dantzil's murder," Raina Lambert said. "We've picked up one bright, promising clue after another in this case, and all of them have run like those strange desert

312

rivers that suddenly vanish underground. Now I'll see if I can exorcise something else."

She left, and McCarney started to follow her. He paused in the doorway. "What are you doing this evening?"

"I'm going out to eat — not at Lon's. Not at Diamond D's, either. Then I'm going to bed."

"You aren't working on anything?"

"No."

"Thank God," he said. He left, closing the door firmly.

16

Anyone who has a genuine aversion to gambling, glitter, and hype can enjoy a healthy, pleasurable, fascinating, and even educational vacation in Nevada without entering a casino. The scenery is beautiful; history can be pursued in all of its infinite variety from nineteenth century mines and ghost towns to geological eras measured in millions of years. Several companies run sightseeing tours out of Las Vegas for the use of the anti-casino crowd and also for those wanting the best of both worlds. The tours radiate in all directions, starting with Las Vegas itself and moving outward to Hoover Dam; to Lake Mead, for boat excursions; to the Colorado River, for rafting; to neighboring communities and their museums; to nearby natural wonders. Air or overnight tours take tourists as far as the Grand Canyon or Death Valley.

A fleet of coaches ranges through Glitter Gulch and along the Strip each morning, calling at the various hotels to pick up sightseers. I had seen the coaches as well as the posters and stacks of circulars, but I had paid little attention to them.

Leda and her detective arrived at Diamond D's shortly before eight-thirty the next morning, and I handed her directly from his car into the waiting coach. She wore a brightly flowered dress, and she looked much too spirited and alert to be a Las Vegas tourist. "How do you manage to be so wide-awake when you entertained a man all night in your apartment?" I asked.

"It requires severe conditioning. What will they do to him while we're frivoling? Send him to Siberia? He doesn't know a word of Russian."

I told her the bodyguard had been assigned to less exciting duties for the day. Actually, he had been given the day off.

The coach picked up tourists at several hotels and then took us to a central depot — in the slum behind the Strip — where the sightseers were assigned to their respective tours. Ours headed north on a fifty-mile jaunt. The driver delivered a continuous, folksy commentary, first on Las Vegas and Nevada, and then, as we approached the Valley of Fire, on the wonders we were about to see, but I had a knowledgeable guide of my own closer at hand. The valley had long been Leda's favorite place. It was a magnificent surrounding in which to study the history of the Mojave Desert, its geology, its flora, and its fauna. Leda could wax as ecstatic over technical details concerning the various cacti as Professor Quilley had over electrostatics.

Stark beauty lay just outside our coach windows, where sandstone outcrops had been sculpted into fantastic shapes and colors by that greatest of all surrealistic artists, nature. Several times we stopped to admire them close up and even climb over them. Far up a mountain, cavorting desert bighorn sheep looked the size of mice. They were leaping and running about, clearly conveying the message that it was a fine day to be a sheep. It was also a fine day to be a tourist, and our group chatted in friendly fashion, lent binoculars, showed pictures of grandchildren, and exchanged addresses.

We enjoyed lunch on the shore of Lake Mead, and then we visited the Lost City Museum to see artifacts of the region's Indians. Finally we headed south again, and after a ride of several miles, we entered Nevada 2100's parking lot. Twenty-five or thirty cars and several other coaches were there ahead of us. We climbed out awkwardly, which is the only possible way to emerge from a touring coach, and stretched our limbs. Stretching mine, I found I had received no physical sensation of arriving in the future.

The driver presented each of us with an admission ticket, wished us a pleasant time in the year 2100, and asked everyone to be back at the coach by three-thirty. Beyond the parking lot was a sprawling cluster of geodesic domes and solar panels arranged on different levels of the humped south side of a craggy hill. At first glance it looked like something blown in by a freakish cosmic wind. In the center was a towering misrepresentation of a spaceship; another spaceship, much shorter and stubbier, stood on the upper level at the edge of a playground.

The central and largest section was called "The Museum of the Future." For would-be athletes, there was a future exercise room that featured strange-looking equipment and offered gymnastics under "simulated zero gravity." There was a room full of optical illusions. There was a computer room for games and computer art, and it even contained a computer that for five bucks would print the front page of your choice of fifty newspapers with your own name in a banner headline.

I asked Leda politely, "Would you like to see NEW LEDA RAUCHMAN SCANDAL on the front page of the *New York Times*?"

"No, thank you," she said. "If I can't make it on my own, I'll leave it to someone more talented."

In the next group of domes, we found a snack bar unfortunately named the Rocketeria, a book store, and a shop that sold souvenirs and handicraft items. There was one singularity about the book store's offerings. I had never seen such a formidable assortment of right-wing propaganda, including a large number of handsomely printed books about

317

that sterling patriotic organization, Americans All. In addition, a short videotaped propaganda film that dramatized the glories of Americans All ran continuously on a TV set suspended overhead.

The largest dome was a theater where science fiction or science fact motion pictures were shown and where meetings were held. I marked it down as the probable site of the meeting attended by Joletta Eckling and von Mach.

We paused in the Rocketeria for a glance at the menu. A glance was sufficient. Broiled algae burger or a Martian fish fry didn't appeal to either of us, though we learned later that these were fanciful names for ordinary fast food items.

The snack bar's tables and chairs convinced me that the future according to Nevada 2100 would be a thoroughly uncomfortable place to live. The human animal has been making and using chairs and tables for several thousand years, starting with crude chunks of wood or rock and eventually achieving splendid artistic creations fashioned for beauty as well as for comfort. Designers of Nevada 2100's furniture of the future directed all of their skill and ingenuity at devising something strange looking. The chairs were metal loops slightly broadened on top as a concession to human anatomy and set in concrete. A table consisted of loops supporting a board, and the board was a mere shelf, too narrow for putting things on or for holding hands under. The appearance was striking, but those who tried to sit down and eat found themselves struck in a different way.

The tall spaceship proved to be an observation tower with a spiraling staircase for the use of energetic tourists intent on a broader view of one of the more monotonous stretches of Nevada desert. At the top was a bilevel observation lounge that looked out on nothing in particular. We rested there while sipping preposterously expensive drinks and debating whether a bird's-eye or a worm's-eye view of the scene would be more depressing.

After we had toured the future, we made our way to the bar and casino on the lower level. A strictly enforced Nevada state law says no one under the age of twenty-one can gamble, and at least in this respect, Nevada 2100 was scrupulously legal. Even septuagenarians had to show IDs with birth dates. The bar offered drinks with cutesy names — a Solar Fizz, for example, or a Drunken Robot. The slot machines accepted dollar tokens only and were far noisier than those in the Las Vegas casinos. Lieutenant McCarney had mentioned a complaint that Nevada 2100's slots didn't pay off. On the evidence of my own eyes and ears, they did — a little, at extremely long intervals. Whether or not the gamblers won anything, they certainly received plenty of electronic agitation for their money.

The atmosphere seemed vaguely familiar to me, but for a long time I had difficulty in placing it. Suddenly I remembered. The attitude of the employees, the haughty way in which food and drinks and merchandise were sold, the outlandish prices, the brusque response to queries and complaints, brought to mind the old-fashioned tent carnival where every game, every souvenir, every entertainment was a fraud.

Suddenly Leda exclaimed, "That's him!"

I hushed her, but it was too late. Everyone in the room had turned to look at us.

She whispered, "Sorry about that. It took me by surprise. That's one of the men I saw with Harley Dantzil."

It was a young attendant in space uniform, and he did indeed look like a defensive halfback whose face had been run over regularly for several years. "Noted," I whispered back. "Don't look at him again."

I didn't mention that I had made a discovery of my own. One of the bartenders was the muscular young man with the misshapen nose who met me at Fremont and Main the day I arrived and gave me the number of a pay telephone to call. Nevada 2100 was full of surprises. I wondered whether we would next encounter Hayseed pushing a broom or Win Upway selling futuristic cosmetics.

The establishment's one complete success was the upper level, which was for kids, and kids loved it. So did adults. The uproar from the large electronic games room, where it was possible to fight a minute of your own private space war for a dollar, completely blanketed out the joyful shouts from the playground. Many of the combatants were adults who had managed to figure out that the principal payback of Nevada 2100's slot machines was in noise, and they could get more of it for their money here.

The surrealistic playground outside featured parabola teeter totters and a merry-go-round that wound itself up and then ran in the reverse direction without pushing. For a price one could descend an undulating slide in a submarine sled that swooshed *under* pools of water along the way. There were electric cars to drive. A ride was expensive, but the kids received a generous cross-country trip for their money. Even the smaller spaceship was a plaything. It offered two spiraling slides that could be used for racing.

In open areas — around the central tower, near the playground, or out by the parking lot — there were periodic laser gun duels and electron sword fights, which were Nevada 2100's version of the gun duels featured at pioneer towns. There also were fake psychic exhibits of mind reading, telepathy, and telekinesis, some of them pathetically crude.

Following Raina Lambert's instructions, I scrutinized all of this for something that seemed out-of-place in a tourist attraction. Several of the features were unusual in a humdrum way. All were aimed at separating tourists from their money, but that wasn't what she had in mind. Otherwise, I had no idea what to look for, so it wasn't surprising that I didn't find it.

I said to Leda, "It's just a tourist trap with a different backdrop."

She shook her head. "It has a sinister purpose."

"So do all tourist traps. They're designed to rob you without your knowing it. The fake past you see in those replicas of the Old West is just as phony as the fake future that Nevada 2100 shows you."

She shook her head again. "There's a difference. The tourist trap versions of the Old West show you pioneer towns where most of the buildings are souvenir shops and the only residents are buffoons in cowboy costume who wander about shooting off their guns. They can be pretty bad. The proprietors of one sham village I visited had a magic formula for transforming pyrite, which is fool's gold, into real gold. They were selling tiny pieces for a dollar each. But those places are a breath of fresh air compared with this. These people don't merely want your money, they also want your mind. All the time you think you're being entertained, they're brainwashing you. Nevada 2100 uses the future like a Venus's-flytrap to catch live meat for their crummy right-wing political group. That's why these creeps have such a contemptuous attitude toward their customers. They have no ethics at all."

She was right, of course, and Nevada 2100's hospitality was as questionable as its ethics. Shortly after we arrived, we acquired a tail — a man in the usual space uniform. As far as I could tell, we were the only tourists accorded such an honor. After Leda's outburst, he was joined by a spacewoman. I didn't know how many others were following us. I would have felt surrounded had it not been for an extremely attractive girl with red hair who managed to keep close to us despite the fact that her spaceman escort kept urging her in other directions. The spaceman was delivering an unbroken monologue on the glories of Americans All and Nevada 2100, and the girl was listening avidly. She seemed totally naive and innocent, but then — so had the serpent in the Garden of Eden. She was Raina Lambert.

We played electronic games to pass the time until we had to return to the coach. When we started back toward the parking lot, there were several laser gun duels in progress. These were impressive to watch. The duelists agilely pretended to catch the beams of their opponents on their shields while firing back between their legs or over their shoulders with their own laser tubes. The shields emitted a loud *crack!* for each supposed hit. The whole performance was faked, of course, but it was acrobatic and made a good show.

Near the parking lot, several spacemen were

playfully attempting to entice tourists into their game. One of them offered me a laser tube and a shield. I said, "No, thank you. I couldn't hit the target with a searchlight."

Another joined him, and the two planted themselves in front of me. "Give it a try. Point the tube, press this button." Several tourists paused to offer encouragement without actually volunteering themselves for the role. Raina Lambert and her escort circled to avoid the crowd, and then they stopped a few paces away to watch. I persisted in my spoil-sport attitude, and finally the spacemen turned away. Leda and I walked slowly toward the coach while I kept my eyes on the laser action.

One of the duelists tossed his tube aside and picked up another that was lying at his feet. He raised it to an aiming position, leveled the tube on his opponent, and then absently let it swing to one side. I had lengthened my stride, but when it finally steadied, it pointed toward Leda and me.

I wanted to make certain I was right before I acted, and I almost waited too long. As I dove, taking Leda to the ground with me, two shots rang out almost simultaneously, one a loud "crack" and the other a muffled "pop." They were followed by two loud cries of pain. One came from a tourist who was standing nearby. He was clutching his arm. The bullet that whipped over us had nicked him. The other came from the spaceman who fired the shot. He had dropped his weapon to inspect a bloody hand.

Two male tourists rushed forward to take possession of him and his laser tube. They identified themselves as police officers. The spaceman stared at them open mouthed. He protested, "Somebody shot *me!*"

The wounded tourist had only been grazed; he had a burned arm and a hole in his shirt. The spaceman's hand was a mess, and the officers couldn't figure out where that shot had come from. A crowd began to gather, other officers identified themselves, and one began questioning tourists about a second gun. He found out nothing at all. Raina Lambert's accuracy with her .22 automatic is difficult to believe even when seen, and no one had seen it because she fired through the bottom of her purse. I had known what was going to happen, but even I hadn't seen her do it.

Because the gunman fired before she did, and because my dive had already upset his aim, her shot had been unnecessary, but I knew better than to point that out to her. If I had, we would have argued about it for months to come.

Other spacemen came at a run to demand what the police thought they were doing on private property, and for a moment a riot seemed imminent. The spacemen actually thought they were going to forcefully evict the officers, papers or no papers.

Then someone bellowed, "You idiots! Get back to your stations!" It was Joletta Eckling's von

Mach. He was a Presence — tall and ruggedly good looking, with an erect and imposing figure. He had the bearing of one accustomed to commanding and being obeyed. The spacemen drifted away immediately, the wounded tourist was hurried off for first aid and apologies, the wounded spaceman was taken to a doctor, and von Mach began to explain to the police how this incredible accident could have happened.

There was more to explain than he realized, and the posture of leadership that so impressed his followers wasn't going to be of any help to him. What we had seen was the beginning of a full-scale raid by the State of Nevada Gaming Control Board reinforced by the Las Vegas Metropolitan Police. It would have been interesting to watch, but Raina Lambert reminded me, with a jerk of her head, that I was supposed to be impersonating a tourist. I hurried Leda toward the coach.

Leda had been absolutely superb. She took in everything that happened, but she said nothing at all, not even when I knocked her down. When we were safely aboard the coach, she finally spoke. "I just thought of one more way Nevada 2100 is different from places celebrating the Old West."

"What is it?"

"In the pioneer towns, the cowboys use blanks. Was that character actually trying to shoot us?"

"One of us," I said. "I hope he wasn't foolish enough to think he could pull the trigger twice and call it an accident."

"You mean — if he shot only one of us, he could get away with it?"

"If he could convince the court that it happened accidentally, he might be let off lightly."

"Then which of us was he shooting at?"

I grinned at her. "Me, of course. Why would he shoot you?"

Witnesses are far more important than detectives, but I didn't want to frighten her. Not until later did I remember that both of us were witnesses.

I was furious with myself for exposing Leda to danger. I took her home and waited with her until her police officer arrived. Then I left, hoping he would look after her better than I had. Raina Lambert was still at Nevada 2100, but she had installed a telephone answering machine, and I recorded a brief report.

When I called McCarney, Raina had just talked with him. "She wants a meeting," he said. "My office at nine tomorrow morning. The three of us. She must have turned up something."

I told him about Leda's identification of one of the men who had met Dantzil and my identification of the young man who had handed me a telephone number that first afternoon.

"Then Nevada 2100 *is* involved," he said. "But what did the guy expect to accomplish by shooting you? Something must have gone wrong."

"Yeah. He missed."

"And hit a bystander and got shot himself. Very peculiar. Are you certain he was aiming at you?"

"A laser tube with a rifle barrel inside might not seem like a precision instrument, and he wasn't even sighting it, but for all I knew, he'd been practicing with that thing for years and won metals. Did Miss Lambert say anything about Nevada 2100 conducting secret electrostatic experiments?"

"No. No doubt she'll tell us all about it in the morning."

I went to Diamond D's casino — I hadn't been there since I checked out of the hotel. I wandered through the slot machine maze and watched a blackjack game for a time. I had forgotten what a noisy and nerve-wracking place a casino could be. The music pounded; the slots beeped and honked and whistled; the PA system announced winners, none of them large; waitresses came and went with free drinks; keno runners brushed past me carrying tickets and money.

I tried to play the slot machines, but I was driven away by smoke. Ardent gamblers tend to be nervous, and if they also are smokers, they will smoke a lot. The main problem in casinos is not with smokers, however, but with burners. Burners may smoke very little, but they have a psychotic compulsion to hold burning tobacco in their hands. This sounds like an especially dumb habit, but burners are in fact very bright people. They know better than to hold cigarettes near their own noses where they might inadvertently inhale poisonous smoke. If they are playing the slot machines next to yours, they will hold them under your nose.

Some casinos are far better ventilated than others, but only a few of them have really confronted the problem of smoking and burning gamblers and tried to provide smoke-free areas. The action is long overdue. By midevening, smoke hung so thickly over Diamond D's slot machine arena that the air could have been bottled and used as an insecticide. I thought of Harley Dantzil and his emphysema with a touch of sympathy.

Finally I went to the keno lounge and watched the staff call game after game. Our investigation had taken us a long way from where we started, and I had lost sight of what all the fuss was about: this simple gambling game, numbers 1 through 80, pick your favorites and see how many you can catch. Some numbers seemed to come up over and over again while others never came up at all. I took a keno ticket and started marking the results of each game. No sooner did I establish that three or four favored numbers were turning up every time when they vanished from the board completely and several that hadn't been caught all evening suddenly began to appear.

I had heard mention of a publication that listed the winning numbers for every keno game played in every Las Vegas casino. Serious students of the game could sort through this mountain of statistics with computers and achieve a superbly logical new betting strategy that would bankrupt them in about the same length of time it would have taken if they had gambled without one. I wondered whether Professor Quilley could study such a publication and tell me which games were being influenced by electrostatics.

Clyde Goodler presided at the high table behind the keno desk. He didn't smile all evening. The tension had to be telling on him. My own inclination was to confront both Goodler and Fernard and try to make them talk, but Raina Lambert wanted to wait until she was certain they were ready. Goodler knew by now that I was a detective, and he must have been having nightmares trying to figure out what I said to him that first night. Fernard surely knew he was being followed everywhere. Raina thought we had only one chance at each of them, and she was holding back to make it more effective.

Probably it didn't matter. I doubted that either of them knew anything at all beyond the roles they had played and their contacts with Harley Dantzil.

Eventually I returned to my decrepit apartment 212A and went to bed.

17

THE NEXT MORNING THERE WAS A FRONT page headline about the State of Nevada Gaming Control Board's raid: GAMERS CLOSE 2100 CASINO. The accompanying story was careful to point out, however, that Nevada 2100 was not closed — only its "Adults Only" gambling level, and I wouldn't have dignified that by calling it a casino. The Gaming Control Board had seized relevant records and sealed the slot machines. Nevada 2100 was accused of skimming profits to evade state gaming taxes and of falsely reporting jackpot payouts. The investigation had been in process for months.

McCarney had the newspaper spread out on his desk when I walked into his office at nine o'clock. "That's the best way to enjoy a raid," I told him. "Read about it afterward."

Raina Lambert arrived. Normally she projects her own special aura of a confident, cynical detective, always ready to dazzle with dramatic revelations, but on this morning she looked thoroughly disgusted. "I have never invested so much time and energy on clues that came to nothing," she said. "I want to dispose of these characters so we can get on with the case. Mind you, I have no proof, but I'm ninety-nine percent certain about what happened."

We have worked together for a long time, and that was as much hint I needed to know exactly how her Nevada 2100 investigation had gone. "If you don't insist on proof, I can do this myself," I said.

"Go ahead."

"Von Mach hasn't decided whether he's going to lead a revolution or get himself elected president, but either one will be expensive. He's taking money wherever and whenever he finds it without too much attention to legalities, which is vividly demonstrated by the way the Nevada 2100 casino was run. When Joletta found out about the keno losses, she showed the figures to von Mach, and the two of them agreed it was a shame to have Diamond D's losing all of that money to strangers when they could have been stealing it themselves. It was exactly what his war chest needed. So they started their own investigation of the keno scam — not with the intention of stopping it but of taking it over.

"At that point Harley Dantzil must have done something that made Joletta and von Mach suspicious of him. My guess is that he and Clyde Goodler carelessly allowed themselves to be overheard. When they discovered what they'd done, they began avoiding each other so conspicuously that Mildred Comptom thought they were feuding, but the cat was out of the bag as far as Joletta and von Mach were concerned. They demanded a cut. Joletta met with Harley, she brought von Mach to see him, and a tough young spaceman was assigned to keep up the pressure on him. Harley played it with a shrewdness I wouldn't have expected. He protested innocence while giving the impression he was about to cave in.

"When Eckling decided to hire a detective, Joletta was one of the first to know. It was bad news for her and von Mach. They didn't want the scam stopped; they wanted it kept going with the money coming to them. They must have thought they could exercise some control over the investigation, or at least keep track of what I was doing, if Harley became the casino's liaison with me. Joletta suggested it, and Joel Eckling agreed. It was another of those jobs no one else wanted. What happened after that makes sense only if we consider yesterday's events at Nevada 2100. When von Mach isn't keeping a firm hand on things, his cohorts tend to run amuck. This is understandable. If they hadn't already taken leave of their senses, they wouldn't have swallowed his warped philosophy in the first place.

"Several of them were assigned to tail me from the airport. They may have had some wild notion of abducting me and trying to buy me off. They gave Harley orders about the flight I was to take and about my wearing a yellow flower when I got off the plane so they wouldn't miss me. Harley passed their orders along, and then he crossed them up completely by warning me about being tailed and giving me a ridiculously complicated route that was guaranteed to lose them.

"I messed everything up by arriving on a different plane. They met the plane I was supposed to be on. When no yellow flower marched out of the exit gate, those assigned to tail me tried to telephone Harley. Harley was dead, but they didn't know that. Consternation followed. They suspected a double-cross. They kept trying to locate Harley and couldn't. They knew nothing about his secret apartment, but they did know where he intended to meet me and when, so they sent a spaceman in mufti to warn me off before Harley could make contact with me. I walked east on Fremont; the Nevada 2100 man went across the street to the Plaza, found himself an observation post, and watched for Harley.

"When he saw me return and resume waiting, he telephoned Joletta and told her she had to get over to Main and Fremont and lure me away. It's only a few blocks from Diamond D's, and usually there's a cab waiting at the door. She came in a rush, probably inventing Harley's telephone call along the way.

"The comedy at the pay telephone was an over-sight. When they gave me that number to call, they'd stationed someone at the phone to answer it. Then they switched plans and sent Joletta to meet me, but they forgot to cancel the watch on the telephone.

"They got onto Leda Rauchman when the young man spying from the Plaza saw me ditch her there. Naturally he wanted to know who she was. He described her to Joletta, who identified her at once, and when Joletta saw Leda leaving Diamond D's that night, she had her followed. Leda eased her concern by going directly home, but the next night she left the casino with me, which put both Joletta and Americans All in a panic and started the Grand Slam. That sort of thing — carloads of young thugs with radios — is an ideal operation for those people as long as none of them have to think. Of course they didn't know the Las Vegas back alleys as well as our cab driver, and they lost us. By the next morning, Leda had a police escort, which must have unnerved them. They left her alone after that.

"As for what happened yesterday, Leda loudly identified one culprit, and perhaps I wasn't as pokerfaced as I should have been when I recognized another. The two incidents together made them think Americans All was about to be tied to a murder case, and they panicked again. Naturally it didn't occur to them that their attempt to avoid

335

trouble would put them in far worse trouble. The normal human safety valve of common sense is missing in every one of them, and that's what I find terrifying about Americans All. They make me think of the original Nazis, or of Arab terrorists willing to blow themselves up with their victims, or of combatants in Northern Ireland indiscriminately slaughtering women and children. Anyway, that's one view of what happened. Without a scrap of proof, of course. How does it agree with your version?"

"Fairly well except for a couple of minor details. Nevada 2100 was like a hungry dog slobbering over the beef roast it saw in a butcher's display case. It very much wanted a piece of the keno action. It got nothing at all. I had a talk with von Mach yesterday. He's not admitting anything, but he let slip as much as I needed. Let's leave Americans All to the state and federal authorities and give our attention to things that are relevant."

"Not so fast," I said. "That was *your* scenario I just played. I can give you one just as good with Nevada 2100 as the high-tech element trying to get a bigger piece of the action. Would you like to hear it?"

"Not without some evidence. Before we can make any progress at all with this case, we first must put Harley Dantzil in his place. Right at the beginning, you tagged him as the scam's go-between, but 'go-between' has several possible interpretations. One of them had Harley virtually running the scam — looking after day-by-day details, giving orders, keeping in touch with everyone, keeping people in line, dividing the money: A straw boss or even a supervisor. Now tell me this: Was Harley Dantzil the sort of person you would confidently put in charge of an organization like that?"

"In the beginning, I wouldn't have put him in charge of emptying ashtrays in the keno lounge," I said. "But maybe he seemed inept because no one ever gave him a chance. That would explain his pathetic behavior in the casino — he desperately wanted to do something worthwhile. The scam was an opportunity for him. Someone finally made him responsible for something, and he was doing a good job and getting rich."

She shook her head firmly. "Diamond D's had him tagged correctly, and those running the scam tagged him the same way. He was their errand boy. Literally. And that's all he was."

"He was murdered," McCarney protested. "Who would bother to murder an errand boy? And if he was no more important than that, why did the scam come to a sudden stop when he was eliminated?"

"I've seen the details concerning the trust fund Harley set up for Betty Varnko and the kids," Raina said. "There'll be a tax fracas, but that has nothing to do with us. I was able to convince the attorney that we were looking for insights on Dantzil's mur-

337

der and not snooping for Internal Revenue. Last June first, the fund had twenty-eight thousand dollars in it. By July first, it had doubled, and it built rapidly from there. As you know, it now has more than four hundred thousand dollars. Whence this sudden prosperity on the part of Harley Dantzil, alias Brian Varnko, who was a mere lacky and go-between?"

"I've wondered about that from the beginning," McCarney said. "That's why I say he had to be more than an errand boy."

"An errand boy who applies himself can learn a lot about a business," Raina said. "Harley learned enough to set up for himself and run his own keno scam on the side. Once his boss got the operation running, with the electrostatic device — or whatever — in place, it took no organizing genius to make use of it. All Harley had to do was recruit an employee on a different shift from the one the scam was using. Since there were no higher-ups grabbing outsized cuts, he had only three people to pay: the casino employee; Fernard, who had no difficulty in creating an infinite variety of tourist characters to make the bets and collect the winnings; and whoever forged Fernard's documents. It left Harley an enormous surplus to keep for himself. And *that* is why the trust fund grew so rapidly. It is also why the scheme came crashing down. Suddenly there were too many winners taking too much money."

"And *that* was the motive for his murder," I said. "There's a Big Boss out there who was furiously angry when he found out what was going on. I told you that days ago. Either he supplied the high-tech expertise himself or he has a high-tech contact, and he used Dantzil to recruit casino employees to work for him. The only other thing I know about him is that he — or his high-tech assistant — smokes a pipe. It was a pipe smoker who left the bug in Leda Rauchman's apartment, and that may be the biggest mystery of our case. I have yet to encounter a pipe smoker, anywhere. I looked all over Nevada 2100 for one. I'd very much like to identify him."

"I'd rather have a better discription of Win Upway," Raina Lambert said. "I'd like to know what she would look like wearing a bushy brown male wig and overalls."

McCarney sat up with a jerk. "Are you saying Hayseed disguised himself as a blonde female to rent the apartment? Or that the blonde disguised herself as Hayseed?"

"Either is possible. That blonde hair certainly sounds like a wig. The well-preserved figure could have been masculine, suitably padded, and the face that had been around the track a few times could have been a male face trying to look feminine. All he had to do was switch wigs and put on a dress and a padded bra. We already suspect that Fernard collected keno winnings disguised as a woman.

There could be two men in this gang who can play female roles."

"How much of this can you prove?" McCarney demanded.

"Not a thing — yet. Our accumulation of evidence hasn't kept pace with our understanding of this case."

"I think we've come as far as we're going to until we get the high-tech angle figured out," I said. "Which is why I would very much like to meet that phantom pipe smoker."

"I agree," Raina said. "I'm continuing my investigation of Edwin Morabin. I'd suggest that the police take a closer look at Darnell Condellor."

"Condellor — in a high-tech role?" McCarney asked wonderingly.

"People I've talked with say much of his business concerns high-tech industries in Las Vegas," Raina said. "Not only does he write advertising copy for them, but his work has given him extensive high-tech contacts."

This was news to both of us. "An advertising writer who produces high-tech copy has to be highly qualified and know his clients' businesses well," I told McCarney. "He'd be likely to develop close working relationships with his clients' employees. A close relationship with just one — if it were the right one — would be enough to start a keno scam."

"I'll find out who his clients are," McCarney

said.

"There's another curious thing about Condellor," I said. "He's a friend of Wes Zerin's. Zerin is an engineering student who was acquainted with Harley Dantzil. It's one more dratted merry-go-round, and when I get some of these graver issues resolved, I'll take a ride on it."

"Your next assignment will be to lean hard on Ford Fernard and Clyde Goodler," Raina told me. "If they know anything that might be useful, now is the time to find it out."

"It'll be my pleasure," I said. "I'm not optimistic about the result, but I'll certainly enjoy leaning on them."

I wanted to tackle Fernard first, and we agreed that the best time and place would be his home, early, before he left for breakfast. The next morning at eight o'clock I made a leisurely stroll along Ewell toward the court where he lived. There are times when I have the tingling sensation of having the solution of a case at my fingertips. I didn't feel that way about Fernard, but I thought I might be able to set something in motion.

The first thing I noticed was that the police stake-out was gone.

A stake-out in such a location quickly becomes conspicuous, but McCarney had solved that problem by getting permission to paint the window and door trim on some of the houses. He kept a detective on that job during the daylight hours. The trim very obviously needed painting, and no one was likely to suspect a man mucking around with a paint brush of being a policeman. He wore his painter's cap with the bill turned toward the back when Fernard was at home, and it was useful to know that at a glance. The other officers kept out of sight. Now all of them were gone, even the house painter.

So was Fernard.

There had been no reason for him to skip. I called McCarney; he was out. His office telephoned me two hours later when the officers on the stake-out finally reported in. Three elderly friends had picked up Fernard shortly after seven. They drove down to Laughlin, a small gambling town a hundred miles south of Las Vegas, with the police on their heels. It seemed to be a carefree outing; probably they would be back that evening. I called Raina Lambert and suggested cornering Fernard in Laughlin, but she vetoed the notion.

"You only have one shot at this. Do it right."

"Then it'll have to be Clyde Goodler first, and he isn't due at work until five. Shall I try to see him at home?"

"Better not," she said. "Catch him on a break."

"Did anything turn up on Edwin Morabin?"

"Inventing is neither a hobby nor a profession with him. It's a religion. His current passion is transportation. He says we're still using nineteenth-century technology to move people around.

To his way of thinking, automobiles and airplanes are nineteenth-century technology. The railroad is eighteenth-century. He thinks it's time we started looking ahead."

"Don't tell me. He's going to move people with electrostatics."

"He did mention something about revolutionizing rail travel with magnetism."

"I'll be darned," I said. "That was my idea for the keno scam. Professor Quilley vetoed it."

It left me with nothing to do, so I went to police headquarters to see how McCarney was making out with Darnell Condellor.

"Technicians who have worked with him say he has a gift for describing things once he understands them," the lieutenant said. "Making him understand them can be an ordeal. Opinion is divided as to whether he's as moronic as he sometimes acts or just very, very careful to get things right."

"As far as the keno scam is concerned, it doesn't matter how moronic he is. All he had to do was meet the right kind of technical expert, and that could have been an employee of a client, or a former employee of a client, or a former client's employee, or someone any of those accidentally introduced him to."

McCarney covered his face with his hands. "Don't. I already feel as though I've been investigating this case forever. We're checking out the list of clients Condellor has worked with."

I wished I had a list to check out. I went back to apartment 212A, looked out the side window toward the apartment Win Upway had rented, and tried to envision exactly what happened the night of the murder. Harley and Hayseed went through their act for me at high speed, at normal speed, and in slow motion. I got Hayseed into the apartment and out again with no problem whatsoever, but my imagination still refused to supply a name for him. He could have been Darnell Condellor, or Betty Varnko — or even Manfred von Mach, since I wasn't as ready as Raina Lambert to write off Americans All. I had the feeling there were undercurrents in this case we weren't yet aware of.

Diamond D's keno lounge was always busy in the evening. Shortly after 7:00 P.M., I carefully picked my way through the crowd, found a chair, and sat down to look around. The two men working at the high table behind the counter didn't interest me since Clyde Goodler wasn't one of them. Two men seated off to one side did. They were Darnell Condellor and Wes Zerin. I watched for half an hour. Goodler didn't appear. Condellor and Zerin were behaving very chummy indeed. They seemed to be having long technical discussions about the numbers they were playing. Goodler had priority, so I had to settle him before I could corner them.

I went up to the counter, waited until the crowd of customers with tickets had thinned out, and asked about him.

"He's off today," a keno writer told me cheerfully.

"So am I," I said. The girl smiled vaguely, perhaps wondering why I sounded so disgusted about it. When I turned around, both Condellor and Zerin had disappeared. They must have run the moment they saw me. This made me far more interested in them than I had been a few moments before, but there wasn't much I could do about it. Las Vegas is a large and complicated place in which to start an impromptu search for a couple of missing persons.

I went back to my chair and watched the keno play for a time. I had already done my day's futile thinking about the case, so I thought instead about the high percentage of keno players who were elderly. Senior citizens are vacationing in Las Vegas in ever increasing numbers, and they are certain to have an impact on the casinos' high-roller bias. They are far less likely to throw money around. Many don't toke — or tip — at all. The senior who hits a small jackpot after losing next month's grocery money isn't likely to feel that he owes something to the person who pays him off. Not only did he earn that jackpot all by himself, but he urgently needs it.

Finally I went home. It was almost eleven o'clock when the duty officer called from police headquarters to tell me Ford Fernard had returned from Laughlin and was having a late dinner at

Lon's. I decided to postpone our interview until morning. It was the wrong hour to be intercepting him on the street or trying to talk my way into his house.

It had indeed been an off-day — not only for me, but for everyone. Neither McCarney nor Raina Lambert had picked up anything worth mentioning, or they would have mentioned it. I confidently expected the next day to be better for all of us if only because it couldn't be worse.

18

W HEN I ARRIVED AT THE COURT OFF EWELL
Street the next morning, the young officer in white
overalls looked up from the trim he was painting
and gave me a smirking salute with his brush. I
went up to Fernard's door and knocked.

He opened it in his undershirt with a razor in
one hand and a towel over his shoulder. He had
slept later than usual after his Laughlin outing, and
he looked and behaved like an aging matinee idol
taken unawares. I studied him for a moment before
I spoke, and he grunted impatiently, "What is it?"
He was expecting a sales pitch, and he had his
refusal ready.

"I know you well, but I don't believe we've met,"
I said.

Suddenly he wasn't sure of himself. He said
hesitantly, "I think I've seen you around."

"You're in trouble," I told him bluntly. "All of us
are in trouble. I'm taking Harley's place. We've got
to work together and try to find a way out of this."
I pushed past him into a decrepit living room, and

he stumbled after me. He really was living the role of an impoverished pensioner. I sat down in a worn overstuffed chair that sagged worse than the one in Dantzil's apartment. He stood staring at me until I sternly pointed at the chair across the room, and then he sank into it.

"Without a doubt, you are the world's most asinine idiot," I told him. "Why did you bring those jerks Smith and Bolt into it?"

His jaw dropped. He tried to speak and couldn't.

"They've been talking, and the police are onto them," I said. "You can't expect that quality of thug to keep his mouth shut. Not only are we in big trouble, but Harley left things in a mess. I'm trying to pick up the pieces. Did he give you an emergency phone number to call?"

Fernard shook his head.

"Come on," I said impatiently. "I know you've met the boss."

"I met Butch."

"Fellow with brown, bushy hair, always wears overalls?"

He nodded.

"He doesn't give the same name to everyone," I said, "for obvious reasons. To you, he's Butch. Who do you get hold of in an emergency?"

"I don't. Harley took care of everything."

"That's damned poor organization," I rasped. "No wonder we're in trouble. I'll see that it runs differently from now on. Have you had contact with

348

anyone else?"

He shook his head.

"And you have no way to get in touch with Butch?"

He shook his head again.

I got to my feet. "That certainly was a stupid move, bringing Smith and Bolt into it. You had a real good thing going, and you blew it."

He jumped up and took a stride toward me. "I'm worth a lot more than what Harley was paying me," he protested bitterly. "He wouldn't even talk about it."

"Of course you're worth more. You did a damned good job for Harley. I'm worth more, too. So is everyone. There are smart ways and dumb ways of doing something about it. You picked the dumb way. How much money have you taken in lately?"

He maintained an uncomfortable silence.

"I'll be in touch," I said. "Don't do anything until you hear from me."

He followed me to the door and closed it after me. For an actor, he had done a very poor job of ad-libbing.

So I drew a blank, and the fact that I expected it didn't improve my mood. Neither did the unproductive day I spent trying to find out for Raina Lambert whether Edwin Morabin had ever shown an interest in casinos or gambling. I prowled about the University of Nevada, Las Vegas, pretending to be researching an article for a trade journal while I looked for former colleagues of Morabin's to talk with. One said Morabin indulged in a little social gambling — perhaps he meant those weekly bridge sessions with Florence Stevens-Dantzil. Another said gambling was against Morabin's religion. A third said Morabin gambled whenever he got the chance, which would be a genuinely tragic affliction for any resident of Las Vegas.

Late in the afternoon, I stopped by to see Mc-Carney. The police had little to show from another day's work on Darnell Condellor's clients. "It must be someone else," McCarney said.

I didn't know enough to have an opinion. I wished him well and returned to my own problems.

I knew Clyde Goodler would be back at work that evening; I had checked with Mildred Comp-tom. The keno lounge was crowded, the writers were furiously busy, and for once Condellor and Zerin weren't sitting together. They were on opposite sides of the lounge. It was after eight o'clock when Goodler decided to take a break. He turned things over to the second shift boss and strolled toward the restaurant. He didn't notice me following on his heels until a waitress tried to intercept me. I told her, "We're together."

He was startled, but he said nothing. We went to a booth at the back of the room and ordered coffee. Neither of us said anything until the wait-ress brought it. Then I leaned toward him and spoke quietly.

"Have you heard anything from anyone?"

He shook his head. He had aged since I first encountered him. His hair looked grayer. There had been three weeks of hellish suspense for those who had participated in the scam. Probably several of them would be willing to talk, but I doubted whether they could tell us more than we already knew. We wanted the boss, and the casino workers would know him only as Butch, who had brown, bushy hair and wore overalls.

"We're in trouble," I said. "I'm trying to pick up the pieces and get this thing going again. Did Harley give you instructions about what to do in an emergency?"

"Butch did."

"What was it?"

"Telephone."

"Do you have the number?"

He nodded. He fished out his wallet, took out a business card — it was actually a dentist's appointment card — and showed me a telephone number scribbled on the back.

I took the card. "Who do you ask for?"

"Butch."

"When are you supposed to call?"

"Any time between 8:00 p.m. and midnight. If there's no answer, I'm to keep calling until there is."

"Have you ever used it?"

He shook his head.

I pocketed the card. "I'll give you another number as soon as I have one. This is obsolete anyway, and it wouldn't be safe to use it now. Sit tight until you hear from me."

I walked away. Neither of us had touched his coffee.

I returned to the keno lounge, determined to settle Condellor and Zerin and make it a clean sweep. Both of them had left. They must have seen me leave with Goodler and decided to clear out before I returned. I wondered why they were so certain I would return. I resolved to confront them the next time I saw them, wherever it was.

McCarney and Raina Lambert were at police headquarters commiserating with each other on their own unproductive days. I hailed them cheerfully. "The Big Boss finally made a goof," I said. "In some petty crisis a long time back, he gave Goodler a telephone number and forgot about it."

McCarney responded with an elegant shrug. "The phone certainly was listed under an assumed name, and he probably had it disconnected long ago."

I refused to abandon my cheerfulness. "I'll soon find out. I'll telephone right now."

McCarney told me to wait until he had the number checked. To our immense surprise, it was still current. It was listed to Lincoln Washington at 2812 Valhalla. None of us had ever heard of a

Lincoln Washington. The name sounded like a pseudonym someone in Americans All would choose. "Where is 2812 Valhalla?" I asked.

McCarney went to the map on the wall. "Here," he said pointing. "It's a street that's going commercial. Business firms and professional men have taken over some of the large houses for offices. Doctors, dentists, photographers, public relations people . . ."

"Advertising agencies?" Raina Lambert asked. She reached for the telephone directory and began flipping pages.

"Possibly. Why?"

"Here it is — 2812 Valhalla."

"Here is what?"

"Preswick and Lyonce. The advertising agency Condellor works for." She switched her attention to the map. "It's also within walking distance of Edwin Morabin's home. Not that that matters. Morabin owns three cars, and there's no reason why he should walk anywhere."

I asked them to please give me elbow room to think about the call I was about to make. McCarney demanded, "Are you sure you know what you're doing?"

"No, but if this doesn't work, we'll be no worse off than we are now."

I insisted on privacy for my performance. I didn't mind if they listened in, but I didn't want an audience in the room. McCarney gave up his office to me and had extensions hooked up in the next room for himself and Raina Lambert. He announced, "It's all yours. Good luck."

"Don't sneeze and mess it up for me," I said.

I made myself comfortable at the desk, performed a few practice whispers to get the intonation I wanted, and dialed Goodler's emergency number. The phone rang unanswered.

While we waited, Raina Lambert described her own frustrating day. She had assembled a quantity of inconsequential information about Edwin Morabin to add to the inconsequential information the police had collected on Darnell Condellor. She did have one item she thought interesting — she had managed to track down another friend of Florence's, a Hilda Grimston, whom she described as a very, very bright woman of fifty-five. Grimston also was an engineer, and she had her own firm with a large ad in the yellow pages under "product development."

Raina called on her in the guise of a free-lance writer preparing a magazine article on the psychology of product design. She pretended to be especially interested in the possibility that gamblers are influenced by the design of the gambling apparatus. They had a most interesting discussion on the merits of the two keno systems. Grimston considered the RAFFSCO, or wire cage system, superior in the unbiased selection of numbers, but she thought the design of the goose, the transparent fish bowl with a blower, more acceptable to the public because the ball selection appeared to be less susceptible to tampering. She was a keno enthusiast herself and was in fact designing her own system, but she wasn't ready to publicize it.

"Come back in a year or two, darling," she said brightly, and Raina promised to do that.

"Hilda Grimston lives in Henderson," she said, "which is a long, long way from Valhalla, but probably that's no more important than the fact that Morabin lives close by."

Half an hour later, I called the number again. This time the phone was answered on the first ring by a male voice that sounded as though its owner was speaking around a mouthful of mush with his teeth clenched. It announced, "Yeah."

"Butch gave me this number," I said in the whisper I'd practiced. "Can you hear me?"

"Yeah."

"I'm suppose to call in an emergency. We got one. Can I talk with Butch?"

There was a long pause. "He ain't here."

"Can you get a message to him?"

There was another pause. "Yeah."

"A friend on the police let something slip. There'll be a raid tonight. On that address. At two o'clock. They'll dig things up or tear things apart if they have to. They know what they're looking for, and they know where to look. They had a tip. Someone talked. Understand?"

"Yeah."

"Anything connected with gambling is a giveaway. You've got to get rid of it. Can the stuff be moved to a safe place?"

"Yeah."

"What'll you do with it?"

"Break it up."

"They'll find the pieces and put 'em back together. If they find anything at all, we're in trouble. Look. I can borrow a truck. I'll meet you at midnight. You help me load the stuff, and I'll drive it to a place I know up by Mesquite. I'll bury it in the desert where they'll never find it."

There was no response. I added, "You can come along and help me dig if you want to. We'll wrap the stuff in plastic so we can dig it up later if we need it again. How large a hole will it take? Five by five? Six by six?"

There was another silence. Then the voice said, "Somethin' like that."

"That's a lot of digging. Too much for one person. If you can't come yourself, you better send someone. I'll bring shovels. Will you have the stuff ready at midnight?"

"Yeah."

"Remember — anything that has to do with gambling. Where do you want me to pick it up?"

"Twenty-eight twelve Valhalla. Follow the drive around the house. I'll wait for you at the garage."

"Right. I'll try to be there exactly at midnight.

The password is 'Butch.' Got that?"

"Yeah."

"When I drive up, if the first person I meet doesn't say 'Butch,' I'll get the hell out of there. I don't know this place, and I'm not going to walk into a trap. Understand?"

"Yeah."

I hung up.

McCarney and Raina Lambert joined me. McCarney was shaking his head. "Clever of you — making *him* use the password. You're a very good actor."

"All it takes is the ability to lie with deep sincerity," I said.

"Did you recognize the voice?"

"No. It could have been anyone. It was disguised, of course, but even if it hadn't been, it isn't easy to identify someone from a telephone conversation when he mostly says 'Yeah' through his teeth."

"What are you expecting to pick up?" McCarney wanted to know.

"Gambling equipment. Weren't you listening? In order to perfect that keno scam, they had to have a keno machine to experiment with. I don't know where they got it, but I do know they wouldn't just throw it away when they finished with it. For one thing, they might need it again. If the casinos introduced countermeasures, they'd have to perform more experiments. For another, a keno machine

357

would be an awfully awkward thing to try to dispose of in Las Vegas — especially by someone who didn't want it known that he'd ever had one. If he put it out with the garbage, it would get talked about. If he tried to sell it, he might be asked where he got it and why. So there's a good chance that he kept it along with a lot of other stuff. He may be trying to develop scams for other gambling games. Now all you have to do is find me a pickup truck."

McCarney wearily reached for his telephone.

"A pickup truck with an extended cab," I added. "I can't drive it myself — this may turn out to be someone I've been seeing daily ever since I arrived here — but I'm certainly going along. Just in case I have to surface in a hurry with all of my limbs functioning, I want enough room behind the seat to hide in comfort."

"I suppose I've also got to supply you with a foam pad like those they sell for dogs."

"Cheer up," I told him. "With any luck at all, we'll wind this thing up tonight."

"Don't I wish," he muttered. He dialed a number.

I selected the truck driver myself — a rather elderly detective, bald-headed with a graying fringe of hair, slightly stooped, obviously rheumatic — and briefed him carefully. The person in charge at 2812 Valhalla might be expecting a familiar face. An elderly stranger would be less likely to arouse suspicion than a young one.

The truck McCarney borrowed had plenty of space behind the seat. We assumed that it would be driven into the garage to be loaded, so I planned to hide in the cab and be the detective's first support gun — the two of us inside the garage against whatever chanced to be waiting there. As soon as the garage door closed, a small army of police would surround it on the outside ready to break in if that seemed necessary. We might need an army if von Mach's Super-Americans were involved.

I was in my hiding place, peeking out as best I could, when the truck followed the drive past the large brick house that was now an advertising agency. It coasted to a stop in front of the garage, and the detective turned its lights off. It was precisely midnight. There was no light in the garage, but when the detective rolled his window down, a shadowy figure stepped from the garage's side doorway.

"Butch," the figure hissed. The whisper carried through the cold night air with startling clarity. It was the same tight voice I had heard on the telephone. "When the door opens, drive all the way in."

The detective started the motor again. As the garage door lifted, he flipped on his lights and edged forward. The door closed a moment later and lights came on inside the garage. The detective turned off the truck's lights and motor, opened its door, and jumped down. Outside, McCarney and his men — shivering because January nights in Las Vegas can feel frigid — would already be surrounding the garage. Everything had gone exactly as planned.

Then the plan suddenly collapsed.

I heard a snarl, "You're a cop, damn you!"

Our elderly detective had been recognized. Sounds of violent combat followed. I immediately began to scramble out of my hiding place. It was a contortionistic process — getting over the back of the seat, getting a door open, getting my feet in place so I could keep my balance when I hit the garage floor. In the few seconds it took me to manage all of that, the combat continued. The detective's assailant fought as though he had grown up brawling in the streets. The detective was no slouch himself in spite of his age, and while he fought, he talked.

"Of course I'm a cop," he huffed. "Where do you think your information comes from? How do you think I found out about the raid? I've worked for Butch for a long time."

If I had stayed in the truck, he might have talked his way out of it, but the moment I joined the party, the game was up. My face turned out to be as memorable as I had feared, and there was no way I could pretend to be working for Butch. The detective and I suddenly had an infuriated madman to contend with. He staggered the detective with a body punch, missed me with a wild swing, missed me again with a kick, and then gripped me and flung me backward, grunting curses all the time. He turned on the detective again; I leaped forward and took several body punches. His rage made him invincible, and when the side door was finally smashed open with a splintering crash, and the police came pouring in, I was ready to put my bruises and abrasions in retirement and let them have him.

My first glimpse of him had been a revelation in the same way that lightning illuminates a dark night, and all the time I was fighting, I had a vision of swift, sure fingers reassembling a lawnmower.

It was Thad Yaegler.

McCarney led the police charge and was promptly and severely kicked in the shin. He swore and retired to rub his leg while others subdued Yaegler and applied handcuffs. My topcoat had lost two buttons in the fracas, and several of the officers were battered. "Cheer up," I told McCarney. "If you can't think of anything else to charge him with, you certainly have him for resisting arrest."

A detective returned from a quick examination of the garage. "This is quite a place," he said. "There's a whole machine shop back there. Who is this guy?"

"He was top man in the keno scam that was defrauding the casinos," I said, speaking loudly. "Florence Stevens-Dantzil told us all about him. If

361

they tag him with one count for every game that was rigged, he'll get life."

McCarney and his officers were immensely surprised. Their captive was astonished.

"Now just a moment!" Yaegler shouted. He'd been allowed to get to his feet, and he stood staring at me, handcuffed hands held stiffly in front of him. *"Florence* told you all about it?"

"She sure did — about the way Harley and Ford Fernard worked for you — Harley lined up the keno shift bosses, and Fernard used a million disguises to play the numbers and collect the winnings. She says she has no idea what you did with your share of the money. It must amount to a fortune. Want to tell us about that?"

Yaegler tried to lurch toward me. McCarney intercepted him. "Take it easy," he said. He started reading him his rights. Another officer had a tape recorder going.

Yaegler paid no attention to either of them. "What *I* did with the money! I never had a smell of that money! Florence kept it all! I'm not like those house pets of hers. I don't take money from a woman."

"That isn't her story. She blames it all on you. She also said you murdered Harley. Now why would you do that?"

"That was her idea, too. She planned the whole thing. That bitch is the most ungrateful . . . look! She had plenty of money, but instead of living

362

sensibly, she had to waste it on those young dandies she kept picking up. And Harley, he had plenty of money — a good salary, a share of the keno take, and no expenses — but he had to have another woman. Sex is no good. If it wasn't for sex, there wouldn't have been any trouble."

An outpouring of profanity followed. Finally he broke off and said bitterly, "You tricked me."

"Nope," I told him. "Florence tricked you — into thinking you could get away with it. Probably she tricked herself, too."

A police car drove up, and Yaegler, who had begun to struggle again, was roughly forced into it. I went to look at the machine shop. There was a large, conical ashtray on the work bench, the duplicate of those I had seen in Harley Dantzil's suite in the mock castle, and the butt of a hand-rolled cigarette was still burning in it. I sniffed the smoke.

"Ready or not, here's another revelation," I told McCarney. "He's our phantom pipe smoker, too."

"What do you mean?" McCarney demanded.

"He rolls his own — with any scraps of tobacco that come to hand. Sometimes he uses pipe tobacco. That explains the smoke he left when he planted the bugs. Now you'd better get Florence Stevens-Dantzil out of bed and search her house immediately before she hears Yaegler's been arrested. We should have suspected her the moment we realized she had an unbreakable alibi. A clever wife *always* arranges an unbreakable alibi when she has her husband murdered."

19

Even though the murder victim and the confessed murderer had both lived in the mock castle, McCarney went about getting his search warrant with the gloomiest of misgivings. Accessory or not, Florence Stevens-Dantzil still had enough influence to cause an uproar. I told him he was being silly. An uproar over a legal police search would cause a scandal regardless of the outcome, and Florence would avoid that at any cost.

I was wrong. Florence shattered the local decibel record and threatened mayhem when the police walked in. That didn't happen until morning. It took that long to get the papers in order. McCarney was afraid Yaegler would tip Florence off and give her a chance to tidy up the entire house, but Yaegler refused to talk to anyone and also refused the offer of a phone call. Florence still hadn't missed him when the police arrived.

The moment she erupted, McCarney telephoned her attorney and told him to get his client under control if he didn't want her hit with a list of

charges. The attorney arrived in a rush and persuaded Florence that the less the police were har-
assed, the quicker they would leave. He offered to
supervise the search himself, and — despite the
cool morning — he finally got her and all of her
retinue bundled up and comfortably settled in
chairs in the back yard.

Raina Lambert and I heard nothing about that
until afterward. McCarney wanted no strain placed
on his search warrant by the participation of outsiders, so we didn't take part. Neither of us
minded. I had unfinished business of my own, as
did Raina, and she also wanted to report to Joel
Eckling.

At eight o'clock I was ringing the doorbell of
Dr. Harold Quilley, the physics professor. I had no
appointment, but Quilley couldn't have received me
more graciously if he had got out of bed early that
morning in the hope I might drop in. Perhaps twentieth-century physics has surprised its devotees so
frequently as to inure them to the unexpected.

We arranged ourselves in his office as before —
with him in his throne-like reclining chair — and I
said, "Our case is solved. We have the murderer,
but we still haven't figured out the technical aspects. Eventually someone will talk, but right now
we're extremely puzzled. From what you told me
about the possible scientific complications, and the
hundreds of difficult experiments that would be
required, we rather expected to find an accom-

plished scientist behind the scheme. It turned out to be a handyman who had no scientific education at all. He lived with a relative and repaired lawnmowers and appliances for pocket money."

The professor tilted back and laughed heartily. Then he said, wiping his eyes, "I'm sorry if I mislead you — but surely you're aware that some of the greatest inventors in history had little or no formal scientific training. Look at Thomas Alva Edison. We attach entirely too much importance to the letters scientists put after their names. We forget these only signify attendance at an institution like a term in prison. Capability and accomplishment don't have Ph.D. measurements. There's no reason why an untrained person can't solve scientific problems if he has aptitude and persistence. Many do. The basic materials for a technological education are available to anyone who has access to a library."

He went to the blackboard and wrote the same scientific formula I'd seen before:

$$\mathbf{F}_{12} = k\frac{q_1 q_2}{r^2} \; \mathbf{n}$$

"Beautiful, isn't it?" he murmured. "A physicist can do that for you. A physicist can demonstrate its mathematical applications. But an observant person wouldn't need to know Coulomb's Law in order to make use of it."

He opened a desk drawer and took out a Ping-Pong ball. "I forgot to return this," he said, looking

367

guilty. "I hope the Savard kids haven't missed it. They keep losing Ping-Pong balls behind the washing machine."

He rubbed his comb on his sleeve and extended it toward the ball. "One doesn't have to have a scientific educaton to notice that the harder the comb is rubbed, the greater the distance at which the ball will respond to it. The moment a person observes that, he is applying Coulomb's Law even if he's never heard of it.

"Twentieth-century developments in electrostatics are every bit as complicated as I implied, but I should have stressed the fact that this has always been a prime field of experimentation for the amateur. Benjamin Franklin was a magnificent amateur experimenter, and he's had successors right down to the present. There are excellent books available that describe simple electrostatics experiments for beginners. One of them, by A.D. Moore, is a classic. Your amateur could have begun with something like that and gone on to devise his own experiments. Many people get started in science that way.

"But you must avoid the mistake of thinking that the keno scam was simple and easy to do because an amateur thought of it. It was neither, and while he may have gone at it differently, and used trial and error to a much greater extent than a trained scientist would have, he had to be no less competent in his mastery of electrostatics. With that kind of problem, a person who is extremely skilled at building things and working with his hands might be far better qualified than one who is merely a scientific theorist. Today's physicists tend to concentrate on the exotic — quarks, plasma physics, lasers, fusions, and so on. A bread-and-butter subject like electrostatics may be almost totally neglected." He paused. "I'm not a gambling man, but I'd be willing to bet a substantial sum that your handyman is an excellent lawnmower and toaster repairman. Few Ph.D.s could make that claim."

I next went to see both Ford Fernard and Clyde Goodler. Fernard refused to say anything until he had talked with an attorney. Goodler was disposed to cooperate. He offered to go to police headquarters himself, taking an attorney with him, and make a statement. When he did, the police would finally find out how the scam had been worked.

With that taken care of, I went to see how McCarney was doing with his search of the mock castle. Raina Lambert arrived shortly after I did, and we waited in my rental car, which I had parked down the street. "What do you think they'll find?" I asked her.

"Thus far, everything has gone Florence's way. She made only one slip, with the telephone number. I'm hoping she's made another. One more should be enough."

When McCarney finally appeared, his face was a blank study. He said, "Would you two come in, please." He put it like an order.

We followed him down the drive to the house, through the house to the curving sweep of a long flight of stairs, and up the stairs to Florence Stevens-Dantzil's private suite of bedroom, bathroom, and boudoir.

Sanding, the young black officer who had helped me search Harley Dantzil's rooms, had been at work there. He was proud of the skill with which he was applying the lessons I taught him.

"There's a concealed area at the back of the closet," he said. "The partition is cleverly done — see how it opens? I took measurements and there was extra space there, so I fussed until I found it."

Hanging there were a woman's blonde wig; a man's brown wig; overalls; and several rather flamboyant dresses that possibly went well with the blonde wig but seemed highly unsuitable for a Florence Stevens-Dantzil.

"Then Florence was Hayseed *and* the blonde!" I exclaimed.

"Then there's this," Officer Sanding said. It was a compartment under the closet floor, and it seemed to be filled with records.

"And cash," Officer Sanding said, beaming at me. "Fifty grand, at least."

I took a moment to look the suite over. Florence enjoyed the same ingenious arrangement I had seen in Harley's rooms. By opening a panel and swiveling the TV set in her boudoir, she could watch it from her bed. It was a custom job, very expensive and just as unnecessary as Harley's had been. The fake partition in the closet looked like the same kind of work. I wondered if Yaegler had added these touches himself.

"Come downstairs," McCarney said. "I have something more to show you."

"Just a moment," I said. I wanted to compare the view from Florence's suite with the one I had seen from Harley's. It was the same, but Florence had larger windows and a direct view of the pool area. She and the other residents of the house were waiting there now, seated in the grove where I had talked with Yaegler. A police officer was watching them with polite alertness. She sat tensely on the edge of her chair, her red face at the boiling point. Mrs. Gabble, the cook, and Selena, the maid, looked as though they enjoyed having a little time off. Darnell Condellor, the alleged nephew, had returned from work in a rush when Florence telephoned him, and the police had invited him to join the others. He was as angry as Florence, but his face had turned white instead of red.

"Did you find anything in the handyman's quarters?" I asked McCarney.

"A disassembled food mixer."

"I don't suppose it's an electrostatic food mixer."

McCarney looked startled. "Is there such a

371

thing?"

"I'd have to ask Professor Quilley. What about Condellor?"

"He has a choice collection of pornography in his room, but I can't arrest him for that."

"Nothing else?"

"A stack of magazines and a filing cabinet full of advertising copy. Not only is there nothing incriminating, but there isn't even anything that's very interesting."

"Mind if I take a look?"

"Why?"

"Because he's a nonentity in this case. I haven't been able to place him at all."

"Go ahead."

He led the way and then stepped aside at the bedroom door to let Raina Lambert and me in ahead of him.

I first looked into the closet and whistled softly. I had never seen such a prime collection of expensive suits outside a clothing store. The quality was superb. I gave him credit for trying even though I knew every one of them looked better on its hanger than it would on him.

The pornography — book collections of photographs — could have been entitled *Sexual Acts Illustrated*. It provided belated proof that Condellor's interests were heterosexual, but we were no longer interested. The magazines were a miscellany. The filing cabinet was packed with proofs of advertisements, some of them for high-tech industries. They looked extremely technical.

"I still can't place him," I said.

"That's because he didn't have a place," Raina Lambert said. "I talked with Wes Zerin this morning. It seems evident that Florence sent Condellor to snoop around the casinos and find out whether it was safe to operate the scam again. It's also evident that she told him so little he had no idea what to look for. While he was hanging around Diamond D's keno lounge, he overheard Zerin talking with someone about Harley Dantzil. He immediately deduced that Zerin must know all about the scam, so he attached himself to the kid. The questions he asked seemed so odd that Zerin thought Condellor must know something about Dantzil's murder. Zerin decided to do a bit of detective work on his own with the result that each of them was trying to pump the other when neither of them knew anything. They must have had strange conversations."

"Will Condellor talk?" McCarney asked.

"It doesn't matter one way or the other," Raina Lambert said. "He certainly doesn't know anything important."

"What about the current resident gigolo?" I asked.

"He left yesterday," McCarney said. "He's described as having dark, curly hair."

"The one I saw was blond."

373

"This one is the blond's replacement. She only kept them for a few days and then threw them back. Come downstairs — I still have something to show you."

In a stand by the door was a plaid cloth umbrella. "There are rust particles clinging to the inside," McCarney said. "It won't take the scientists long to tell us whether they match the ones found in Dantzil's skull."

"You've got your case," I said. "Florence ran the scam and employed her husband. When she found out he was double-crossing her and running his own scam, she arranged an impeccable alibi for herself and sent Yaegler to murder him. Why haven't you arrested her?"

McCarney asked gloomily, "Why would a wealthy society woman get herself involved in a mess like this?"

"That's the wrong question," Raina said. "You should ask yourself — how rich is a rich wife?"

"If you're referring to Florence Stevens-Dantzil, she's plenty rich. Any list of donors to local worthy causes is certain to have her name in a prominent place, and she doesn't give piddling amounts. This house would cost a fortune at present-day prices, and it cost plenty when she bought it."

"Would it surprise you to know she's broke?"

"Yes. It would more than surprise me. It would astonish me. Where did you get that notion?"

"From her banker," Raina Lambert said. "Information reluctantly and confidentially divulged to avoid the turmoil of a formal police investigation — which, unfortunately, he is going to get anyway. Four years ago, her banker thought she would have to sell this house in another year or two. There was discussion of a mortgage, which — since she had no prospects for new sources of income — had to be viewed as a first step toward destitution. Somehow she managed to stay afloat without the mortgage. Her banker thinks she must be making frantic manipulations that somehow keep her one jump ahead of the sheriff. Actually, she's been clever enough to sock her money where snoops like us — and Internal Revenue — can't pick up all the details and start wondering where it came from. If you check, though, you'll probably find an account in another bank where she deposited some of the scam money, properly declaring it as income — perhaps income from gambling winnings. She couldn't pay for everything in cash. She'd have to run a fair amount of money through a bank for routine expenses and charitable donations."

McCarney was staring at her speechlessly.

"How else can you account for her miraculous financial survival?" Raina demanded. "She's always been considered a tightwad — no charitable contributions for her unless the donors were well publicized, no new Mercedes as long as the old one could be kept looking new — but what it really meant was that she was never as rich as people thought. She cleverly got the maximum show from the money she had. The last few years she has kept the show going with very little income, and that requires something more than cleverness."

We met with McCarney in his office that afternoon. The investigation was shaping up nicely. The rust in the umbrella did match that found in Harley Dantzil's scalp. Just to cinch things, a hair follicle with a bit of skin had been transferred to the umbrella from the pipe. Florence was refusing to answer questions, which seemed ironic since she was being held for questioning. The news of her arrest had been released to the papers, but they were certain to handle it with asbestos gloves while waiting suspensefully for further developments.

Raina Lambert ceremoniously opened a package she was carrying and placed the contents — a large, conical ashtray with push buttons — on the lieutenant's desk.

"What's this?" McCarney demanded.

"It's evidence to hold in reserve just in case the jury seems doubtful that Yaegler is a scientific genius. He's known as a ne'er-do-well, almost a ne'er-do-anything, who's been living with and on his cousin for as long as anyone can remember. He drove her Mercedes for her and did odd jobs around the house and yard. Probably he never held a full-time job in his life. All he ever wanted to do was putter."

"I know all about that," McCarney said. "When

she bought the mock castle, he built the addition onto the garage himself so he could have a private place of his own. It's better constructed than the house is. He could do anything, but as you say, he preferred to putter. The really peculiar thing is that she made a fortune with his keno scam and still didn't give him any money. She kept the whole net profit for herself. As you say, the jury may have trouble believing Yaegler did it. We have his keno machine and some suggestive stuff from his shop, but it's possible that the scam will be played down at the trial. There's plenty of murder evidence, plus the bits of confession Yaegler has given us, and the Gaming Control Board may not care to let the public know how to cheat at keno successfully. But one never knows, so I'll take everything I can get."

"This ashtray," Raina Lambert said, "was a Christmas gift that Florence Stevens-Dantzil gave to Hilda Grimston at least ten years ago. Florence distributed a number of them. Hilda mentioned this yesterday. This morning I had a twitch of curiosity, and I went back for·more information. The gadget was invented and manufactured by Thad Yaegler. He applied for a patent on it or was going to. I don't know whether he actually got one."

McCarney looked at the ashtray as though it were a bomb someone had just placed on his desk. "The hell you say."

"Yaegler was always tinkering, and he had a

number of inventions to his credit. Both he and Florence had great hopes for several of them, but like this ashtray, they came to nothing."

"There were two of those things in Harley Dantzil's suite at the castle," I said. "I wondered why a non-smoker with emphysema needed ashtrays. They didn't look as though they'd ever been used. I suppose they were put there to get them out of the way. There also was one in Yaegler's workshop on Valhalla, and he used it himself."

"You didn't mention them," she said reprovingly.

"At the time, I didn't connect them with anything. Expensive gift shops often stock unlikely gadgets like this on the theory that if a thing is ugly enough, they can charge a high price for it."

"They were handmade by Yaegler, and Florence tried to promote them for him. She demonstrated them for her guests, and she gave a few to friends. They certainly are ugly, but we mustn't judge by appearances. Get someone in here who's smoking a cigarette."

McCarney went to the next office and came back with Sergeant Dunkor. Raina Lambert gave the sergeant a sweet smile. "Would you sacrifice your cigarette to this ashtray in the interest of science? Don't snuff it out — just lay it here."

Dunkor stared. "That thing is an ashtray? Don't tell me, let me figure it out myself. It has a built-in gyroscope that gives the manufacturer an excuse to charge ten thousand dollars for it. It was developed for the space program. Or for the Navy. Right?"

He good-naturedly laid a half-smoked cigarette in it.

Raina Lambert pushed the top button. The burning cigarette disappeared. "It dropped into a small airtight compartment," she explained. "The diminishing oxygen and accumulating smoke will quickly put it out."

After a short wait, she pressed the button again so we could look inside. The compartment was filled with smoke, and the cigarette was indeed out.

"When the next cigarette is ready to be disposed of, the second button is pressed . . ." She did so. ". . . and the extinguished cigarette is dropped into the large bottom storage compartment. Then the air-tight compartment is ready to extinguish another burning cigarette. It's the world's only scientifically effective ashtray."

"If he made those things by hand, they must have been expensive," McCarney said. "How much did he think people would be willing to pay to be able to dispose of a cigarette without putting it out first?"

"I don't know what he charged for it. Grimston's was a gift. Both Florence and Yaegler were proud of it, Grimston said, but as you say, it was a lot of fuss and expense for a rather feeble result. There's very little demand for scientifically effective

379

ashtrays."

"He seems to be a slow-moving and slow-thinking person," McCarney said.

"But extremely clever with his hands," I said.
"I saw him working on a lawn mower. He must be
a great repairman. And 'slow-thinking' doesn't
mean he isn't brilliant. I've thought of something
else. There's a small speaker above the castle's
doorbell button, and when you press it, Florence
Stevens-Dantzil's voice informs you that this is the
Stevens-Dantzil residence, deliveries at the rear
door only and solicitors shot at dawn. If you want
to chance it, you are instructed to ring the bell a
second time. That must be more of Yaegler's
work."

Raina Lambert looked at me severely. "You
never mentioned that, either."

"An expert gadgeteer should go over that house
from top to bottom to see how many more items
Yaegler scattered through it," I went on. "The
bugs were another impractical invention. Did you
find out how he happened to rent the garage behind
Condellor's advertising agency?"

"Condellor told him it was available," McCarney
said. "He had another place, but it was farther
away, and he needed more room. About those
bugs. Yaegler put the receivers and their tape
recorders inside plastic cases from discarded
smoke alarms. He installed suction cups on them.
Clever of him — he could fasten what looked like

a smoke alarm to the wall at any convenient place and come back and remove it later, and no one saw anything suspicious about it. Fortunately for us, the technology of the thing was far beyond his competence. The bugs mostly malfunctioned, and our audio lab got nothing at all from the tapes we found." He turned to me and said resentfully, "You said the bug in Harley's apartment proved the high-tech element didn't murder him. You were wrong. Yaegler put it there because he wanted to know what the police were up to."

"He seems to have made a full confession."

"He talked some when he heard Florence had been arrested. The night Dantzil was murdered, he drove her to that ball in the Mercedes and parked it conspicuously. Then he walked a few blocks to where he'd left the Toyota earlier that day. He had told the maid and the cook he was taking it in for repairs and a tune-up, and the day after the murder he did just that. The night of the ball he drove it to a place near Win Upway's apartment where Florence usually parked. He put on Win Upway's wig in the car, just as Florence always did, and then he went to her apartment and changed to Butch's overalls, wig, and gloves, also just as she always did. The iron pipe in the umbrella was his idea; he borrowed Florence's umbrella and put it back without her knowing he'd used it, which was a break for us. Florence had made an appointment with Harley, and Harley let him in thinking

381

he was Florence. They look a little alike and have the same build, and the apartment is poorly lighted. Yaegler was back at the Plaza long before the ball was over. We have the 'how' down pretty well, but I still would like to know 'why.'"

"He was protecting his home," Raina said. "He loves that little apartment behind the garage, and he'd have been evicted along with Florence if she'd lost the castle. It wouldn't surprise me if he perfected this keno scheme years ago and then filed it. Money meant nothing to him, and he could work for years on a problem just for the pleasure of solving it. When he heard Florence was broke, he revived it for her. Shall I sum up?"

McCarney nodded.

"The scam worked because the two cousins were unexpectedly gifted. Yaegler's genius was for making things. Edwin Morabin has a high regard for his ability, and Morabin isn't lavish with praise for others. He says Yaegler has a genuine gift for gadgetry. Unfortunately, few of his ideas were practical. When Florence was hosting those bridge sessions, Yaegler would wait in the background for a chance to corner Morabin with highly technical questions, and he often borrowed Morabin's technical journals."

"Did he ever ask him questions about electrostatics?" I asked.

"Morabin doesn't remember any. Florence's gift was for organization. She used her no-good husband to make contacts and arrange meetings for her. Harley was actually very good at that. He had no friends, but he had huge numbers of acquaintances. He probably knew Ford Fernard. He certainly knew a forger — he'd used one himself. Some of Brian Varnko papers were forged.

"Florence was very, very careful to make certain no one could identify her in her Butch disguise. She kept an apartment just to have somewhere to put it on, and as you noted, she always slipped on that synthetic Win Upway wig in her car before going to the apartment. She was careful to meet her helpers in places where the light was poor — either in taverns where dimness was part of the décor, or in an apartment where small light bulbs could be used."

"She also made Harley report to her at the mock castle," I said. "What an irony! At this stage of their marriage, they finally were paying each other nocturnal visits, but only so he could deliver money and receive new instructions! I wondered why he would spend even one night a week there. The answer is that he didn't. He waited until the household had gone to bed and Florence could come to his room for a meeting or he could go to hers. Then he left. I suppose she paid her collaborators as little as possible. Even Yaegler admitted she was a cheapskate. Harley was like Fernard. He got tired of handling all that money when Florence let him keep so little, so he set up on his own —

383

and proved to be just as much a cheapskate as she was."

Raina nodded. "In the end, greed ruined both of them. Florence eventually became suspicious of Harley and had him tailed — maybe by Condellor or one of her other 'nephews' — and found out what he was up to. She also found out he'd carelessly let outsiders know about the scam. She was furious. Yaegler must have been furious, too. Harley was threatening everything he valued — his place to live, his freedom to putter.

"So Florence told Harley she wanted to discuss something and arranged to meet him at his apartment. There was no reason for him to take alarm. That sort of thing happened frequently. The charity ball provided an alibi for her in case she needed one. In the Butch costume, Yaegler looked so much like Florence that Dantzil didn't suspect a thing."

"Yaegler did make one special gesture at disguising himself," I said. "He shaved off his mustache. When I saw him the following Sunday, it was just starting to grow back. All of us owe Harley an apology. It wasn't until Florence tried to get the scam going again, using Condellor, that she realized how valuable he'd been. He knew the casino scene perfectly, he had contacts at all the casinos, and he must have been a highly astute judge of people. If just one person he approached about the scam had talked, the whole scheme would have gone poof."

McCarney scribbled a reminder for himself to find out whether anyone else had noticed the shaved mustache. "Yaegler blamed the scheme's demise on sex. Maybe I should explain to him that greed is no good, either. Anything else?"

"One more oddity," I said. "Why did Yaegler bug Leda Rauchman's apartment? As I see it, Harley must have noticed her following him and mentioned it to Florence, and Florence thought Joel Eckling only pretended to fire Leda so she would have more time to investigate the keno scam. Yaegler bugged Leda's apartment to find out what she knew."

"I'll ask Yaegler about that," McCarney said.

Before we took our leave of him and the Las Vegas Metropolitan Police, he made me promise I would never again bother him after hours or on weekends. Walking toward the parking lot, I asked Raina, "How did Eckling take it?"

"He was pleased," she said. "Very glad to have it over with. Grateful that Joletta wasn't more deeply involved. Surprised but not too distressed about Florence. He's known her all his life — her mother was his family's housekeeper — but I don't think he ever liked her. Are you still determined to see more of Las Vegas?"

"I want to know what it's really like. Except for the casinos, I've hardly seen any of it. I haven't had time to look."

"Surely you don't expect me to believe that. You've met an alluring female."

"How could that be?" I demanded. "The only females I meet while I'm working are either witnesses or suspects. By definition, they are not alluring."

"You can have three days."

"Nope. I want a whole week plus the following weekend. I want some of those 320 days of sunshine for my own use. I want to go water-skiing on Lake Meade, which I'm told can be done the year around."

"The water will be icy."

"I am not going to fall in — much. From water-skiing, I want to dash out to Lee Canyon, wherever that is, and go snow skiing. On the same day. I want to go to Hoover Dam. I may take an aerial excursion to the Grand Canyon. I want to see a couple of shows — I've been in Las Vegas for three weeks without seeing even one, which is un-American. I want to visit museums and see the car once used by Hitler and the piano once played by Chopin. I want to see animated dinosaurs, which sound far more interesting than Vegas Vic. I may go horseback riding. All the time I've been here, I've been admiring that ring of mountains that surrounds the city. I want to see them close up and maybe even climb one of them. On Sundays, I'll attend church in the city that has more churches per capita than any other city in the world. I'll be back in Los Angeles a week from Monday."

She chuckled. "If you can get all of that done in one week, you're welcome to it."

I drove her to the airport. Then I checked in at a motel. My idea had been to find one as remote as possible from either the Strip or the Casino Center, with no casino, no shows, no crowds of tourists, not even a stray slot machine. Then it suddenly occurred to me that most of the Las Vegas visitors came here to enjoy those very things, and I might be able to enjoy them myself if I could experience them without their cluttering up my work. I found myself a motel smack in the middle of the Strip's heaviest action. For a day, at least, I would become one of the motion picture extras and join in the fun. If the fun proved to be unfunny, I could always look for another motel.

I made a phone call as soon as I checked in. There was no answer. After I had unpacked, I telephoned again. Leda Rauchman answered on the first ring.

"I just got back from police headquarters," she said. "It was ghastly. I can't understand why I thought she was a man."

"It was the dim light. You never got a good look at her. She was canny about that — no one got a good look at her when she was disguised as Butch."

"Are you really staying on for a few days?"

"Absolutely. Our program for this evening is

387

already arranged. I've made the reservations. First, a German dinner. Weiner schnitzel, sauer-braten, fleischrouladen . . ."

"I've never eaten German food. I don't know any of those things."

"That's an exceedingly strange confession for a young lady with worthy German ancestors. I will undertake your education."

"I was hoping you would."

"Afterward, a bar where we can listen to old-fashioned songs and singalong with whomever or whatever. From there, we'll go dancing — any place you like."

"Good. And after that," she added firmly, "we will have the next drinks at my place. I have finally got rid of that damned policeman."